ALSO BY ANTHONY SWOFFORD

**Jarhead: A Marine's Chronicle of the Gulf War
and Other Battles**

EXIT A

A NOVEL

Anthony Swofford

SCRIBNER

New York London Toronto Sydney

SCRIBNER
1230 Avenue of the Americas
New York, NY 10020

This book is a work of fiction. Names, characters, places, and incidents either are products
of the author's imagination or are used fictitiously. Any resemblance to actual events or locales
or persons, living or dead, is entirely coincidental.

Copyright © 2007 by Anthony Swofford

All rights reserved, including the right of reproduction in whole or in part in any form.

SCRIBNER and design are trademarks of Macmillan Library Reference USA, Inc.,
used under license by Simon & Schuster, the publisher of this work.

For information about special discounts for bulk purchases,
please contact Simon & Schuster Special Sales:
1-800-456-6798 or business@simonandschuster.com.

Text set in Granjon

Manufactured in the United States of America

1   3   5   7   9   10   8   6   4   2

Library of Congress Cataloging-in-Publication Data

Swofford, Anthony.
Exit A: a novel/Anthony Swofford.
p. cm.
1. Americans—Japan. I. Title.
PS3619.W64E95 2007
813'.6—dc22   2006044394

ISBN-13: 978-0-7432-7038-0
ISBN:10: 0-7432-7038-X

The Akahito epigraph comes from *One Hundred Poems from the Japanese,*
edited by Kenneth Rexroth (New Directions Paperbook, 1964).

For my mother and sisters

EXIT A

I wish I were close
To you as the wet skirt of
A salt girl to her body.
I think of you always.

 —Akahito,
 One Hundred Poems
 from the Japanese

This boy is an American, born on the third of July, 1972. While his mother spat and screamed through the life-endangering birth, his father and the orderlies and janitors lit illegal fireworks in the hospital parking lot. The men drank from bottles of bourbon and beer while leaning down to light Bottle Rockets and Flaming Marys and Wailing Jennys. His father supplied the armament and the devil's milk, and the matches, and most of the boisterous ranting and raving about God and Country and the Founding Fathers and the *Mayflower* and Plymouth Rock and the Salem witch trials and the Red Threat, that ungainly, bloody bear from the East.

The doctor held the boy upside down, and the safety of the womb became history. The room above the mother spun one hundred times, and she went under.

No one found the father, not even the orderly sent to look. So they slapped the boy's bottom and placed him in a crib, where he waited for someone with his same blood to come to consciousness. His aunt Mirtha was the first to appear at the hospital, and after cursing the father's name, she picked up the boy and performed an auntly show for him, baby talk and ego stroking and burp and bowel sounds. Because his aunt was present and cogent, and the nurses wanted to get down to the parade grounds for the base general's midnight fireworks display, they asked her to name the boy, and she did. This boy's name is Severin Boxx.

•   •   •

This girl's name is Virginia Sachiko Kindwall. She is the daughter of General Oliver Kindwall and Mrs. Oliver Kindwall, once known as Olive, though that was not her given name but simply a shortening of her husband's. Her given name was Nakashima Sachiko. Olive died on the birthing table at Travis Air Force Base in California, in July 1972. While she died giving birth to Virginia Sachiko, her husband, a major at the time, paced the base morgue while overseeing the identification and shipment home of the newest dead boys from Vietnam, some of the last. Later, Kindwall would tell his daughter that on the day of her mother's death and her own birth, the dead boys from Vietnam seemed much more dead than usual. He spent that night wide awake with his back ramrod straight, flat against the gray concrete floor of the hospital morgue, while his daughter, a few buildings away, slept with other military babies, some born to mothers whose husbands had died in Vietnam.

The maternity nurses that night paid extra attention to Baby Kindwall, Baby and not yet Virginia Sachiko Kindwall, because her father had been too distraught to remember what name he and his deceased wife had decided to call the child if the ball of love entered the world as a girl. The nurses rocked Baby Kindwall in their laps and called her "sweetheart" and "precious" and "lamb," and the nurses wept and cursed God and Vietnam, as they did every night.

On the floor of the hospital morgue, Kindwall dreamed of his wife in twenty years, in a church dressing room, preparing their daughter for marriage. The women's faces were made of shattered glass, and they could not find the wedding dress, so the daughter decided to be married in the nude. The dream ended with Kindwall walking his naked daughter up the church aisle, but the altar was absent priest and groom. Flames shot from the tabernacle. Kindwall awoke in the morning without recalling the dream.

The next day he volunteered for his third tour in Vietnam.

EXIT A

The day he left, he noticed a yellow piece of paper affixed to the refrigerator door with a watermelon-shaped magnet, these words written on it in his wife's penmanship: *Girl=Virginia Sachiko*. So his daughter had a name now, but no mother, and a father back at war.

PART I

Tokyo, November 1989

ONE

Severin Boxx rode home from football practice in the back of Coach Kindwall's van. In the front passenger seat, the coach's daughter applied a French manicure to her nails. The coach was also the base general of Yokota Air Base, Japan, and Severin's father's boss. These facts made Virginia Sachiko Kindwall untouchable and even more desirable than had she been a sergeant's daughter. Severin didn't wish to cause trouble for his father, and he intended to start the remainder of the season as outside linebacker, but he also wanted five minutes alone with Virginia, five minutes to speak in a calm and controlled voice, to practice his Japanese with her, five minutes at a ramen shop, slurping their noodles, laughter, together. The back of the van smelled of pigskin and wet gridiron and the still sweet sweat of boys. In a year or maybe in months, the boys Severin's age would begin to sweat like men, and stink like men, and maybe even suffer and want and love like men. But for now they were boys.

The van passed the flight line and the jet-fueled, mind-blowing birds of human prey. In the dark the planes looked harmless, like linked parts of a playground that young children might scamper on and under. But Severin knew, because his father had told him, that within twenty minutes General Kindwall could strike North Korea with a rain of bombs and fire more effective and impressive than ever unleashed before. All of this firepower idled within a half mile of the football field and two miles of Severin's front door.

Severin stared at Virginia's profile and felt his desire for her flush his face and his chest. Coach was talking about the power of the linebacker blitz, but Severin ignored him and stared at Virginia's beautiful nose and lips and the wisps of hair that floated above her head like strands of God. The car arrived at Severin's house in the officers' suburb of the base, and Severin jumped out with his gear in both hands and said good-bye to Coach and his daughter. He could barely pronounce her name.

"Hold up, Severin," Kindwall said. He put the van in park and walked around the front of the vehicle and faced Severin. Kindwall was a massive man, six foot four, over 250 pounds. The general's face looked as though two pit bulls had played catch with it. His scars were from his third tour in Vietnam. A bouncing Betty made from ball bearings and gunpowder had rendered his face a combat zone. The general's carriage invoked the competing sensations of victory and humiliation. Severin knew the general could use rhetoric to turn breakfast into Pershing's European campaign.

Kindwall stooped and aligned his eyes with Severin's. "Tomorrow we will win a football game. It is all a part of the march of history. Only a few names are remembered in the end, only a few names make it into the great score sheet of history. Eat right, sleep well, and hit hard."

"Yes, sir," Severin said.

Kindwall grabbed the back of Severin's head and pulled him into the crook of his arm and, with his other hand, vigorously slapped the boy on the back. Virginia looked at Severin as though to apologize for her father's historicized, militarized vision of everything, even a hug. She blew Severin a kiss.

He nervously extracted himself from Kindwall's embrace.

Inside, Severin's dinner waited on the Formica kitchen counter. From the mudroom, he eyed the plate and guessed that it was chicken-fried steak and potatoes. His dad liked chicken-fried steak, and Dad was home from somewhere in the world—Taiwan, Diego Garcia, Turkey?—so they would eat chicken-fried steak.

And his mother would drink less coffee, and her girlfriends, the mothers of his friends, would not hang around as late at night complaining about their absent husbands.

Severin stood at the counter and ate, wearing his grass- and mud-colored football pants and a half-shirt stained with sweat and winning. He was not tall, five foot eight, but he carried a solidly muscled 175 pounds. An admiring coach from an opposing team once said, after Severin had clobbered his quarterback ten yards behind the line of scrimmage, "That kid is made of bricks." His sweaty bangs fell across his brow and into his blue eyes. His eyebrows, dark black like his hair, grew in an arched pattern that gave his face a constant look of youthful surprise. His nose was thin and straight, and his thin lips pulsed cranberry red. He looked his age, seventeen. He felt younger. He needed to prove something.

His mouth bulged with steak and potatoes and gravy, and he breathed riotously through his nose. Mrs. Boxx entered the kitchen. "How many times must I tell you to shower before you eat? It smells like the fifty-yard line in here. And please sit at the table."

He swallowed hard. "Sorry, Mom. I'm hungry after practice. I can't wait." He fell into a chair at the kitchen table.

"I make your father shower when he comes in from the flight line. Are you suddenly the power around here?" She tousled his sweaty hair and then smelled her hand, her son.

"What's for dessert? Cookies? Ice cream? Both?" He turned his face toward her with an expectant smile.

"Pistachio ice cream," she said after a quick survey of the freezer.

"That stuff is nasty. How about some green-tea ice cream?"

"Your father doesn't like it. Too Japanese for him."

"But we're in Japan! Dad! We are in Japan!" he yelled toward the living room. "Eat the ice cream!" Severin was truly angry. His father preferred a teriyaki burger from McDonald's to a bowl of ramen.

"Your father is asleep. Jet lag. How does a pilot get jet lag?" She sat down next to her son.

Severin briskly stirred his potatoes and gravy. "When is he leaving again? Midnight? He's always gone. He never sees my games."

"How's the team looking?"

Severin dropped his fork and it rang against his plate like a bell. "Practice sucked. He ran us through two extra cycles of calisthenics. But he gave me a ride home."

"He must be stressed out over the accident this morning."

"What accident?" Severin hadn't heard of an accident.

"A troop transport truck ran over and killed Yoshida's son, riding his bicycle home from school. It's horrible. The driver didn't even know it happened until he got to the front gate and an MP stopped the truck because a bent bicycle wheel was hanging from the bumper." Mrs. Boxx shook her head.

"Yoshida, like Yoshida Electronics?" Severin's eyes pleaded with his mother to say no.

"Yes, honey."

"Mom, he's so nice to everyone. He lets us hang out in his store as long as we want, watching TV or listening to music. I can't believe this. What's going to happen?"

"The liberal papers will call for a withdrawal of American forces. I can't say I think otherwise." Mrs. Boxx leaned back in her chair and sighed.

"How old was Yoshida's son?"

"Seventeen."

My age, Severin thought. My age and dead. "The general didn't say anything at practice."

"I wouldn't think so."

"Can I go to the Base Square? The guys are hanging out there until football curfew. I think Johnson knew Yoshida-san. He's probably messed up."

"On Sunday I'm attending a memorial mass. I hope you'll go

with me." Mrs. Boxx looked out her kitchen window at the darkness.

At seventeen, Virginia Sachiko Kindwall wore pearls around her neck and diamonds in her ears, combat boots, and mostly black clothing. She was a *hafu,* a dark-haired Faye Dunaway from a punk-rock remake of *Bonnie and Clyde. Bonnie and Clyde* was her favorite movie, and it often played at the Yokota base theater. She'd covered her bedroom walls with still photos from the film: Bonnie and Clyde in bed; Bonnie, framed in bars, pointing a revolver at a bank teller; Bonnie, Clyde, and C.W. living in their car.

Virginia tried on clothes and scrutinized herself in the mirror, full-length, attached to the closet door. A crowd of rejected skirts and T-shirts gathered at her bare feet. She clenched a pink silk skirt between her toes. She chose black knee-highs, a Catholic-school-girl skirt, and a black concert T-shirt. She approached one of the posters of Warren Beatty and kissed him on the lips. Standing in front of her dresser, she applied makeup, looking at herself in the round vanity mirror. She'd bought it at a thrift store off base. Two of the lights were burned out, so her face was half in shadow.

She opened the top drawer of her dresser and pulled out a blond wig and tried it on. She smiled at her blond self and removed a .38-caliber pistol from the drawer. She put the wig and pistol in her purse and went downstairs to tell her father she was hanging out with friends in Shinjuku after attending the eight P.M. movie at the base theater.

The base kids crowded the Base Square, an area near the center of Yokota Air Base meant to replicate the downtown in Anywhere, America. The kids called the area the mall, even though their parents called it the square. The kids were correct. American food and retail chains had bought the rights to sell their wares on the base, so indeed at Yokota Air Base, Tokyo, Japan, the children and mothers of American military men spent American dollars in a strip that looked as though it had been transplanted from Montclair, New Jersey, or Dickinson, North Dakota, or Sacramento, California. You could buy hot dogs on a stick after purchasing sneakers at the Athletic Shoe Factory, which was located next to a Baskin-Robbins counter, across the way from a Pizza Hut. Some of the kids had lived overseas for so long they didn't know that what lay in front of them was a replica trading center that could be found in thousands of American towns. They lived the suburban American dream without knowing it. The difference was that this mall was always safe. There were no abductions, no girls lured into rape vans with promises of modeling careers or screen time, no burglaries in the parking lot.

Severin Boxx and the other members of the defensive squad for Yokota High School sat at a picnic table in the middle of the food court.

John Duncan said, "Coach thrashed us because he's pissed about that truck killing Yoshida's son."

Connor Johnson said, "I called Yoshida's house, but there was no answer. My mom is going to take me over there tomorrow. He was cool. He was teaching me Japanese."

Severin Boxx said, "Why didn't Coach say anything? I'm really sorry, Connor."

Connor said, "Me, too. But all we have to worry about is playing football. That's what we do, right? The general asks us to win, nothing else."

"Winning is garbage," Severin said. "We should dedicate tomorrow's game to Yoshida-san. Let's have our moms sew red patches on our uniforms. Everyone cool with that?"

All the boys agreed, and Connor took responsibility for calling the rest of the team.

"You better keep your eyes off of winning Virginia," Leon Frank said to Severin. "That's the only thing I'd worry about. The general seeing you take off his daughter's clothes with your eyeballs."

The boys all started making grunting noises and slapping Severin on the head and punching him on the shoulders.

"Back off," Severin said. "You guys look at her the same."

"We look at her the same, but we've got *sanity*. You don't have sanity on your side," Leon said. "I bet Boxx knocks up Coach's daughter before Christmas. Or he breaks in the house to steal her panties and gets caught."

High fives for everyone, and the other boys danced circles around Severin and continued to berate and cajole him. He couldn't respond, he couldn't tell them they were wrong, that they had no idea what he was made of, because they knew, and they were right, and he would have to do whatever it took to keep his sanity, to not break into Virginia Kindwall's house and steal her panties. To do whatever it took not to ask her to his house to listen to music or allow his mother to do the same. Maybe no one would care, and maybe Coach already knew of Severin's ardor for his daughter, probably Virginia, with a name like that, wasn't even a virgin—he'd watched her camped at the theater with the old sergeant Focheaux, watching *Bonnie and Clyde* three times in a week, that old man had gotten her virginity a year ago, Severin guessed, and the coach knew and his own mother knew and the world knew and he knew nothing about anything, least of all Virginia Kindwall and love. He considered himself a simple, brutish boy who excelled at monkey-jumpers and other kinds of nonsense—the linebacker blitz, the safety rush, wrapping his arms around the opponent when tackling, holding on until he ground the bastard's body into the turf, punching the ball out for the fumble on the way down, kicking the quarterback in the head when the referee had his back turned—simple, brutish acts that placed him on the same ladder rung as the ape. There he sat on the ladder, smiling stupidly, swinging his legs in unison with the ape, awaiting a synaptic tug toward the civilized world. He was deep in the cave of unknowing, and he knew it. Perhaps knowledge of his low-down location was progress. He longed to take his first step out. No, he longed to leap out.

Severin caught sight of Virginia across the square. The tips of her hair teased her chin, and she smiled—at everyone or at him, he couldn't tell.

Virginia walked toward the football players. They stood between her and the eight P.M. showing of *Bonnie and Clyde*. She knew Severin Boxx was madly in love with her and that he didn't have the courage to tell her. She also knew that all of his friends and even her father knew. And she liked Severin, she'd liked him since seventh grade. But he was a boy, like all of them, for God's sake, even her father was a boy. The boys stopped talking as she approached, and one of them, she could never remember his name, pushed Severin toward her and whispered obscenities in his ear. The kid had extreme acne; someday he would have scars and be ashamed of them, she thought.

"Hey, Severin," she said. "You left a book in my dad's van when we dropped you off. Why don't you come by tomorrow morning and pick it up? Ten too early for you?"

She didn't stop walking, and Severin failed to answer her. She had no idea if he would show up or not.

The reason *Bonnie and Clyde* played so often at the base theater was that the theater manager, Master Sergeant Leroy Focheaux, suffered a dangerous crush on the base general's daughter, and she knew how to expertly use it to her cinematic advantage. Not only did he play the movies Virginia wanted to see, when she wanted to see them, but he also paid her for watching the movies with him. Focheaux was afraid of Virginia's father. She knew he didn't want to touch her; that he simply liked to look at her and think impure thoughts—fantasies he'd take home to his marital bed, high-water marks of onanism that old Mrs. Focheaux, head cashier at the base commissary, could never reach.

Master Sergeant Focheaux welcomed Virginia into the theater with a flourish. He'd ordered *Bonnie and Clyde* again because she'd asked him to. Really, she didn't ask him for anything, she told him to do things, and they both knew it, but she still used the words "please" and "thank you." For more than a year, Focheaux had been receiving complaints in the theater comments box about the constant repetition of movies, but he told Virginia that his job was secure and he threw away all of the complaints. She was the BG's daughter, and he'd been placed on this earth to please her.

Virginia settled into her seat next to Focheaux. She loved the opening credits: the genesis of the cult, the making of the imagery of the outlaw life.

The opening scene, close-up on Bonnie's lips. Pure sexuality, an animal clinging to the screen. American. Was that directed or natural? And calling Clyde "boy." Putting the man in his place. Clyde, smiling. And the ride begins. Later, the foreclosed farm: Here she always thought of her father. Midlothian, Texas, the dust-busted town her father grew up in. By the time his parents raised him, they lived in town, the farm gone, four generations of labor lost. In his closet, her father had pictures of the lost farm and his Texas youth. Mud-faced boy on a squalid porch, smiling. Can you ever know a man from a photo of his boyhood? She'd tried.

On-screen, the old farmer shooting out the windows of his farmhouse, now owned by the bank. What kind of world makes a man shoot out the windows of his former home?

As Severin walked away from his teammates and toward the theater the boys made sucking and grunting noises. Savages, he thought. He bought popcorn and licorice and a soda.

"The movie started thirty minutes ago," the counter lady said. "I guess you've seen it before."

He knew that if Coach caught him gorging junk food the night before a game he'd be condemned to monkeyjumpers hell for the rest of the season, for the rest of his football life. When the counter lady turned her back to him, Severin jumped the rope that cordoned off the balcony. He sat in the center seat of the first row and trained his eyes on Virginia and Master Sergeant Focheaux.

Severin hated Focheaux because the old sergeant was sitting next to Virginia, in a dark theater, and what a waste, Severin alone in the balcony, the spy, the loner, the private investigator doomed never to touch the girl because of his own great incapacities. Language left his body whenever she was near. He knew the words: Virginia, I love you. But was that how you said it? Virginia, I have strong feelings for you? Virginia, can I be alone with you? Virginia? Virginia, may I speak? No, that certainly wasn't it, don't ask if you can speak, just speak. If you ask she might say no, she might say, I know what you're thinking, but it isn't a good idea. And then you'll die with the thought and desire dead in your brain, in your shorts. Virginia, I want to kiss. Yes, that seems right. Let's kiss, Virginia. Virginia, let's kiss.

His favorite scene in the movie: the Texas Ranger caught by the gang, Bonnie getting sweet with him, the gang posing for pictures with the defeated lawman. He spits in her face, and they put him out on the river in a rowboat. Down with authority. He liked the movie. But he couldn't relate to the romanticism of the outlaw. Robin Hood was still a thief, even if he gave to the poor.

Here the outlaw's horse was replaced by the V-8 engine. Life on the road, life in a car, escape and violence. Ride.

Clyde couldn't get it up at first. Severin remembered this. But later, in a field, they made love. That's how it should be, in a field, honey, you and me, sticking together.

After leaving the theater and exiting the base, Virginia boarded a train at Haijima station. At Shinjuku, she switched to the Ikebukuro Metro line. A middle-aged man seated across from her stared at her legs. She mouthed the word *sukebe,* pervert. Her knees were scarred from spending most of her youth playing rough boys' sports with the sons of her father's subordinates. She pulled the rosary out of her shirt and thumbed Jesus' face. She wished she knew some Catholic prayers. The rosary had belonged to her mother, an unlikely convert from Buddhism. She blamed her father for this conversion, but she liked the way, in rhythm with the subway car, the rosary bounced against the taut T-shirt between her breasts, where Joey Ramone's silkscreened face was eating Jesus. She'd seen the Ramones the prior spring. A gray-haired Japanese punk rocker had bought her the shirt and then sung Ramones songs to her all night in the back of a shot bar called the Crane. She drank too much Kentucky bourbon and eventually vomited in the man's lap.

Tonight she was nervous because this was only the second evening of her life as a criminal. She tried to convince herself that no man could match her in speed, and no man could match her in wit, and no man could match her in cunning.

She thought the blond wig was a dumb idea, but the Boss had insisted that it would throw the police off the trail. Generally, a victim forgets all aspects of a crime other than the barrel of the gun you point in his face, or so the Boss had said. And why on earth would she point the barrel of a gun at someone? Because she wanted to feel alive. Her life on base was boring and dull, and her father expected only the best behavior from her. But how did he behave? Wasn't he a hypocrite? Didn't hypocrites deserve what they got? How many handguns existed in the entire country? And she carried one of them in her purse.

She stopped around the corner from the *konbini* store, affixed the wig, checked her makeup, and walked quickly into the store, not looking at passersby. She grabbed a basket and proceeded to the rear of the store. She picked one carton of tofu. At the freezer she selected a bag of frozen *gyoza*. In the dry-goods aisle, she grabbed two bags of rice crackers and a tin of green tea. She walked to the counter, set down her basket, and waited while the clerk figured her total.

She read his name badge: Haruki. It was like being named Mike in America.

Haruki said, looking up from his calculator, "Are you hungry tonight, miss?"

"I'm shopping for my *obâchan,*" Virginia said.

"Sweet of you," he said. "Where does she live?"

"Nearby." She waved her hand toward the door and the dense nothingness of the city beyond. Nearby meant anywhere. And why did he care? She could have told him: I don't know where my *obâchan* lives because I have never met her, because I am a *hafu* and the Japanese half of my family rejected me. But she did not.

He smiled as he moved the items into plastic bags. She moved her weight from foot to foot and frantically opened and closed the snap of her purse. The noise attracted the attention of the young boy on the stool next to Haruki; probably his son. As Haruki began to speak the total, she opened her purse and, instead of her wallet, removed her .38-caliber handgun and pointed it at Haruki's stomach. He gasped, and the little boy put his hands over his eyes, the see-no-evil monkey.

In slow, deliberate speech she said, "Haruki, I need you to give me all of the money in the cash register and to empty the safe underneath the counter. And I need you to do this now."

"I am unauthorized," Haruki said, but she cut him off by cocking the gun.

He complied.

She thought: This is happening too easily. She wanted another customer to walk through the door. She wanted to tell someone to shut up and lie facedown. Or, like an incredulous Clyde Barrow in a 1930s dust-bowl grocery, she wanted to fight a fat white guy who attacked her from behind with an ax. "That guy attacked me," she'd scream. In a very small corner of her brain, she wanted to pull the trigger while pointing the weapon at someone's head. She had no idea where this desire came from. Probably from her father. Men who volunteer for combat three times must pass on the killing gene to their children. Haruki placed all of the cash in a bag, along with the tofu and the other goods she'd gathered in her basket.

He said, "I hope your *obâsan* is ashamed of the trash she has brought into the world."

She reached across the counter and slapped the clerk. His son finally began to cry.

She felt bad about taking the groceries. She hadn't even asked for them, and now they'd be wasted. "Sit on the floor and count to one thousand," she said, and left the store.

At Exit A of Ikebukuro station, she handed the bag off to Yumiko, a fifteen-year-old girl pretending to be homeless. She'd met Yumiko at her recruitment lunch and had liked her. Yumiko was having sex with the Boss. Virginia wanted to tell Yumiko to wait a few years before having sex again. She wanted to say, Hey, I'm a virgin and I'm seventeen and I'm doing all right. Of course, she wasn't sure that she was doing all right; she'd been considering getting rid of her virginity and seeing what life looked like without it.

In exchange for the shopping bag with stolen groceries and yen, Virginia received an envelope with fifty American dollars in it. The Boss's agreement with his cadre of young female thieves was that for each robbery, they received fifty dollars, and at the end of the month, they also received 2 percent of the net take. Costs included rent of the apartment that the operations center ran out of, phone lines, recruiting expenses such as lunches and gifts, and the aspect of his operation that the Boss claimed set him apart from other hoodlums—the flowers and card he sent to his victims a week or so after the robbery:

WE APOLOGIZE FOR THE INCONVENIENCE OF OUR CRIMINAL ACT

This night Virginia robbed two other *konbinis,* one near Ginza station and one near Tokyo station. In perfectly orderly fashion, the victims performed the tasks she'd asked of them, she exited the establishments without incident, and she handed her shopping bags to Yumiko at Exit A of each station. Between her robberies and watching the film with Focheaux, Virginia had made $250 in five hours. She had no idea what to do with the money.

Her friends planned to party all night in Shibuya and Roppongi, hustling GIs and German tourists for drinks, maybe doing some drugs if they could find them for free or cheap enough. But she didn't want to be out all night. She boarded the last Chuo-line train and returned to Yokota.

She'd told Severin to stop by the house at ten in the morning, and she intended to be there. Her intentions for him were not all good. She knew the Boss needed an American kid with muscle, and that was Severin. She had no idea what the Boss needed him for, but she felt certain she could convince Severin to participate—such was his simplicity and, well, his longing.

Virginia's father ate a late dinner with his girlfriend every Friday night at a small sushi restaurant in Yokota. He'd never introduced the two. As far as Kindwall was concerned, Virginia didn't have knowledge of his relationship with Miyoko. But Virginia knew: she knew Miyoko's name, where she lived, that she worked as an auto mechanic at the Suzuki shop next to her apartment complex, and that Miyoko was a *hibakusha*—a Hiroshima survivor—unable to get an office job because of the prejudice bomb victims suffered, especially in Tokyo.

Virginia regularly spied on the two lovers while they dined at Mikuni.

And there they were, at their usual seats, stage left of the sushi bar. Virginia watched from outside the restaurant, sitting on a barrel of sake, sign of good luck and plenitude. The owner prepared fish behind the refrigerated counter, his knife slicing through *saba* like a shooting star through a new-moon night. Her father wore civilian clothes, the casual attire of a banker on his weekend: a white oxford shirt tucked into khakis, brown deck shoes, brown belt, a blue jacket with epaulets. Miyoko wore a dark blue pencil skirt, a red blouse, and a silk scarf with a blue-and-cream flower pattern. Virginia thought that her mother had been prettier than Miyoko, but Miyoko was still pretty and elegant—two qualities Virginia admired and found so rarely in the militarized world of her father. Virginia had more than once walked by the Suzuki shop to watch Miyoko work on cars: Bent over an engine, wearing blue overalls and rubber surgical gloves covered with grease, Miyoko retained her elegance and beauty.

Miyoko fed Kindwall a piece of *maguro*. Virginia had seen enough. Some nights she followed them through the city, to a pachinko parlor, to the Pretty Getter for drinks, home to Miyoko's apartment. But now she wandered the city alone, following no one. Again tonight she'd broken the law without being caught. She wondered if, in some perverse way, her father would be proud. Aren't fathers supposed to be proud of their daughters no matter what they do or fail to do? My daughter the criminal, my daughter my love.

TWO

Coach Kindwall awoke at four A.M. on game days. In fact, he rarely slept, so it was less like waking and more like rolling over in bed, sitting, and sliding his feet into his slippers. He hadn't slept much since his first tour in Vietnam, and that was many years ago. Sometimes he thought about retirement, but it worried him that, after leaving the military, his body and mind might suddenly need to catch up on years of lost slumber, and that he'd sign his retirement orders and fall over right there at the desk, not dead but asleep for a decade.

He stepped out of the shower, shaved quickly, and combed his hair with a straight black comb and water, the white line of the part like the perfect delineation on a landing strip. Now he needed to wear his glasses to shave and comb his hair. Sometimes he considered this demoralizing, but usually, he gave it no thought. He knew that a few doors down, his daughter was sleeping soundly, that she was a sweet girl with a bright future as long as she kept her drug use to marijuana and locked the swarming GIs and Japanese kids and punk dependents out of her pants for long enough. He thought he knew all of this.

He didn't want her to stay a virgin forever, but he considered thirty a nice round number. By that time she'd have a career and her own money, and she wouldn't have to grant the every wish of some wiseass husband who would despise and disparage her father. He didn't want her to have daddy issues, but he did want her to love him until the day he died and longer. His job mattered, the air force mattered, the Cold War mattered, but none of those things was worth a single hair on his daughter's legs. Fathers had killed for their daughters, and they would continue to.

But *did* the Cold War matter? The Berlin wall was down, but he could turn things hot in a matter of seconds. All it took was one phone call and he'd have two dozen bombers dropping five-hundred-pound balls of flaming death and metal on Pyongyang, no questions asked. Let the exchange of fireworks begin. Why did people constantly want to wreck his day? It would seem the world would want to keep General Kindwall in good spirits.

Yesterday it was a half-blind airman from the motor pool driving a five-ton truck over a perfectly innocent Japanese kid on his way home from school. The son of Yoshida, the guy he'd bought his TV from. Would Yoshida kill for his son? It was possible. Public Affairs had already put together a Sunday service at the chapel. He needed to visit the family. Flowers. Sake. Visit the temple. Eventually, a check would arrive from the U.S. Treasury. He'd already requested a quarter of a million dollars for Yoshida, an amount equal to nothing when measured against the loss of a son. He wondered how many Japanese nationals had been killed in American military accidents since the end of the occupation. The protests would begin anew. Okay, then.

He'd fallen so far from the comfort of a cockpit. From that great height, you never heard the wailing of the dying and their families.

It had been too long since he'd forced his way into a bomber—now he simply told the young guns where to fly—but that was where he felt most alive, in the cockpit. Early in his career, he'd lost the sensation of flight: In the air he *lived,* on the ground he walked. The world was always down, and heaven up, and the people you were dropping bombs on were always the soon-to-be-dead, never the living. That was the god of the bomber's mission. Burning through the sky in his B-52, sighting a target, he knew the future. He could lean down and whisper into their ears: *Soon you will be erased from this earth. Travel well.* A mind-numbing amount of destruction at his fingertips. Every pilot thought he was God; if you didn't, you'd know you were the devil. They'd grounded him during his third tour in Vietnam because he took his plane up when he wanted, he didn't attend bombing mission briefings, and he found his own targets. They were always the same as the old targets. In 1972 he bombed the same hills he'd bombed in 1966. His freelancing lasted for three weeks, and then they pulled him out for a month of R&R in Taipei. He returned to a desk job in Saigon, counting bombs. But he could not sit. He banded with his cousin, a Special Ops cowboy from the army, and that's how he caught the shrapnel in his face, way deep in the jungle, on foot, a place a bomber pilot should never land. A pilot should die before he hits the earth. That is the best death, in the air. Now he tasted war, in the form of metal ball bearings, every day. No matter what he ate, he experienced the sensation of chewing on burning metal. I would like an omelet with onions and burning metal. Thank you.

Back to football. It's Saturday. Pigskin and leg, as his college football coach had said, that's what Saturdays are for. Tackling and screwing.

He opened the playbook and wrote his game plan. Football, even high school football, was much like war. Men had been beating the hell out of one another since they first pulled themselves from that swamp somewhere in Africa, and they would always do so, and football, a controlled game with rules and officials, was one of the more civilized modern equivalents of killing your neighbor and satisfying the crowd.

His team always won, and the entire base population, even the single GIs, celebrated the victory in the dark corners of the base and just outside, in the space that he'd often inhabited as a young man, the streets and alleys and crevices and small dank apartments where cultures collided and the roll call of victims never ended— prostitutes, junkies, drunks, reefer kings, the *yakisoba* woman punched in the face for shortchanging a GI by five yen, the thirteen-year-old gang-raped by four marines, the electronics-store owner greeted with empty shelves on Monday morning, and the perpetrators of all these crimes, they, too, victims, victims of moral and cultural meltdown and their own ever-increasing stupidity and desire. He could not forbid Virginia entry into the alleys and crevices, because she knew they were there, and they called constantly, and she would wander in regardless of his protestations. He could forbid entry to a private who'd caught the clap fourteen times, and he could forbid his football team, but he couldn't forbid his daughter. The world of Japan was half hers anyway, though he'd never helped her claim it.

This afternoon they would air it out. He wanted at least two hundred yards in the air. That running back Johnson was getting on his nerves. He'd limit the kid's game time, turn him into a blocker and a diversionary presence, beat Ikebukuro with the pass, and the next week he'd be so keyed up, he'd run for two hundred yards, set a Far East record.

Kindwall wrote ten passing plays. Ten plays: all he needed to beat a team, any team. Perfect offensive execution, finesse. Eleven kids on defense who resembled baboons. Minimal penalties. Monkeyjumpers and good-night Eileens all night if they were penalized more than twenty yards. Make their mothers cry.

Dim early-morning light began to appear through the kitchen window. Beyond, still in shadow and mist, Mount Fuji tortured the population with its hidden beauty. Who was the famous printmaker? Hiroshige, *Thirty-six Views*. Kindwall assumed he'd tried so many times because he hadn't considered any of them perfect, and at thirty-six, he'd given up. Kindwall had been looking at that mountain for twelve years, and it hadn't changed. What did he expect? During the same twelve years, his daughter had grown from naïf to young woman with a drawer full of bras. No lace on the bras, he'd commanded her, but he'd never looked. That's the work of a mother.

The grandfather clock in the living room struck six, and he called Miyoko. He didn't expect her to answer. He didn't necessarily want her to answer; he'd dialed more out of curiosity than need, though the need was there. She picked up.

"Moshi, moshi," she answered sleepily.

"Miyoko. Mr. Kindwall here."

"Oliver? Why do you call so early?"

He hung up. He'd only wanted to know that she was home and alone. They had been on a date last night and ended the night at her house, as always. At three he drove home. She resented that he would not introduce her to Virginia, and he resented that she never understood why. He considered it an act of respect for the memory of Virginia's mother. No one would ever replace the girl's mother, so why try? Miyoko wanted to offer Virginia an intimate view of her maternal culture. This was the argument. Kindwall never bought it. He had been with Miyoko for seven years. Miyoko had never met Virginia. It was one of the few things the two of them fought about. And they fought about it constantly.

He decided to walk the perimeter of the base. During the first few years of his tenure, he'd walked the perimeter often. The troops thought he did it to catch a private sleeping at faraway Post Fifteen, or to discover the sergeant of the guard on a long-distance phone call to Omaha, and indeed, he'd caught the sleeping privates and the long-distance sergeants, had caught the same men again and again, but he'd never busted them. He knew that sleeping and conversations with the girl back home were essential to morale.

He pulled on a pair of GI green trousers and combat boots and a flight jacket. He was a general and this was his base, and he owned it, he owned the whole motherfucker. But on Saturday mornings, he removed his stars from the lapels of the jacket.

The canal on the other side of his residence was a favorite spot for lovers to gather during nice weather. The waste from the prior night's couples littered the slope above the canal: empty bottles of whiskey and vodka, a bra, and used condoms. At least the bastards are using condoms, he thought. How many times do we have to give them the horror stories about super-clap, tell them AIDS isn't just for butt-ringers, play the doctored videotape of the private with hamburger dick, before they decide to pull the latex over their sticks?

For the past five years, he'd been participating in a high-dollar VD betting pool with the commanders of other Far East bases: The officer with the fewest number of reported cases per quarter won the pot, with an even bigger payoff at the end of the year. He'd won the winter quarter of 1989, it was about a grand, but he'd lost the spring and summer, and the last time he checked with the chief pecker doc at the hospital, his numbers did not look good for the fall. Even some of the female personnel had begun to appear on the VD dockets, a new and shocking occurrence, and bad for the quarterly numbers. The admiral at Yokosuka would win the final quarter and the year. And wasn't he a charmed bastard, that squid, a leader of sailors who proudly admitted to having had his bore punched more than twenty times during stints in Pusan and South Vietnam.

Kindwall was walking toward the concertina-topped chain-link fence that surrounded a flight-line weapons bunker when he heard his name called. He turned around and saw an MP and, next to him, Miyoko.

"Sir, she said it was important. She threatened us with, well, with bodily harm if we didn't let her in. I thought I should escort her. I knew you'd be walking the line."

"Carry on, Sergeant Blake. I'll take the detainee from here."

The sergeant smirked and let go of Miyoko's arm.

She approached Kindwall and said, "Do not call me the detainee. Do not insult me in front of those men. Those killers." Her face was flushed red with anger and shame.

"Don't call my boys killers. Their daddies might have been

killers, and their granddaddies, but these boys haven't killed anything, not yet."

"I heard that a man at the gate is the grandson of Jones, the
Enola Gay gunner. Is that true?"

"Yes, it's true. Jones's grandson guards my base. What are you
going to do, crucify the poor kid? His grandfather dropped the
bomb over your head. His grandfather is sorry, his father is sorry,
hell, he's sorry. Leave the poor kid alone."

"You want to forget it, but it is not forgetting us." She pointed
at herself.

Miyoko was fifty-five but could have passed for a woman twenty
years younger. She ate a Japanese breakfast every morning—miso
soup, *shioyaki* salmon, rice, *tamago,* pickles—and swam laps six
days a week. She gardened at the community plot, she went to
temple, she helped her older neighbors up the stairs with their groceries, and during extreme heat and cold, she looked in on them and
sometimes had a few of them over for dinner. Her eyes were deepest black—the kind of black Kindwall imagined was at the bottom
of the sea when you died of drowning. Her eyebrows were painted
on perfectly: They looked like a sketch of the perfect eyebrow by
Hiroshige. Her nose was shaped like a teardrop. Her lips she
painted dark red every morning and throughout the day. Her neck
was muscular and inviting at the same moment. He wanted to
kiss her neck. He wanted to kiss her damaged face.

But instead he lashed out. "Why are you here? Where is your
boyfriend?" His voice hit a cruel note intended to hurt. Three
months earlier, they'd split for a few weeks, and she'd dated another
man.

"You are my boyfriend. You have to stop calling on the phone all
hours and asking my name and hanging it up. I do not sleep with
other men. I am the older woman, yes? The older woman does not
run around. She waits for her young lover!"

"I am not so young." Kindwall approached her and pulled her

near. He unzipped his flight jacket and tucked her head against his chest while she wept.

She spoke into his chest. "But you are the younger lover of me. So I wait. I put up with your selfishness and I wait. How do you like that?"

Kindwall realized that in fact he was tired of his own selfish shit. He did not like to see Miyoko cry. They'd had this fight hundreds of times. She pointing out their age difference, ten years, he claiming it didn't matter, he claiming he kept her away from his daughter in order to protect Virginia. But who was he protecting? Himself, of course.

Kindwall lifted her chin and looked into her eyes. He said, "Come home with me and meet my daughter."

Back in his kitchen, he poured two cups of coffee. He looked at Miyoko, who sat at the kitchen table, a red wool shawl thrown artfully around her shoulders. How to wear a shawl, what a simple matter! Something he never would have been able to teach Virginia. Now she might know! He'd isolated the poor girl in the world of men and the world of the military, the world of power, of white America. Her Japanese was flawless, but language did not equal culture, he knew. The grandparents on her mother's side had refused to recognize his marriage to her mother. Later, they refused to recognize Virginia. One of Olive's sisters had visited when Virginia first arrived in Japan, but that was the only time; she had refused his other invitations. He wondered if he'd have had a softer daughter now if he'd introduced Miyoko and Virginia five years ago. Virginia was not soft. For so many years, he'd been proud of this. Why? And what about himself? What if, for the last five or seven years, Miyoko had been sitting at this table for breakfast each morning? What would that have meant to him? The thought of what he'd ruined disgusted him.

Above him he heard the shower running and he knew that beneath the water his daughter stood cleaning her body.

"I will make a large breakfast for us all," Kindwall said. "The First Breakfast."

Miyoko rolled her eyes. She was used to his bad jokes. "Even in your own house, you aren't funny," she said.

"It's a house from the outside, I want to make it a home. What do you think of it?"

"It's nice, Oliver. A nice American house. Everything is so big." She gestured toward the dining room and the living rooms beyond. "I might get lost in here."

"You know Americans; we make it bigger, faster, and stronger. But I want to make a French breakfast. Omelets," he said. "French omelets. Virginia will be happy." He opened a cookbook to the index and scanned for omelets. "My mother gave Olive this cookbook when we got married. Western cuisine was not to her liking. I think she used it twice—once to burn a turkey, once to burn a cake." He laughed at the old fond memory. Then he asked Miyoko, "Is there such a thing as a French omelet?"

"Of course." She removed her shawl. "According to the French, there is a French everything. Let me help."

"Oh, no. This is my show. I'm the chef. I want a French-American omelet, not a French-Japanese omelet! Gruyère and seaweed? Hah!" He embraced her, picked her up, and spun wildly around the room.

He set her down and kissed her forehead.

She looked at him and said, "Be careful."

But he didn't understand her. He smiled. "Anything we break, we will fix. You wait in the dining room. When Virginia's out of the shower, she'll come down and want some coffee. I'll sit her down and explain it. I'll tell her that things have changed. That we're going to start a family."

"Whatever you think is best." She hugged and kissed his massive arm and went back into the dining room.

He looked out at Mount Fuji. Officers' housing had been designed so that every kitchen had a view of the mountain. He'd climbed Fuji once with some of his junior officers. Now he'd take the girls on a trip. The girls. It sounded great: the girls, the two ladies, the two women in my life. He almost forgot about tonight's football game. Hell, the assistant could run the team with his eyes closed. The guy was probably a better coach. Maybe he'd take the game off and drive the ladies to Fuji for the day. Or to the coast, to Kamakura, sushi lunch, fish fresh off the boats, one minute the salmon is a mile out in a net, and ten minutes later, the poor boy's lined up pretty in mini-fillets on sweet rice. And they'd spend the night, yes. A family weekend at Kamakura. Who on earth could argue against the purity and beauty of that?

He discovered that the French omelet was simple, two lightly beaten eggs and one added ingredient, or none, even. But he found some chives and chopped them finely. The French-omelet technique supposedly took some practice, but he was a handy guy, and he had no doubt he could master it with one try. He viewed the handle of the skillet as he used to view a plane's throttle. It was all in the motion. He laughed at himself, an American general making a French omelet. He had a cook for three meals a day during the week, but he gave her the weekends off. Fried-egg-and-cheese sandwiches, and Scotch, lasted him the weekend, and Virginia ate most of her weekend meals with friends. Time to change that.

Virginia descended the rear stairs that spilled into the kitchen. It was fair to say that General Kindwall was in love with his daughter.

"Virginia," he said. "Breakfast? ETA of five minutes." He smiled at her.

She looked at him suspiciously. "I just want coffee. I hate eggs. They're gross."

"You can't drink only coffee. Do you want to run around like an enlisted wife, juiced up on diet pills and caffeine, hair in curlers, three kids humping each leg?" He laughed at his own joke.

"You are so crass." She poured herself a cup.

"I'm sorry. These aren't simply eggs. I'm making French omelets! Woman can't live on coffee alone. Put some milk in there." He pointed at her coffee cup. "That tar I make will eat through your young stomach."

"What about you? Four pots of black a day?" Her face, still damp from her shower, had the fresh look of a meadow at dawn. "Who was here? Sussman? Damage control? I heard voices."

"I have a lifer's stomach. I could live on coffee and tobacco for forty days." He ignored her questions. He knew she'd want to talk about Yoshida's son, but he needed to avoid hot topics. He poured two beaten eggs into his buttery skillet. He had to stir the eggs lightly with a fork, just barely touching them with the tines while shaking the pan back and forth until the eggs achieved a custardy consistency. "It was just me reading the recipe aloud, a briefing for the troops," he said, keeping his attention trained on the pan.

"No. I heard a woman's voice." She looked around the room, as though she'd see a woman crouching in the corner or behind the door.

"I was doing Julia Childs."

"Why are you actually cooking? What happened to fried-egg-and-cheese sandwiches? I like them sometimes." She crossed her arms over her chest and sank into her seat.

He rolled the omelet out of the pan and onto a plate, topped it with a sprinkle of chives, and held it at arm's length for Virginia to inspect.

She said nothing.

"Perfect!" Kindwall said. "I hope you are impressed with your old and uncultured father. I have created a French omelet as good as any you will ever eat in Paris, when you finally get there." He placed it in the oven to stay warm.

"We need to taste it before that judgment can be made," Virginia said.

But she did seem impressed. He loved this kind of banter with his daughter. It rarely happened, and he was eating it up. She was a smart kid, bright and a quick thinker, a bit of a pessimist, but she'd gotten that from him. No, maybe she was just a healthy skeptic. All of her beauty and grace came from her mother. They shared responsibility for her temper.

"You are right, my dear. That was the practice run, but it was good enough for the real thing. It'll be mine. One down, two to go."

"Two to go? What does that mean?" She finally noticed the red shawl on the seat next to her. "Whose is this?" She picked up the shawl and smelled it.

"Virginia, it means we are making a family. Miyoko? Please come here and meet my daughter."

Miyoko entered from the dining room and smiled at Kindwall and then Virginia. She offered a slight bow.

Kindwall looked at his daughter. He wanted her to speak, he wanted her to run over to Miyoko and hug her, he wanted her to instantly love this woman he'd loved silently for so long. But Virginia didn't move. She sat with her arms crossed. Her face became dark red, like the desert sky at sunset.

"'Please meet my daughter'?" Virginia repeated. "Just like that? You run around and hide something from me for years, and then one morning you decide to make some French omelets and ask her to please meet your daughter? You think it's so simple? Present her like you presented your omelet?"

He leaned against the kitchen counter. "I don't think you understand what I'm trying to accomplish here."

Miyoko stood next to Kindwall with her hands crossed in front of her and her head lowered.

"Accomplish? Like a mission? I understand. You're trying to buy back seventeen years of guilt with one simple gesture—so now you can live with her in this house, and I'm supposed to feel good for you?"

"I'm trying to make a family, sweetheart. I'm trying to give you a mother. Miyoko knows a lot about you. I love her. She's a refined

36

woman. You're a young woman; she'll teach you the things I never could."

"Like what? Putting on makeup and fixing a radiator? She's a mechanic. I've watched her fix cars."

"What are you talking about?" Kindwall said.

"I've followed you on your dates. I know where she lives and works. Why didn't you do this when I was twelve?" She burst into tears. "You are such a horrible man," she screamed. She grabbed Miyoko's shawl and ran out of the house.

Kindwall reached for Miyoko. The huge man needed her to steady him, or he would fall.

Severin waited for someone inside the Kindwall house to respond to his knock. He had never knocked on the door before. He hoped that Virginia and not her father would open the door.

"Hi, Severin," General Kindwall said.

Severin looked up, surprised. The general did not look good. He looked as though he'd been crying. But that seemed impossible.

"Hello, sir," Severin said. "Virginia told me to come by this morning."

Kindwall spoke. "I don't know where she is. She ran off an hour ago. I can't go chasing her. What would that look like? Will you find her and tell her to come home?"

"I don't know where she hangs out, sir. But I'll go to town and look around. I think we were going to hang out or something."

"Or something? What is 'or something'? What is 'hang out'?" Kindwall leaned down toward Severin.

"I don't know, Coach." Severin thought that calling him "Coach" would cut some of the anger. He was right.

"Just find her, okay, boy? You have two things to do today. Find my daughter and win a football game. You have all of my confidence." Kindwall slammed the heavy wooden door.

Severin walked toward the main gate. He passed the enlisted

barracks, where guys were in the parking lot washing their cars and blaring music from the radios. Some of the guys had girlfriends with them, both American and Japanese. Most of the black guys had Japanese girls, and the white guys had white girls. The men were playing catch with a football and generally messing around, a lot of profanity, a lot of talking trash. His father had told him never to hang out with these guys. They were uneducated, and they were trouble. But his father had once been uneducated trouble, an enlisted guy, so Severin didn't know what his father's problem was. They seemed like cool guys. Many of them were good athletes. Severin respected feats of athleticism. He liked the guys except for the ones who hit on his mom at the Base Exchange. He always remembered their faces.

From behind, he heard his name being called, or some mangled version of it. "Severo. Severo." It was Virginia. He felt his feet lift from the earth.

She was in the parking lot, leaning against the door of a big Chevrolet, using it as a prop to assist with the image of herself that she constantly, unerringly, and with minor effort projected: the image of a sexy beast. Severin knew that he was the small piece of prey being torn asunder within the beast's jaws. A pleasant sensation.

"May I start calling you Severo? Doesn't that sound slick? It could be your street name, your punk name." She batted her eyelashes.

"You can call me Severo."

"Let's get out of here. Let's go downtown." She pointed to the other side of the main gate.

"What about the book I left in your van?"

"You didn't leave anything in the van. I was asking you out on a date."

Severin smiled, embarrassed.

The GI whose car she'd been leaning on interrupted. "I

thought you and me was going on a date? Come on, I never got me a general's daughter yet!"

Virginia looked at the guy, a young man with a permanent farmer's tan from decades of work on his family's farm in the Midwest. She smiled. "Next time, hayseed."

The men erupted in cheers for the general's daughter.

"Severo, since we're going on a date, I assume you brought some money?" She raised her eyebrows and led him away.

"I have ten American, that's my two-week allowance. My mom just gave it to me." He shrugged, assuming this sum would be met with disapproval.

"That's really sweet. Ten bucks. Don't worry. I'll pay. I'll always pay for you, Severo."

"Okay. I mean, you don't have to. I have more money at home. I have a lot of money. Let me get some. But do you have to say my name *every* time you talk to me? It's kind of weird, dude."

"Severo, I like your name. Let me say it as much as I want. And, Severo, please don't call me dude. I am not one of your muscle-headed football friends. I'm not going to slap you on the ass or say, 'Killer, dude.' I'm a girl, Severo. Treat me like one. Here, this is how we'll do it. I'll give you the money, and you pay."

She handed him a wad of fifties and twenties. He'd never touched a fifty before, and he tried not to act nervous. He attempted to count the bills before shoving them into his jeans pocket. He fingered the bills. He thought that maybe a fifty was thicker than a twenty, but this was not the case; all the bills felt the same. What dead president was on a fifty, anyway? Whatever the case, he had more money in his front pocket than he'd ever touched before, and he was walking off base with the general's daughter, one Virginia Kindwall, and she was holding his hand, not simply holding but *gripping*. How did this happen? He imagined that on either side of the street, the people from his life were lined up, blowing noisemakers, lighting fireworks, shouting messages of goodwill. Severo, he said to himself, don't blow this date.

But wait. He had found the general's daughter, and he was walking the wrong way with her. He was supposed to bring her home to her father. He needed to stop this wonderful date that had only just begun and turn her around. This sickened him.

An MP cruiser passed the young couple, slowed, shifted into reverse, and pulled even with them on the shoulder of the road. It was the Jones guy, Severin noticed. He was somewhat of a legend and a curiosity. He made Severin nervous.

"Hey, guys," Jones said. "Great day for the race, yeah?"

"The human race, Jones," Virginia said. "That's my dad's joke. It's not very funny."

"Boxx, how many sacks you gonna make tonight? I'll give you twenty dollars if you make four sacks. I'll give you fifty if you make five. If you guys win by more than five touchdowns, I'll throw the whole team a party in the ville. Tell your boys. And your mama."

Jones accelerated. The engine growled, and the tires clawed into the earth, kicking dust and gravel into the air. He slowed and backed up, his car even again with Severin and Virginia.

"You see what happened in Germany last week? That's the power of America, my friends. That's democracy knocking down the evil doors of totalitarianism. It's gonna happen all over the world, one way or another. China, Cuba, North Korea, the rotten prison of communism will crush under our weight. Watch out. And I'll keep you safe, Virginia!" He sped away.

"That guy is a freak," Virginia said. "He must have a death wish. General order number one is you don't try to screw the general's daughter. Same with that hayseed who spent five thousand dollars to get his Chevrolet shipped to Japan. Car is three times as big as any Japanese car. He can only drive it around base, ten square miles, at fifteen miles an hour. Where do they find these guys?"

"Have you told your father?"

"That Jones wants to sleep with me? I don't have to tell him. He knows everything. A sergeant over in the enlisted ghetto yells too loudly at his dirty-diaper kid, and my dad knows. That's how he became a general. He knows how these guys think. And he thinks for them first, so they don't blow up the world or kill someone when they aren't supposed to. At least that's how he and his general buddies talk about it. Next time they're all over, I'll invite you. Half of the world's largest military is dangling at the ends of their fingertips. They are not the sharpest tools in the shed. But they know how flyboys and squids and army doggies and jarheads think. That's why they're in charge. Between them, they've got about one hundred and fifty years of war and ten thousand corpses. And now that they've got Jones, one hundred thousand more. You know Jones's grandpa dropped the bomb on Hiroshima, right? The general eats that up. Can you believe his girlfriend is a *hibakusha*?"

"I didn't know your dad had a girlfriend."

"Today you will learn a lot."

Severin stopped walking and let go of her hand. "I went to your door. Your dad asked me to find you and bring you home."

"My own private bounty hunter. How much did he offer you?"

"Nothing," Severin said. "He's the general. He told me."

"Next lesson for today: Generals don't always get what they want. Let's get off base before he really catches me."

The pair walked briskly across the pedestrian crossing, moving from militarized zone to de facto occupied zone. They glanced at the main gate below and saw Jones staring. Virginia flipped him off, and then Severin did, and they laughed, and Severin yelled, "Stay away from my mother," and Virginia shoved him, and they laughed, and they ran the rest of the way down the pedestrian crossing and into the mad world of noodle shops and pawnshops, porn stores (video or paper, take your pick), strip clubs, whorehouses, gentleman's houses, family sushi joints, *konbini* stores, gas stations, gin and beer houses, whiskey shrines, sake fountains, military surplus stores (where the gear was not surplus but stolen, military surplus being the arena in which hundreds of supply sergeants had made their fortunes from the beginning of the occupa-

tion on September 2, 1945, until this very second; this very second
a supply sergeant and his minions were unloading in a warehouse
somewhere in Tokyo—ten dozen pallets of gas masks, two tons of
olive-drab wool blankets, four hundred cots, one Jeep, canisters of
mustard gas), tattoo parlors, hash bars, gay bars, hetero glory holes,
lesbian bars (the tough butch air force chicks loved going down on
Japanese women, lotus-flower honey, they called it), comic-book
stores, pachinko parlors, barbers, butchers, fish shops, flower shops,
and the alleys, the alleys that all led somewhere, usually down.

They caught their breath. At the nearby station a Japan Rail
train lumbered to a stop. Horns sounded everywhere. The streets
smelled like fish and flowers and sewer. It was a calamitous and
vomitous smell, and refreshingly foreign to Severin. He needed to
take a piss. He looked down the alley. It was empty. He squeezed
Virginia's hand and ran down the alley, disappearing into a smaller
alley, a tunnel, really. He leaned against the wall and pulled himself out and pissed against the opposite wall. There was a shower
window just above his head. Steam escaped from the window, and
also the sounds of two people having sex, loudly. Damn them, he
thought. They were both Japanese; he could tell by the accent in the
woman's moans and by the things the man was saying. Severin
didn't know what the man was saying because these weren't
words they taught him in elementary Japanese and cultural
exchange classes, but he knew it had to do with sex. He buckled his
belt and returned to Virginia, skipping.

She was speaking to an age-warped Japanese woman. The
woman wore a daily kimono, gray, with light green silken scenes of
cranes landing and clouds floating above. The woman's hair was
gray and gathered just below her shoulders in an enormous knot. As
Severin arrived, the woman hobbled away without looking at him.

"What was that about?" he asked.

"She is part of the Yokota Citizens' Action Committee. She
reports GI infractions of civility to my father. Disturbances and
such. She said she has further complaints. She always does.

Yoshida's dead son, major complaint. To the victors go the spoils. My dad has a budget of fifty thousand dollars a year in shut-up money. Usually, that's enough. Not this time. Protests begin next week after the funeral."

"Did you know Yoshida's son?"

"Some of my friends knew him. His parents are angry. I don't think my dad will be able to buy his way out of this one. It's too much. I can't believe it. He was our age, Severo. I'm tired of living on a military base. It's such a brutal system."

Severin had never heard anyone talk like this about the military. It was the only system he knew. "I'm sad about Yoshida's son. But it was an accident."

She looked at him with rage in her eyes. "An accident? No. They don't let the hayseed drive his Chevrolet in town because it's almost as wide as the street. But they drive those big trucks through town, tearing up the street, ripping down stop signs and business signs and finally killing a teenager. It was not an accident, Severo. That was neglect. And my father is going to pay for his neglect!"

"It's not your father's fault."

"You play football for my dad. What does he constantly tell you guys? 'Take responsibility for your actions.' It's his turn to swallow the responsibility pill."

"Your father will." Severin grabbed her hands. "He will. He's a leader. He'll take care of Yoshida."

"Can we stop talking about my father? I need to just be on a date with you."

"Do you know your way around Tokyo?" Severin asked shyly. "I only know Yokota, sort of."

"How often do you come downtown?"

"Usually with my mom, once a week to the butcher. Yoshida's, to check out electronics with Connor. My dad doesn't like to leave base when he's here. But my mom likes the shops and the food. I go to that Korean barbecue place with the football team."

"Severo, you are living in the dark ages. Do you ever go to Shin-juku or Roppongi?" she asked, her eyes wide with amazement.

He blushed. "I've never been. I mean, I know about them. My dad has to go down there sometimes to pull one of his guys out of the police box or to convince a private that he shouldn't marry an Indonesian prostitute or get her name tattooed on his forearm. But that's all I know about those places."

"Next Friday we'll go. There's more to Roppongi and Shinjuku than GIs getting bad tattoos and trying to marry hookers. My favorite *yakitori* restaurant is in Roppongi. And there are some beautiful neighborhood temples."

"What are we doing now?"

"Shouldn't you decide? You're the one with all of my money!" She playfully pushed him against a wall and pinned his shoulders. He didn't resist. He could smell her shampoo and feel her slim fingers grasping his shoulders.

"Where did you get all this money?" He reached into his pocket and pulled out a few bills.

"It's my allowance. Generals obviously give better allowances than colonels."

"Let's get some noodles. And then I'm going to have your name tattooed on my forearm." He escaped her grasp and ran down the street.

She pursued. "No, you won't, Severo," she yelled, laughing. "Your dad will kill you! My dad will kill you, too."

"I'm not hungry yet. Let's find a tattoo shop."

This was not hard for them to do. Tattoo parlors were every-where, as was the case in most of the edge communities that existed within the overlapping regions of the U.S. military and a local culture that predated the military presence by decades or even centuries. During the occupation, any guy with a sharp needle and ink could put up a tattooist's shingle. The same was true forty years later. Whether he was good or not didn't matter. If, with needle and ink, he could create a U.S. flag, the flags of the nearby military units, naked ladies with big tits riding missiles to North Korea or Russia, *with love,* and any number of cartoon characters, the tattooist was guaranteed a healthy monthly income. If, on payday, a drunken military kid wanted the Hulk but the tattooist was better at Spidey, the drunken kid would end up with Spidey. Friends would ask him why he didn't get the Hulk, his favorite comic-book character, and he'd answer, "I don't remember."

Virginia told Severin that she'd heard of a place that was good; she'd been told about it by a Japanese guy who was a recognized delinquent and had been getting tattoos since he was four.

Severin laughed. "Where do you meet these people?" He couldn't imagine knowing someone who got his first tattoo at four.

"Out here, Severo, in the world. The base, my father's fiefdom, is not the world." She pointed in the direction of the base, the place that for Severin meant safety and home. He recognized the immense gulf between the two of them, two kids who lived a mile away from each other in officers' housing. He must do the work to close that gulf.

"But I'm happy to know," she said, "that you aren't just another one of my dad's knuckle-dragging football players. Do you like those guys? They're animals."

"I like Connor and a couple others. I've known them forever. They're like brothers. Sometimes I want to beat their asses. I guess that's what brothers do. Like last night, when you walked toward me and they were playing around. But it's nice to talk to you. I've never really talked to a girl before. Except in science, for a lab, when I have to."

"I refuse to dissect a frog with you. Why do you watch me watching movies? Why don't you ask me to watch a movie with you? Wouldn't that be easier? And possibly more pleasurable for both of us?"

He was surprised she knew this. He thought he'd been so careful. "You sit there with old Sergeant Focheaux. It's weird. Like you're on dates or something. You tell him what to play, don't you? It's like your own theater. You should hear the enlisted wives bitch about that. Connor tells me what they say."

"I don't care what those women say." She waved her hand dismissively above her head. "I'm the general's daughter. Everyone talks about me. And none of it is true. Or all of it's true." She smiled at Severin, daring him to choose. "That's one of the perks of being the general's daughter. No one knows anything about me, but they think they know everything. But because they know nothing, and never will, because they will always be wrong about me, I can do whatever I want. And you shouldn't trust your little friend Connor. He's been trying to kiss me since fifth grade."

"That's dangerous. You can't do *whatever* you want. No one can do that. You still have a father who's a general. Connor?"

"Forget him. Severo, my father is a general, but he is also a *father*. I can do no wrong in his eyes. Because of my mother's death, he thinks I am *her*. And he loved her and knew she could do no wrong, that she would never hurt him. The only thing she ever did wrong was die while giving birth to me. He will never forgive her for that, and he will never forgive me for living. My father despises me because I lived. He just doesn't know it."

"Your father loves you. If he didn't love you, he wouldn't take care of you."

"Of course my father loves me. But he's also afflicted by me. He's damaged. He is psychotic. And I can't help him."

"He's a good man. He does so much for the team, for the base." Severin's voice rose to anger, and he pointed at her. "You just don't see it."

"The team and the base are not the point here." She stopped walking and shook her head. "Severin, my dad has broken my heart for the last seventeen years. And this morning he tried to make it up by bringing his girlfriend home so she could teach me how to wear this shawl." She pulled the piece of brilliant red fabric out of her purse, and it exploded against the gray of the city like a bomb. "He was too late. You'll never understand. You have two parents." She wrapped herself in the shawl.

They walked in silence.

They arrived at the tattoo parlor. A young Japanese man sat in the chair. The artist was bent over the man's torso, hard at work on his abdomen.

"That's Silver Oda," Virginia said. "He's my friend."

"Did you know he was going to be here?" Severin asked.

She ignored his question. "Look at him. Isn't he beautiful?"

"Yes," Severin said, surprising himself with his candor. "He is beautiful, strange but beautiful. How do you know him?"

Silver Oda hadn't yet noticed Severin and Virginia. The tattooist and his subject seemed to be settled deep in a coma induced by the buzz of the needle and the sting from the ink and the slowly surfacing image on the young man's abdomen. For a moment Severin imagined that, rather than applying ink to the man's skin, the tattooist was actually erasing his skin and thus exposing the art that already existed beneath the surface.

Severin looked at the examples on the walls while Virginia ventured over to the chairs to talk to the tattooist and his subject and a female tattooist lounging in an empty chair. The proprietor displayed the usual bait for military guys. KILL 'EM ALL, LET GOD SORT 'EM OUT. ON THE 7TH DAY GOD CREATED THE U.S. MARINE CORPS. U.S. AIR FORCE, DEATH FROM THE SKIES. TRAINED TO KILL BY UNCLE SAM, ORDAINED BY JESUS. One wall featured hundreds of different naked ladies. Severin thought that it might make more sense to get a poster of a naked lady rather than having her tattooed on your skin. You could change the poster whenever you wanted, while the lady on your skin was always there; you were stuck with Miss December 1984 for the rest of your life. But he liked the idea of being stuck with Virginia's name on his forearm. His father would be angry. His father had a tattoo of Popeye on his left shoulder. Severin looked at the Popeye tattoos. How foolish, he thought. Virginia came up behind him and breathed against his neck and wrapped an arm around his waist. He felt both heat and extreme cold rush through his body. Virginia kissed his neck just below his right ear.

She said, "Severo, Silver might be beautiful, but you're handsome. And you're strong. After you get my name tattooed on your arm, I'll love you forever."

And what could he say to that?

The female tattooist stood from her chair and beckoned him.

"Do you know my middle name?" Virginia asked Severin.

"No, you've never told me."

They walked toward the chair.

Virginia spoke to the tattooist. *"Konohitono udeni Sachiko te hotte kudasai."*

He sat in the chair as if he were taking a seat at the barber. The tattooist grabbed his right arm and pushed his sleeve beyond his elbow and stared at the canvas of his skin.

"It's Sachiko," Virginia said, "meaning happy child. She's going to tattoo the characters on your right forearm."

He looked at the tattooist, who was wearing black jeans cut off at the knees and a sleeveless flannel shirt. The woman's arms and legs erupted in colorful seascapes and flower blossoms.

"Will it hurt?"

"Karewa tafukai?" the tattooist said to Virginia.

"Tsuyogatteru kedo," Virginia said.

The two of them laughed.

"Only if you want it to," Virginia told Severin.

"Well, no, I don't want it to. How much is it going to cost? What did she say?"

"Fifty dollars. It's my treat. She said you look like a tough guy, *tafugai.*"

"Do you have any tattoos?" Severin asked as the gun made its first pass over his skin. He flinched.

"No," Virginia said. "Of course not. My dad would kill me."

She walked away from the chair and left Severin alone with the tattooist. Behind him he heard Virginia talking to her friend.

An hour later, at the Korean barbecue place, Severin looked at the bandage on his right forearm. Beneath the bandage, in dark green ink, the word "Sachiko" burned.

"Happy child," Severin said. "Are you?"

"I have been." Virginia took a big bite of kimchee. "What does your name mean?"

"Severin is a saint. I guess there are a few named Saint Severinus. One was tortured to death with hot rakes dragged over his back. Another is the philosopher Boethius."

She said, *The Consolation of Philosophy.*"

"But the hot-rakes guy, they named a hotel in Paris after him, it's next to the cathedral named after him. My aunt lived in the hotel with a French guy the spring before I was born. My mom passed out when I was born, they couldn't find my dad, and so my aunt named me. Severin. The location of her hot French love affair."

Virginia squinted and petted her hair. "It's kind of weird. But sexy. I like your name."

"I like yours." Severin smiled. "Enough to sign my death warrant with a tattoo. What am I going to tell people?"

"Tell them it means revolt. At some point you have to revolt. Tonight is the night, Severo. Leave football behind. Walk off the field. Don't take that abuse from my father. I know how he treats you guys, even when you win every week. Stand up. Just like I did."

"But it's different."

"Nothing is different, Saint Severinus. Revolt."

After their heavy lunch, they walked back toward the main gate.

"This is where we part, Severo," Virginia said.

"Aren't you coming to the game? Aren't you going home?"

"If I can avoid it I'm never setting foot on that base again, ever, for anything." She kissed Severin on the cheek. "Come to this party after you quit the team." She folded a note into his hand and ran into the maze of downtown Yokota, her red shawl a wake of fire.

THREE

All around Severin in the locker room, his teammates cursed and screamed, psyching one another up for the game. He was still full with Korean barbecue, and when he bent over to tie his cleats his stomach felt like a thick knot of spiced meat and rice. He inspected the red patch on the shoulder of his uniform. Kindwall called the team to the center of the locker room.

"Tonight," he said, "you're not just winning for yourselves or for me. This win will be for the entire base and the city of Yokota."

The boys screamed and pounded their fists and helmets against the lockers.

"Okay. Quiet down. While I appreciate the gesture of consolation for the Yoshida family, the red patches on your uniforms make you look like members of the Communist Youth. You're going to have to remove them. Coach Barnes has scissors. Get rid of them."

"But Coach," Severin said.

"I didn't mention other options. Get rid of the patches. It's unauthorized adornment."

Some of the players were angry, and others just wanted to play football. Severin reluctantly cut off his patch.

Severin's tattoo bled throughout the first half. His forearm pad soaked up the blood.

The Ikebukuro kids were as tough as advertised, the number

one Japanese team in the city. Coach had lobbied to play the team this year to give his boys some competition before they played the American base league teams from Guam and the Philippines and Okinawa. Most of the Japanese teams were no competition for the progeny of farm-raised and inner-city American men who'd grown up on football and meat and potatoes. But Ike-bukuro was a working-class neighborhood. They were probably gangsters' kids. Their dads ran brothels and sold stolen booze out of beat-up three-cylinder Suzuki vans. The Ikebukuro kids took cheap shots and knew how to run the clock. They played like Americans, insulting the Yokota mothers, threatening to sleep with the players' girlfriends, hitting hard and late without apology, the whole bit. It had thrown the Yokota kids off kilter for the first half.

At halftime, the mothers and fathers argued about Kindwall's treatment of their sons. The Yokota players were winning by only one touchdown, 21–14, and the parents knew that behind the bleachers, on the practice field, Kindwall would soon commence with his brand of halftime motivational speech. This angered the mothers; the fathers pretended to understand.

His boys had been stunned, but Kindwall intended his halftime show to awake the killers in them all.

Kindwall called Severin to the front and center of the locker room. "Put on your helmet," Kindwall said.

Severin put on his helmet and fastened the chin strap. He knew what was coming. Kindwall slapped his helmet hard at the sides, back and forth, back and forth, harder and harder. Severin felt his eyeballs rattling in their sockets. Kindwall stopped.

"That's for missing three tackles in a row." Then he hugged Severin and spoke quietly into his ear through the hole in the side of the helmet, as though into a dark tunnel. "That's for one quarterback sack and a blocked pass. Did you find her?"

Severin couldn't believe Coach would ask him this in the middle of the locker room. All of the other players were silent. He lied. "No, sir. I looked around Yokota. She must've gone into Tokyo."

"Find her," Kindwall said, and slapped Severin's helmet again. "As for the rest of you." Kindwall sniffed the air. "You smell good. You don't even smell like football players. You smell like ladies of the night, like you haven't allowed one drop of sweat to drop from your sweet perfumed crotches."

The players looked at one another. They knew Coach was teasing them. They waited for the fury to descend.

"My dead grandmother has got more spunk than you showed tonight." Kindwall slapped a locker, hard, and his face was full of fury, turning red, his eyes bulging. "Johnson, Hamilton, Green. You're benched. Don't even come to practice next week. You spent so much time on your knees during the first half, I'm beginning to think my star defensive backfield has been replaced with vegetable gardeners." He snatched Green's helmet out of his hands and threw it across the locker room, into the showers, where it bounced around like a bowling ball.

"The weakness you've shown is embarrassing. Do you know there's a scout here from the Guam team? He also scouts for the Pac-Ten. They'll be having some laughs over his notes on Monday and out in California when it comes time to recruit. Pulling it together in the second half does not forgive your sins from the first. Two fumbles. Twenty-five penalty yards. Dozens of missed tackles, missed blocks, missed everything. Do you think this is a neighborhood game?"

Severin looked at Jones. This wasn't as bad as it could've been. Usually, by now Coach had thrown a player or two against a locker.

"If you win this game, you are still undefeated, and there are three games remaining. Guam, Olongapo, and Kadena. If you beat all of them, we'll meet Guam in the championship. Do you want to win, or do you want to lose?"

The players shouted the word: "Win."

"Then let's work, boys. Let's remember what winning is about. Winning is about spending some time in the confession box."

This meant monkeyjumpers at the fifty-yard line of the practice field. As they exited the locker room, their cleats sounded a cadence of fear against the asphalt. With water hoses, the assistant coaches watered the middle of the field and turned the ground into a cold stew of mud and yard chalk.

Coach Kindwall stood the team on line. The stadium lights beamed brightly on the crowd in the bleachers and on the playing field. On that fifty-yard line, cheerleaders from the opposing team were in a cheer competition, and pop music blared. No pop music here, no cheers.

"I smell a football team again, anger and grass and mud," Kindwall said, surveying the players. "Conventional wisdom would tell me not to punish my football team during the halftime break, that I should allow them to save their energy for the rest of the game. But conventional wisdom does not know how tough you are. I know that punishment will only make you hungrier for the win."

In his rush out of the locker room, Severin had lost his forearm pad. He glanced at the bloody ink impression on his right arm. The name of the one girl on earth he loved now lived the rest of his life on his forearm. No one could take that away, not even Coach. Ten thousand monkeyjumpers couldn't remove the ink. Coach sprayed the players with water and called them worthless buckets of mud.

Monkeyjumpers were a complex calisthenics exercise, a hybrid of the most difficult aspect of four different exercises combined into one extreme movement: push-up, lunge, jumping jack, bend-and-thrust. Every step of the exercise looked and felt as though your body might break in half. Behind and in front of the players, the assistant coaches yelled while Kindwall counted the cadence. Between sets, he lectured on the essentials of playing winning football—fit minds and bodies, the killer spirit, sportsmanship but not at the cost of victory.

They'd done two hundred monkeyjumpers. At the other fifty-yard line, the cheerleaders continued to shout their upbeat cheers. The people in the stands clapped for the excellent display of team spirit and school pride.

"Okay, ladies, Wailing Jennys!" Kindwall yelled at his team.

The Wailing Jenny was named after a firework. You squatted and then exploded upward in a jumping-jack motion, only to recoil into the squatting position, where you waited to explode again. And on and on.

The players continued the muddy dance.

"Cherry Pickers, your favorites. Are you about ready to play football? Twenty-four more minutes is all I ask of you."

"Yes, Coach!" the players yelled.

At a pause in the action, Coach stood in front of Severin. Severin had tried to cover his forearm with mud to hide the tattoo, but he had sweated off the mud. He was on his hands and knees. Coach squatted in front of him. He reached toward Severin's right forearm and wiped away some of the remaining mud, exposing the tattoo.

"What do we have here, Severin boy? A tattoo? Have you joined a criminal element? The revolution? Do your parents know? What does it say?" He slapped the tattoo.

Severin knew what he was supposed to say: "Sir, the tattoo means 'revolt.'"

But he had been taught that the lie was worse than the crime. Though he wasn't sure he believed this, he didn't have time to think about what he believed.

"Sir, the tattoo says Sachiko, which means 'happy child.'"

Kindwall stared blankly at Severin. Severin wondered two things: Had he actually said what he'd heard himself say, and if so, how long would it take Kindwall to comprehend this?

Kindwall stood and said, "Why on earth would you get my daughter's middle name tattooed on your arm, Boxx?"

Kindwall never used Severin's last name.

Still, he could not lie. "Because I love her, sir."

Angrily, Kindwall said, "Boy, every swinging pecker on this football field loves her, and half my airmen. But none of those numbnuts ever tattooed her name on their arm. Jesus Christ. What makes you so special?" He kicked mud in Severin's face and walked away, continuing the punishment farther down the line.

Severin licked the mud from his teeth and spit it out. It was nothing he hadn't tasted before. But he knew that Kindwall's mild reaction would eventually boil into full-throttled rage.

"Monkeyjumpers," Kindwall screamed. As the mud ballet continued, Kindwall greatly increased the tempo. The boys prepared to play winning football, he ordered them to stand, and then, at a sprint, he led them back onto the playing field, past the chorus of cheerleaders and their pleading to win, win, win.

On the first defensive play, Severin called a linebacker blitz. He plowed through an offensive guard and sacked the quarterback. It was a perfect tackle: He slammed his shoulder into the kid's abdomen and grasped his waist and buried him in the muddy field.

Severin's face was bloodred.

In the huddle, Connor looked at him and said, "Dude, what's going on?"

"What's happening is we are going to win this football game. Linebacker blitz."

Smith said, "You got her name tattooed on your arm? You moron. He's going to kill you."

"Blitz," Severin whispered with fury.

This time Figgins led the blitz and hit the quarterback hard. He fell on top of the kid and buried his face mask in mud. The ball was loose, and Figgins yelled, "Fumble!" Severin was still fighting with a guard when he saw someone with his jersey color land on the ball.

The Yokota crowd went wild. Severin thought of his father, absent from the bleachers, flying his plane somewhere in the great yonder.

From the sideline, he watched their quarterback go to the air, with much success. A twenty-yard reception. A fifteen-yard reception. A seven-yard toss to the tight end for a touchdown.

He tried to get the attention of Coach, but Kindwall ignored him. The defensive coach walked by and slapped him on the ass. "Keep calling whatever plays you want Boxx. Good boy."

On the kickoff team, Severin ran down the field like a man on fire. His breath was hot, and he felt the sting of blood on his forearm. He looked for the runner, he looked for the runner. He found him cutting cross-field. The runner juked Connor, the runner juked Smith, and Severin centered on him; he was five yards out, he screamed, he was a yard out, he screamed, he hit the kid so hard that both of their helmets flew off their heads. But the kid held on to the ball.

In the huddle, Severin called another linebacker blitz.

"We can't blitz every time," Connor said.

"I'm the captain. We blitz whenever I say. Blitz."

This time they saw it coming. The offensive tackle cross-blocked Severin and knocked him to the ground, and the fullback clobbered Figgins. They completed a pass for fifteen yards.

"Okay," Severin said in the huddle. "Blitz fake."

The linebackers ran up on the line of scrimmage and dropped back at the snap. Severin threw a legal block on the tight end and with the tips of his fingers he intercepted a beautiful spiral meant for the end, and he returned it for a touchdown. The opposing team didn't even breathe on him. Fifty-five yards. His teammates gathered around him in the end zone and slapped his helmet and ass and yelled his name. He looked at the crowd, absent his father. He looked at the sideline and Kindwall, who was walking in the opposite direction, not even looking at Severin, eyes on the ground. The celebration in the end zone was dying off and Severin thought of Virginia, and he thought of revolt and Boethius, and the halftime torture that Kindwall had put them through, and he decided he'd run his last play. He looked into the stands for his mother, usually seated alone or with Johnson's mom near the fifty-yard line, about ten seats up. He wanted to wave to her. But he couldn't find her. The referee was motioning for Severin to throw him the ball. The special-teams guys were lining up for the kickoff. Severin dropped the ball in the end zone and took off his helmet and dropped it. He ripped off his jersey and shoulder pads and his half-shirt. He kicked off his cleats, and took off his socks, and he wiggled out of his football pants, thick with pads. He took off the girdle, with the bulky hip pads. He stood there in the end zone in his jockstrap.

The stadium turned quiet. The referees and the special-teams guys, and the players on the sidelines and the families in the crowd looked at Severin. Under the bright lights of the stadium, he stood naked except for his jockstrap and cup.

Finally, Kindwall spoke. "What in the hell are you doing, boy?" he yelled. "Put on your uniform and finish this game. What are you doing to me?"

Severin smiled. He smiled at the brute coaches and the brute players and for the first time since third grade he thought he might be above the brawl, above the messy punch and counterpunch, above the fray. Love had done this to him. He was ridiculous, he was a nearly naked fool. He knew that love had corrupted the spirit of his boyhood, the valor of his youth, and he felt as though he'd aged a decade that afternoon and evening. Severin was smart enough to consider the possibility that this love was an illusion and that what waited for him at the end of the love alley was humiliation and pain and an old faded tattoo in a language not his own, but he was not smart enough to rejoin the safety of his boyhood on the playing field in front of him. Nor was he smart enough to run away from this girl. Sex love, girl love. His friends, boys he loved with boy love, they were welcome to continue the game. He stood in the chilly fall night and felt the cold mud of the end zone between his toes—his nipples so cold they stung, his balls crawling out of the cup and into his body, the tip of his dick burning cold. Pinpricks of blood continued to rise to the surface of his tattoo.

The silence turned to booing. He surveyed the crowd for his mother but could not see her. The booing was deafening, and he walked toward the locker room, cold, alone.

The kickoff whistle blew and profanity and shrill screams of pain and elation echoed around the stadium like wild cyclists speeding at the upper lanes of a velodrome. Above all of the noise he heard his mother yelling his name. In the dark locker room he showered and dressed and escaped out the back door.

Football players had been banned from airmen parties, not only by Coach but also by their parents, so Severin had never been to one. At the start of each season, all players signed a contract pledging their allegiance to high standards of dress and behavior, a 2.8 GPA, not to use drugs or alcohol, and to avoid all parties where drugs and alcohol were being used, which meant all airmen parties. After signing the contracts, in a ceremony that closely resembled military induction, complete with a U.S. flag and a scratchy album version of "The Star-Spangled Banner," the boys repeated all of the tenets that daily guided the morality of a Yokota High School gridiron hero: discipline, fidelity, sobriety, honesty . . . The list went on for several pages, culled by Coach Kindwall from military officer training manuals.

The riffraff of the high school, the kids who wore black and smoked cigarettes and pot and committed petty crimes in the city, were not members of athletic teams and their parents were absent or too busy raising younger siblings or protecting Japan to notice that their children were pot smokers and petty criminals. Some of the parents were themselves pot smokers and petty criminals, so they might not have noticed the behavior of their children as abnormal or miscreant. These outcast dependents were, of course, members of a minority, but a very powerful minority. Whatever was hip about America, whatever aspect of Americana that Japanese youth wanted to attach themselves to, was owned by the on-base outcasts, both dependents and airmen. The hip Japanese youth did not want to wear khakis and oxford shirts. Leaving the base, walking across the raised pedestrian walkway between the land of the DOD and the land of *yakisoba* stands and sex clubs, the outcasts became socialites: for some, the pedestrian walkway was the Birth of the Cool.

Severin clutched the directions in his left hand and a can of green tea in his right.

He crossed the pedestrian walkway and looked for the address that Virginia had given him that afternoon. It was only eight P.M., and the streets of Yokota were bright with neon lights and the drunken swagger and shake of partyers. He could smell the excitement. Earlier in the day, the same street had smelled like rotten fish and sewer, and now it smelled like liquor and love and abandonment. Airmen populated the strip, most of them on dates with Japanese girls. Some walked with Filipino or Thai women. Severin knew that those women were prostitutes from the bars named Manila Action and Bangkok Delight. One July evening, when very drunk, Johnson's father had proposed to take the two boys to Bangkok Delight, and they'd accepted his offer, but the elder Johnson had passed out before putting on his boots, to the boys' great relief.

Severin found the building. The apartment he wanted was on the third floor. Graffitos had colored the stairwell with the names of U.S. military units and Japanese new-wave and punk bands—Pablo Picasso, Go Go Freedom, Momoya & the Lizards, Mirrors, 344th Bomber Squadron—and occasionally, the name of a favorite drug was accompanied by a pictorial replica of someone injecting or smoking or snorting the substance. At the second-floor landing, a young Japanese guy with a Mohawk kissed and fondled an American military woman. The door to the third-floor apartment was open, and Japanese punk music assaulted Severin's ears. He entered. Smoke hung over the heads of the revelers in a green and blue cloud, and he smelled tobacco and pot. A mosh pit had formed in the middle of the main room. The female vocalist was yelling "Monkey dance" again and again. Men ran in circles around the pit, throwing elbows and catching elbows and being castigated and pushed and punched by the encircling crowd. Occasionally, a woman entered the circle and took a few laps and a beating. Severin noticed many American faces in the crowd, all of them younger GIs, men or women who worked for his dad on the flight line, MPs on the front gate who waved his mother in when the Suzuki van was full of groceries and goods from downtown, a nurse, the dental hygienist who had cleaned his teeth last week, a clerk from the general's staff. Severin had never been drunk or high, but he assumed most of these people were one or both. Many of the men were shirtless, their bodies covered with tattoos in the *yakuza* style, with an even displacement of typical military ink as well, cartoon characters and missiles and airplanes and pinup girls. Some wore jewelry in their ears or faces, places where he hadn't seen people wear jewelry. To his left, a thick GI kid with a shaved head, no more than two years older than Severin, was displaying his pierced penis to a young Japanese girl. The girl and Severin winced, and the American kid, from Des Moines or Omaha or Oklahoma City, beamed with pride. Someone passed Severin a bottle of whiskey. He held it at his side as though he knew what to do with it. He had never felt so alone.

The dental hygienist approached him. "Hey," she said. "Didn't I clean your teeth last week? You and your mom."

"Last Friday."

"You got a cavity on number thirty, right? What are you doing here? Aren't you a football star?" She wasn't waiting for an answer. She violently shook her head to the music. "I love Japanese chick punk. It's the next wave."

"I was a football star. I quit tonight."

The hygienist screamed loudly, lifted a bottle to her lips, and slapped Severin on the back. "Your former coach's daughter is here somewhere. She's cool for being a general's daughter. She is definitely not Dependent of the Year. Watch out."

The hygienist disappeared, absorbed by the crowd. Severin held the bottle at his side but didn't drink from it. He'd tried a few sips at Johnson's house the night Johnson's father had passed out after offering to take the boys to a whorehouse. They'd finished the old man's bourbon, about a quarter of an inch of the amber liquid. Severin had felt a little funny for half an hour, and then he'd felt sick for the rest of the night. He didn't consider that having been drunk, just sick and dizzy. He had no desire for a repeat experience. He poured the whiskey on the floor, and no one noticed. Some of it slopped against his socks and into his shoes.

He wore a long-sleeved shirt and decided against rolling up his sleeves and revealing his tattoo of the general's daughter's name, the Not Dependent of the Year. He knew that the tattoo would score him big points, that he wouldn't be just another square football player if the GIs saw the ink on his arm, but he also knew the role Virginia played in the mythos and fear of the enlisted corps, and he had no idea how they'd react to her name on his arm. He could say it meant revolt, but why? Why had Virginia told him to lie? He realized he knew nothing about Virginia and this world.

Okay! He'd find Virginia and convince her to leave with him. He carried the empty bottle at his side like a weapon.

Steven, a stoner kid from his calculus class, bumped into him. "What the hell are you doing at a party like this?" Steven yelled. "I thought you guys weren't allowed to go to off-base parties. If you're looking for Virginia, she's in a back room with some dude named Silver. That guy's crazy. He spray-painted his hair silver. You should see it. I gotta get some more weed. See you later. Dude, loosen up."

Severin watched Steven stumble out the door and down the stairwell. He hadn't penetrated farther than five feet into the party. He wondered what Virginia was doing in the back room. He didn't want to know, but nor did he want to wonder, so he fought his way through the increasingly violent and raucous crowd. Beer and liquor spilled on his body, and the deeper he moved into the crowd, the worse the place smelled, like vomit and sweat and alcohol and dope. The middle of the apartment smelled worse than the street had that afternoon. He was exhausted from the football game and the punishment from Coach, and though he hadn't drunk or smoked, he felt high, he thought. He ventured too close to the mosh pit and caught an elbow to the jaw, but it didn't faze him. He fought his way toward a hallway that he assumed would lead to the bedroom and Virginia. The bathroom door had been ripped off its hinges, and there was a guy pissing in the sink; in the tub a Japanese girl was on her knees giving a GI a blow job. Severin stopped and watched. The blow job recipient insisted that Severin high-five him, so he did. The guy pissing didn't seem to notice or care about the sex act occurring to his right.

The GI in the tub finished and high-fived Severin again and screamed, "I work for your dad! I'm his fuel man! This is my girl-friend, Yoko!"

Severin said, "Nice to meet you," in Japanese. He stood stupidly still for a moment, staring, making certain he remembered every detail of the absurd exchange, and took his leave.

He noticed someone wearing a motorcycle helmet exit the back bedroom, then realized that it wasn't a helmet but someone's hair. It was the guy named Silver from the tattoo parlor, and he'd indeed painted his hair silver.

He said to Severin, "Your girl is in the bedroom. Man, don't do any of the drugs here. GIs buy cheap trash. If you ever want to get high, I'll get clean stuff for you. I want to see your tattoo when it heals." He slapped Severin on the back, like an older brother might.

Silver disappeared into the crowd. The punk music continued to blare. Severin carefully walked down the hallway, stepping over embracing couples and passed-out singles. He opened the door to the back bedroom and found Virginia in bed alone. He closed and locked the door behind him and switched on the light, and she shielded her eyes and pleaded with him to turn it off. Her clothes were in a bundle on the floor, a black puzzle of motorcycle jacket and T-shirt and skirt and tights. He knew what the pieces of the puzzle looked like but wondered who had taken it apart and if he'd ever have that chance. With the lights off, some of the neon from the street infiltrated the room, spilling red on the bedsheet.

"Severo," she said.

"What did you do?"

"Jones gave me some bad pills. I don't know why I took them. They started to mess me up. Silver found out I'd taken them, and he gave me something to make me throw up."

She pointed toward the window, and Severin saw that she hadn't made it all the way to the sill before vomiting.

"What was it? Will you be okay?"

"I'll be fine now. Some kind of speed. He got it from one of the nurses. Silver says the military stuff is bad."

"Why'd you take it?" He shook his head as he asked.

"I know you can't understand. But it's not bad to want to get high sometimes."

"I escaped tonight," he said proudly.

"What do you mean?"

"I quit the football team."

"Revolt! Before or after the game?"

"During. Your dad was angry, and he tortured us at halftime. I knew he'd do the same after the game. I wanted to get out of there and come see you. So I left. I made an interception and returned it for a touchdown. And then I took off my uniform in the end zone and walked off the field naked, except my jockstrap."

"Wow, you really did it in style. What did they say?" She was smiling as she asked.

"The crowd booed me. I heard my mom calling my name when I was in the locker room. She must have been in the corridor, but I left through the back." He was ashamed of having eluded his mother.

"Severo, my dad is going to be so pissed. What about your

dad? What about your friends?" She sat up in bed and clasped her knees to her chest.

"My dad doesn't go to my games. I don't know anything except I wanted to get out of there and come see you and I'm tired of football. Everyone will be pissed. I don't want to go home tonight."

"I don't want to, either. Silver is coming back in a while with a car, and he'll drive us to his apartment in Shinjuku."

"I told your dad what my tattoo means." He pulled up his sleeve and looked at the ink. A scab seemed to be setting on the tattoo.

"What did he say?"

"I told him I loved you. And he said that every swinging dick on the football team and half of his GIs loved you but that they weren't dumb enough to tattoo your name on their arms."

"He has a point, Severo. But I love your tattoo."

Severin sat down on the bed and rested his back against the headboard and pulled Virginia's head into his lap. He realized that she had said she loved the tattoo, not that she loved him. But that was okay. Love would come. Wouldn't it? That was why he was sitting here, why he had walked off the football field.

He could faintly smell her vomit, but he didn't care. The party continued at full speed on the other side of the door. He looked at her clothes in their bundle and almost wept at his confusion. He knew that someday he must understand the puzzle.

She said, "Severo, I didn't sleep with anyone. Silver took my clothes off and put me in the bathtub after I threw up."

"What do you need from me?" he asked.

"I need you here." She moved the sheet down to her waist, exposing her breasts. She took his hands and placed them on her breasts. "God, your hands are so warm. It feels so good."

In the palm of each hand, he felt a nipple growing hard. He removed his hands to her sides, gripping her ribs, because he wanted to look. They were lovely breasts. His heart rate climbed.

His mouth watered. He got hard, an animal response he had no control over. A pretty woman half covered by a white sheet. Beneath the sheet, her hips and legs sculpted the topography of his desire. He knew that few things in the world contained as much beauty and possible fulfillment as the scene in front of him. From above, he looked at her beautiful face and her beautiful breasts and thought he would do anything for her.

FOUR

Colonel Boxx and his wife sat at opposite corners of General Kindwall's couch, and Father Carboy, the parish priest, sat between them. The general sat hunched on a side chair. As the priest's prayer ended, the four people let go of one another's hands. The prayer had been for the safe return of Virginia Kindwall and Severin Boxx. It was now Sunday at four in the afternoon. Colonel Boxx had flown in from Taiwan an hour ago. The general was drunk and had been since the prior night at about eight P.M., just after Severin Boxx walked off the field, disgracing football and the U.S. Air Force and America all at once.

"Well, Padre," the general said. "What we have here is a bogus mission with very little advance intelligence. Should we bomb the bastards or let them come in on their own?"

"General, as your priest and your friend, I advise you to drop the military jargon. We're talking about your daughter, not an enemy supply line. Sir, let's be serious."

"I am one hundred and ten percent serious." Kindwall closed his eyes as if thinking, but really, he was trying to find a sliver of sobriety. "I can send intelligence after the little twirps, or we can starve them out. They've got one set of clothes on their backs. They have neither pillows nor a pot to piss in. Boxx, what do you think?"

"Sir, I say we let them come in on their own," Colonel Boxx replied. "If you call intelligence, then the whole base will know. This could be embarrassing for you and hurtful to your career. Severin is a tough kid, and I know he won't let anything happen to

Virginia. This is an innocent charade." He needed to convince himself and the general of this. He went on, "A little escape, a test of authority, a game."

Mrs. Boxx looked scornfully at her husband. She was disheveled—normally, at four in the afternoon on a Sunday, she would be totally composed, well dressed, ready for gossip and a meal out in town with friends after mass. She said, "We're talking about two seventeen-year-olds. They have run off somewhere together. They didn't run away to play catch."

Colonel Boxx looked at his wife as though he wanted to gag her.

Kindwall said, "Your naked son. What happened to that boy? He better not touch her."

"General," Father Carboy said, "let's concern ourselves with their safety before we worry about touching."

"Bugger you all," Kindwall said. "Get out of my house. I'll call you when I've found the kids. I'm using all available firepower."

Kindwall's chief of staff, Colonel Sussman, and two of his junior officers arrived a short time later and Kindwall ushered them to seats at the dining room table. Miyoko appeared as if out of nowhere with *gyoza,* a large plate of sushi, and a bowl of *yakisoba* and plates for everyone. Then she disappeared. The other men declined her offer of food and sat silently while the general ate.

Kindwall looked at the men watching him eat. "That's Miyoko. The cat's out of the bag. She's my girlfriend. I guess everyone knew anyway. Even my daughter knew. I've lost my stealth touch."

"I knew five years ago, sir," Sussman said.

"Sherlock Holmes," Kindwall said with a dark sigh.

"Why did you take so long?" Sussman asked.

Kindwall knew that Sussman, a good officer and a good man, was concerned about his welfare. But Kindwall ate in silence. He hadn't eaten since Saturday morning, when he and Miyoko had eaten their French omelets in silence after Virginia fled. He hoped the food would sober him up, though he knew this was unlikely.

Still, he needed either to get sober or to continue drinking. He thought about the time, near the end of his last tour in Vietnam, when he and an army major had stayed drunk for thirteen days straight. He couldn't remember why they'd decided to do so, whether there'd been a conscious decision to abuse their bodies and brains in such a fashion, but he knew that in a sick way, he and his fellow major had both been proud of their accomplishment, if it could be called that. When they finally got sober, they celebrated by throwing beer bottles and whiskey bottles through every window in the four-bedroom apartment they rented in downtown Saigon. They each paid the honcho five hundred dollars for the damage. He wondered what had happened to that major. Now he picked up a half-full bourbon bottle and threw it through his dining room window.

"Sir," Sussman said, looking nervously at his men. "What can we do for you?"

"Call the civil engineers and get them to fix that ASAP. My daughter is missing, and you three men are now in charge of finding her. I suspect that last night she went to a GI party in town. I also suspect that Severin Boxx, my onetime star linebacker, attended the same party and that at some point he convinced her to run away with him. It is possible the two of them are using drugs. It's very unlikely that they are armed and dangerous. He is a dumb football player trying to get laid. Please consider the clock to be running as of fifteen hours ago. No one other than the four of us, the Boxx family, and the padre knows about this. Let's keep it that way for as long as possible. Colonel, report to me every four hours. Dismissed."

"Yes, sir," Sussman said, and led his men out of the house.

Kindwall rolled over in bed. He looked at Miyoko. What on earth was she doing with him? It was ten P.M. Sunday, and he'd at last reached a sober state. First he thought about Saturday's game. A few of the plays that had failed ran across his brain, and he thought about the better plays he should've called. He thought about all of his mistakes, the replacements called too late, the pass play that should have been a run. He didn't understand why his defensive coach had let Severin Boxx call the plays, although, admittedly, Severin Boxx had done a fine job of calling plays, not to be confused with his skill in choosing a tattoo. For a moment he thought about the punishment he had handed out to his players, but he never second-guessed punishment. Contrary to popular opinion, he never enjoyed putting the kids through hours of mental and physical trials after a less than overwhelming win. He had been coached that way, and he in turn coached with severe disciplinarian measures as the answer to every mistake. He knew the mothers and even some of the fathers resented his style, but he did not care. Style did not matter. Winning mattered. Slaughtering the opponent mattered. Just like in the military. Helping the VC had not been the mission. Goodwill had not been the mission—killing as many of the enemy as possible with superior firepower and tactical wisdom had been the mission. When the war ended, the enemy could be your friends, your lovers. The same would hold true if Bush gave the call to invade China or North Korea or Russia. And you could continue down the list. People didn't understand the risks. Even his subordinates who should have known better were unversed in the dangers of the year, the threat of the moment, the eternal possibility of being asked to fight and kill. Most of the senior officers across the services had done time in Vietnam, but this was not true of the younger blood, the younger hounds—the actual fighting bastards who'd get bloody in the next one. He did not like that Reagan had pulled out of Lebanon after those poor marine boys had been killed. The bombing was a tragedy, and Reagan had had the steel balls to go in front of the country and accept responsibility for the horrible loss of life, but the withdrawal had promoted the wrong message, a surrender doctrine that could be interpreted as weakness and an unwillingness to fight. The U.S. still stared down the North Koreans. Where would the next war take him? Would it even take him, or was he now so old that he'd simply watch from the stables, chewing hay, scratching his balls, farting? These were the same thoughts that crowded his mind every night. Sleep, you old bastard, he told himself. He looked across his pillow at Miyoko, sleeping on her side, her hair covering her face like a black theater curtain. He was happy to have her in his house after all of these years. He felt sorry for the time they had lost. He wondered if she would want to move in. They hadn't talked about it, he'd just assumed, since she had complained for years about his secrecy. But now Virginia was gone. Was that it, he'd spent his entire life trading one woman for another, his mother for Olive, Olive for Virginia, Virginia for Miyoko? What did this say about him?

But Virginia was not asleep in the back room. He sat up. Where on earth could she be? And why had Severin, one of his most trusted kids, thrown his uniform in the end zone and disappeared, naked? His first thought was drugs. He knew that Virginia experimented, a little pot but who cares; it seemed totally unlike Severin to touch drugs or even alcohol. Could it be that Kindwall knew Severin better than he knew Virginia? He got sick and angry when he thought about his star linebacker and his daughter together in a bed somewhere. Maybe they were in one of those cheap hotels off the Base Drive. Sussman and those LTs better find them. I can't go running around the sluthole motels looking for my own kid. Word would get out I was looking for a street whore. Sussman, you better find her. Out the window, he watched gray light from the city filter through a slight fog. He moved toward Miyoko and buried his face in her thick hair. He breathed in her scent and tried for the moment to forget his daughter and the trouble he had caused. Miyoko moaned herself awake and nudged her body closer to his, and he pulled her on top of him and kissed her deeply and felt her warm heavy breasts on his chest.

She said, "This is what you need."

At midnight the doorbell rang, and Kindwall stumbled downstairs in long underwear. His chief of staff stood under the glowing orange porch light. Kindwall let him in. The two men sat at the dining room table.

Sussman said, "We've got some leads on Virginia and Severin. They're running with a Japanese guy named Silver, small-time hustler. We'll have them in by the morning. Honestly, it sounds pretty innocent. But we've got bigger troubles. I think we've got some North Koreans in-country. There are reports of kidnappings in Matsue, Ikebukuro, Chiba City, and Shinjuku, two men and two females, one in her twenties, one an adolescent. This is the same makeup of the last group the North Koreans kidnapped for language services. All kidnapped in broad daylight, a silver Mercedes without plates, nobody dead."

"What are the leads?"

"I gave you the leads. The FBI is assisting the Japanese police with the search."

"Do the papers know?"

"Preliminary reports are running on NHK radio. The world will know in the morning. It's time for you to call a press conference, to speak about both Friday's accident and what seem to be kidnappings. The bad will from the accident is starting to boil over. Last night in town three airmen got beaten by a motorcycle gang. If we find the missing Japanese, we look like angels and geniuses."

"Angels and geniuses." Kindwall exhaled. "When was the last time anything this military of ours did that made us look like angels and geniuses?"

"Just looking for the spin, sir, the bright side of the darkness we create. That's what you pay me for."

"September 1945 was the last time. Chewing gum and chocolate. Why do we want the kidnappers to know we know they're here?"

"This works with us rather than against us. Deflection," Sussman said. "The only people Japanese hate more than GIs is Koreans, especially Communist North Koreans who are here to steal their children and mothers and fathers."

FIVE

Silver lived in a one room, eight-mat apartment in Shinjuku, eight tatami mats being the floor-space measurement. The eight mats didn't include the half-mat kitchen and the half-mat bathroom.

Virginia woke as the Sunday-morning street life below the window erupted. She could smell and taste the exhaust from idling delivery trucks; the noise from car and scooter horns made an urban music that Virginia was not used to in the morning. Her father made the morning music she knew: grotesque male body sounds, a quick shower, a pot of coffee, the morning paper, cursing at world leaders. No view of Mount Fuji from Silver's window.

Still lying prone, she eyed the two other people in the room, Silver and Severin. Severin would probably stay away from home only for another day or two, three at the most. Silver had work for them tomorrow, she knew. She didn't know what it was. Silver had been running with a Korean gang and had been looking for a big break, and he'd told her that he had found it. This would mean an increase in the danger she put herself in. She wanted this, the danger. What she liked about Silver was that he'd never tried to sleep with her. He'd never asked her for a favor through her father. He'd simply been her friend. That was why she stole for him. It was easy, work for a friend—exciting and totally contrary to everything her father had ever taught her. She had to admit her desire to hurt her father.

Silver sat up on his futon. "Virginia, what do you say we go buy groceries and make some breakfast for the football player? Soon he will be back on the, what do they call it, big iron? Crushing his opponents. He needs nutrition! He also needs some petrol jelly for his tattoo."

"Gridiron," Severin said from under his covers. "It's called gridiron. And I'm not going back to play football. This tattoo hurts, man."

"It's because you dumbassingly played football three hours after you got it. They are right that football players are a certain breed of genius. Cow breed!"

"Okay. Enough football jokes. Can't I go with you for the groceries?" Severin asked.

"I don't want to go grocery shopping," Virginia said. "I hate grocery stores. You men go do it. That would be very forward-thinking of you." She stood and looked out the window onto the small alley crammed with people and machines and goods. "Do the shopping, come back and cook for me, and then do the dishes. We'll run a utopian test world."

"Your utopian test, baby," Silver said. "In my utopia, candy jars of good pills rest on every table, and naked Korean women with big tits feed me the pills and pull down my shorts for a turn. I'm so tired of Japanese chicks. No offense to you, Virginia, you're half American, it's different." He looked at Severin and said, "I'm half Japanese, half Korean. So basically, I'm always at war with myself. But Japanese girls just lean back and moan and let you do your thing. I miss Seoul. Whatsa matter, white boy? Are you afraid of me?"

"No. Let's go!" Severin said.

The two men careened down the stairs.

Virginia took a shower in the stall that was so small she barely fit. It looked like a bowl for cleaning and clipping poodles. She rifled through Silver's cabinet until she found a razor and shaving cream to shave her legs. The same brand her father used; the thick white lather exploded into her hand. It looked like whipped cream. With the shower curtain open, the mirror was just a foot away from her. For fun, she lathered her face. She laughed at herself in the mirror. She wondered if her father regretted not having a son because he'd missed moments like this, the moment when the father teaches the son how to shave. Did he coach football to have all of those sons? Well, he'd never taught her how to shave her legs, and he could have, it was the same science, right? He could have taught her to shave her legs, but one day, after he'd commented the night before that the peach fuzz on her legs looked more and more like a bamboo thicket, a twelve-pack of pink Daisy razors and a putrid girlish-smelling shaving cream had appeared on her bathroom vanity. The only time she'd seen women shaving was on TV commercials. The first few times she'd absolutely slaughtered her legs. Along her left shin, a scar attested to her initial missteps with the lather and blade. Now she began to shave her face. As a girl, she'd watched her father shave nearly every morning before he went to work. He usually didn't shave on Saturdays but always shaved on Sunday before mass. She liked the feeling of the blade running down her cheek. She took care of her upper lip with a few smooth strokes. At her left jawline, just below her ear, she nicked herself, and blood raised to the soft flesh like a blush. She washed her face in the running shower and felt a slight pulse at the wound. She looked at her freshly shaved face and decided that was enough shaved skin for the day, so she skipped her legs and armpits. She applied a small piece of tissue to her cut, just as she'd seen her father do countless times.

Silver let her keep clothes in his closet. She chose a plaid miniskirt. In his clothes, she found a black T-shirt that professed in white block letters I AM A CAT. She'd read a novel with this title freshman year of high school. Soseki was the writer. The first two sentences were "I am a cat. As yet I have no name." She remembered liking the novel and the cat narrator. She was not particularly fond of cats, in fact she did not care for them at all, had never met a real cat that she liked, but she'd liked the cat in the novel. She wondered where Silver had found such a cool shirt. He didn't seem like a reader. There were no books in his apartment.

"I am a cat," she said. "As yet I have no name."

She was pleased with this statement. It seemed to fit her life perfectly at this moment. Of course, she was not a cat and she knew her name perfectly well, but the idea of being a nameless cat still attracted her. She looked at herself in the mirror and meowed.

She said, "I am a cat. As yet I have no name."

Silver and Severin entered. Silver unloaded the groceries and pronounced, "Today, dear Virginia, in honor of your lineage and in apology for my earlier disparaging remarks about how Japanese girls screw, we will eat a good old-fashioned Japanese breakfast. Broiled mackerel and miso soup. Not American Budweiser-and-Marlboros breakfast, like most days."

"Thank God," she said.

"Where did you get that shirt?" Severin asked Virginia.

"From Silver's dresser. Remember reading this book freshman year?"

"I think so." Though he looked perplexed.

"It was my favorite book. I feel like a cat. But I shaved my whiskers earlier!"

"What are you talking about?"

"While you men were gone doing womanly chores, I did manly things. I shaved my face. Look." She proudly displayed her shaving wound.

"You are strange," Severin said. "Why on earth would a girl shave her face? I don't even shave. I mean, I've shaved like three times my whole life."

"Did your father teach you?"

"Yeah. He had me watch him and then do my own face. But it was just like when he taught me how to mow the lawn. You know, he had his way, and it was the only way to do it. There must be other ways to shave your face. But I haven't tried them yet."

"I just thought I'd see what you men do. It was fun. Smell my face."

Virginia leaned toward Severin and offered her cheek for him to smell. He inhaled and lightly kissed her ear. She smiled.

"You smell like my grandpa," he said.

"Hey, Grandma and Grandpa," Silver said. "Breakfast is ready in five minutes."

Virginia set the table.

The pieces of mackerel that Silver placed on the table steamed. They were charred black, alongside a big mound of grated radish. In her bowl of soup, the miso floated in the broth like storm clouds. The sweet smell of miso intoxicated her.

"The test of any Japanese meal," Virginia said, "is the miso soup. Good miso, good meal. Bad miso, get up and leave, don't even waste your time."

"This miso is great," Severin said.

Virginia thought that this might be one of the best mornings of her life. Using her chopsticks, she expertly deboned her mackerel. It was her favorite fish, the fishiest, and not always popular with gaijin, she'd been told numerous times by sushi chefs and waitresses. But she loved the salty taste. She thought that maybe the mackerel went deeper into the ocean, and thus the stronger taste. She liked to think about her fish going very deep, looking for the secrets.

"You like my shirt?" Silver asked.

"Sorry. Do you mind?"

"No. Wear it with pride. An American chick gave that to me. I got her and her friends high. Five of them stayed the night, and she and I had sex in the bathroom while her friends were passed out. We broke my toilet seat. So she gave me her shirt. She had it made in Shibuya. It was her favorite book, she said. But I never read it. The landlord charged me up the ass for a new toilet seat! I never wear the shirt. You can have it."

"It's one of my favorite books, too. You never saw the girl again?"

"No. She planned to come back on her way home but never showed up. I don't think the American dudes she was with liked me."

"Why not?" Severin asked.

"No guy likes a dude who hands out drugs for free and then bangs one of his travel partners. One of those dudes probably wanted her but never had the balls to say anything. Then he sulked the rest of the trip. I see this kind of behavior from Americans all the time. They're very predictable."

The door opened, and two young Japanese guys entered. Virginia noticed one of them from the party the other night. He carried an electric guitar, and his friend carried a small amplifier.

"Hey, you bastards, breaking in to my house! I'll call the police. You can't steal my drugs," Silver said.

"We are the police. We want the uppers and the downers, and we want the *hafu* girl, too!" the guitar guy said.

Silver made a hasty introduction. The guitar player was named Half Blind Lemon, and he went by Lemon for short. He'd been named in honor of the bluesman Blind Lemon Jefferson after being beaten nearly to death by some *yakuza* thugs who wanted him off of a certain block. He'd lost his left eye. The other guy went by Sniff. Silver explained that he was "big into glue." Virginia had heard Silver mention their names before. They were members of a punk band named the Concrete Wall.

"Glue heads burn my ass," Silver said. "Can't make any money from them. All they gotta do is mug a schoolkid, and they got their stuff."

Lemon plugged his amp in and broke into a punk-rock version of "House of the Risin' Sun."

This was one of Virginia's father's favorite songs. Late nights she sometimes heard him singing it in a low moan. She liked this punk-rock version better than her father's Bob Dylan–inspired inflections. When the song was over, the audience clapped. Vir-

78

ginia looked at Severin, curious as to whether he even knew the song. Lemon pretended to smash his guitar.

"Very punk rock," Silver said.

"Let's get to business," Virginia said.

"What business?" Severin asked.

Silver opened a map of Tokyo on the floor, and everyone looked at it. He said, "Virginia, I'm going to send you to shops near Ikebukuro, Tokyo, and Shinjuku stations again. It worked well last time. Lemon and Sniff, your girls go here, here, and here." He marked places on the map near Shibuya, Ginza, and Takanawa stations.

"What is this?" Severin asked.

Sniff said, "Your girlfriend is a robber. Bonnie and Clyde, right?"

"Yes," Virginia said. "Bonnie and Clyde."

"This is how you got all that money," Severin said, thrusting his tattooed arm toward her. "Why are you doing this?"

Silver said, "We're going out for a beer. We'll be around the corner." The three men left the room.

"It's exciting," Virginia said. She grabbed Severin's hands in hers. "When I'm out robbing stores, you and everyone we go to school with are sitting around your houses watching *Dallas* reruns on Armed Forces TV, or you're asleep already. And it's good money."

She reached into her purse and pulled out her .38.

"Jesus!" he screamed. He walked away from her and looked out the window and then turned back toward her. "A gun? Have you shot anyone? I don't even know how to use a gun. Do you?"

"I won't shoot anyone. If I pulled out my gun and someone wouldn't give me the money, I'd leave."

"Will you please put it away? Have you thought about what happens when they pull a gun on you?"

"Not really."

"Well, you should. These guys are crazy. I like Silver, but those other guys are insane. They're criminals."

"This is real life."

"This is your fantasy."

"Well, it's better than real life, then. It beats sitting around base with a bunch of idiots. You have a choice, Severo. You can come with me tonight or you can go home to your mom and dad and watch reruns. I'll be back in a few hours."

Virginia and Silver went to Shibuya to hang out with the teenagers. He told her why he'd wanted her to recruit her big football-playing friend, as he referred to Severin.

"I got a call from a North Korean. Merchandise to move. It's human cargo. Four Japanese. You'll pick them up and hold on to them until you get the instructions on where to drop them off. I want—what's his name? Severin. I want him to go with you. He's muscle. I want you two to do this job together. This is big for me. It will be good for everyone."

Virginia was shocked to hear it was human cargo. She'd listened to a story on the radio about four Japanese being kidnapped and the assumption that there were North Koreans kidnapping Japanese to use as language instructors in Pyongyang, as had happened in the mid-1970s and again in the early 1980s. They forced the Japanese to teach North Korean spies the language, and then these spies infiltrated the Japanese government.

She said, "You know who these people are, right? Half of the Japanese police force is looking for them."

Silver said, "It's not our job to concern ourselves with who the people are. We need to pick up and deliver. The rest of this is metaphysics."

Virginia laughed. "Do you even know what metaphysics is?"

"Yeah, man, it's like outside of the physical." He grabbed her arm roughly, and she pulled away. "Just do what I tell you, okay? You're in deep already, sweet Virginia. Nowhere to go but down. Let's buy you a new wig."

• • •

Virginia and Silver returned to his apartment. Severin was sleeping. Virginia had read once that stress and anger make you tired. She woke Severin gently. He looked at her with sleep in his eyes and said, "I'll do whatever you want me to."

On the train to Ikebukuro, Severin asked Virginia why Silver didn't do any of the jobs himself.

"Someone has to be in charge. The guy in charge takes bigger risks and gets bigger pay. I'm at the bottom of the heap."

"How did you meet Silver?"

"Hanging out at Shinjuku with these punk Japanese girls I know. They were hitting up guys for money in the station, kind of terrorizing old guys. Telling them they'd suck them off and then getting them into the bathroom and jumping them with a gang of girls. It was fun. The guys deserved it. A girl got raped a few months ago, a fourteen-year-old. So these girls were after revenge. And I joined them. Wearing boots and kicking these perverts in the head. A few of the girls would do stuff for the guys or at least get some money before beating them. I never did. Sometimes it was tourists, Dutch and German mostly, some Americans and some Brits. But mostly Japanese salarymen. This one girl, she used to buy drugs from Silver, and I met him, and then he pitched this idea to a few of us. She is crazy. She bit a guy's dick. Silver heard the stories. He knew we were all tough and had been beating those guys up for a few weeks. The guys couldn't tell the cops that they'd been beaten up by a gang of teenagers after propositioning them. So we were pretty free to roam for a while. Next week we're getting together again, maybe at Tokyo station for a change. You can come if you want. You would really help. You could really thrash a pervert. Although we do a good job on our own. A couple of the guys had to go to the hospital. I'd like to know how they explained it to their wives. 'Well, dear, I tried to get a blow job from a thirteen-year-old. And you wouldn't believe it, I went into a stall with her, and about ten little witches came flying over the walls, kicking and screaming and scratching and beating me.' I'd love to hear that."

"Does your dad have any idea you do this?"

"Of course not. He thinks I'm hanging out with friends and practicing my Japanese. I *am* practicing my Japanese, but I'm practicing phrases like 'You dirty *sukebe*.'"

"What does *sukebe* mean?"

"Pervert."

The train arrived at Ikebukuro station. "Here we go, Severo. Breaking the law."

Severin followed Virginia up the steps of Ikebukuro station. At the street level, the city he was starting to know and fall in love with came alive, scooters, a fishmonger, a ramen-*ya,* the bright and lovely neon advertising the world.

"The market's around the corner," Virginia said.

Something in her voice had changed. This was not a voice of love and warmth but a voice of business—transactional, practical, cold.

Severin entered the market to get a feel for the place. An *obâsan* stood at the register, flipping through a gossip magazine, and two dorky kids had their heads buried in comics at the back of the store. Severin bought some whistle gum and returned to Virginia.

"There's an *obâsan* behind the counter," he said. "She's like seventy. You'll probably have to yell, she's got a hearing aid. And she won't even see you. Her glasses are as thick as *mochi* ice cream. Two fat kids are sitting in the far corner looking at comic books and eating candy bars." He offered her some of the gum he'd bought.

"Thanks, Severo," she said. "This'll be simple." But she didn't take any gum.

She affixed her new wig, a blond mod cut. She wore the I AM A CAT T-shirt and the plaid skirt, her leather jacket and combat boots, no socks.

She applied lipstick and said, "I need you to stand outside the door when I go in." She checked her top lip in a pocket mirror. "If someone tries to come in, just say the store's closed. You're big. No one will mess with you. Try to look mean."

"But she's an *obâsan*. She's blind and old. You can't rob her." He glared at Virginia. "Find another store."

She stared coldly at Severin. "This is the first target. No stopping."

"Are you serious?" Severin asked, surprised at the angry tone of his own voice.

"Silver says it's all metaphysics. Just do what you must. After this, he'll bring you in on something bigger."

She pursed her lips—they were bright berry red—and kissed Severin on the cheek.

But this time the kiss was not enough. He knew that whatever Virginia asked him to do, in fact he would not. He didn't want to cause her father and his parents pain, or scare to death the *obâsan* and the nerd kids. He wanted to go home and sleep in his own bed, with his own pillow, and in the morning he wanted his mother to make him breakfast and tell him that she loved him. No electric guitars at breakfast. For whatever reason—because she'd had no mother?—Virginia wanted this alternate life, but not Severin. His desire for her did not yet trump his love of the warmth of his home, of his mother. This thought shocked him: I'm still a boy. So he would let her go to a place where he had no business.

Virginia gave him two thumbs up and smiled. It was a carefree gesture for a girl carrying a gun in her purse. She nodded toward the store. He reached for her hands and closed his hands around hers. He said, "I can't do this. I can't do whatever it is you do. It's not me. And I know I can't stop you."

He ran back toward Exit A, the way they'd come.

While trying to sneak on base via the pedestrian overcrossing, Severin was apprehended by Jones, who booked him as a runaway. Severin was cuffed to a chair next to Jones's desk.

"Yes, sir," Jones said, and hung up the phone. He looked at Severin. "You lucky kid. The general is putting a wall of kindness around you. Kindwall, get it? He wants me to swing you by your parents' house and let you sleep in your mommy's bosom for the night. But first thing in the morning, he and some of his gorillas are going to coax some answers out of you."

"I haven't seen Virginia since the party. I was out with some buddies."

"Don't lie to me. So"—he winked—"how much to spend a night in your mommy's bosom?"

Severin kicked at Jones, nearly knocking himself out of the chair.

"Don't get feisty, little boy. I'll have to restrain you with this billy club upside your silly head. Let's go. Up to me, I'd hang you out to dry."

Severin had never sat in the back of a police cruiser. It was not a comfortable ride—hard plastic seat and no leg room. From the back of the cruiser, the base looked as oppressive as Virginia claimed.

Severin's father opened the front door. The porch light was new and bright.

Severin looked at him in shame. He said to his father, "I thought you were in Taiwan."

His father said, "They tend to cancel orders when your son runs away from home."

Jones said, "Sir, I found him sneaking back on base. General Kindwall told me to—"

Colonel Boxx interrupted. "I just got off the phone with the general. Can you take the cuffs off of my son?" He waved dismissively at Jones. Colonel Boxx was a tall, thin man who stooped slightly. He stood with his feet at shoulder width or wider to offset his height. The deep creases in his brow held years of worry and stress. He'd passed his piercing blue eyes to his son. He was wearing civilian clothes, a plaid shirt and khakis, but they were just as starched and pressed as his formal-dress military uniform.

"Yes, sir. So you know," Jones said.

"We have an appointment with the general in the morning." Severin kept his head down.

"Look at me," his father said.

He refused. "I didn't mean to make Mom worry." He spoke toward the doormat that proclaimed, in white-painted rubber, WELCOME. Free of the cuffs, he shook his wrists.

His mom burst from behind his father.

"Severin," she screamed. She stepped down to the porch and hugged him so hard that she forced the air out of his lungs. "I don't care why you were gone. You're back. Now stay. Where's Virginia?"

"Honey," Mr. Boxx said, "he's not saying. But we'll take care of it in the morning."

Mrs. Boxx stood back and looked at Severin, and then she slapped her son hard across the face. Her slap stung on his cheek. She started to cry and turned and ran into the house. He wondered what would happen when she discovered his tattoo.

SIX

General Kindwall sat in his office, constipated and paranoid. Miyoko had left in the middle of the night, no note. He repeatedly called her home, no answer. He knew what the great psychoanalyst had said about paranoia and the function of the bowels, but he'd never bought it. Theory. The theories behind nuclear weaponry never killed anyone. Einstein was off the hook. The theory of constipation didn't keep you from shitting, actual constipation kept you from shitting. He needed an hour. He needed to go on a fast, as he'd done once with Miyoko: a seven-day green-tea-and-seaweed fast. He'd even allowed her to give him a green-tea enema. To his great surprise and initial worry, he enjoyed the enema, and it had done what he'd always imagined an enema would—it freed him up, mind and body, he felt lighter and smarter, his mood improved, and his vision of the world, as a dark place filled with demons trying always to kill you, changed to a vision of brightness and white light, goodness, even. Virginia left for a weeklong camp at Mount Fuji, and he stayed with Miyoko, showing up at the office after noon every day. A sex vacation, Miyoko called it. "General, let's go on a sex vacation." They watched TV and read books and slept and screwed and cleansed their bodies. She poured tea and he drank it. And she poured more tea. They bathed together in warm goat milk. He felt the toxins and the stress leaving his body. His subordinates thought he'd begun to take drugs or had simply finally lost his mind. He asked his clerks to *please* place this call or type this memo, and *thank you* for doing it. He allowed them to listen to the pirate radio station. He said, "I like this David Bowie guy." But Virginia returned from camp, and in a few days the temperamental changes the green fast had inspired disappeared.

He wanted to run away from the Japanese and international press corps, to hide out in Miyoko's twelve-mat room for a week: sleep and sex and green food and enemas and goat-milk baths. But he couldn't. The press stood on the other side of his office door, and there was only one way out, if you didn't count the five-story-high window.

He'd held hundreds of press conferences but knew this one would be the most difficult of his career—ten million Japanese would be watching, and the Pentagon, and all of the bastards who'd been waiting for him to step on his own dick since leaving the Citadel thirty years ago. He imagined a crew of the guys who'd cycled out after Vietnam getting together for a beer at the American Legion, throwing a party to celebrate Kindwall's Greatest Failure. Fifty-cent drafts. Raffle prizes. Replay at eleven.

He inspected himself in the full-length mirror on the door. His shoes gleamed, shined by hand. The new generation painted the fake shine on their dress shoes, but he still used his own spit and Kiwi polish. There were only a few guys around who had more ribbons than he did. The story of my life, six square inches on my chest, he thought. Did the entire story fit there?

He entered the corridor, and the flashes blinded him. His first instinct was that he'd tripped an entire jungle of toe poppers and that the room had exploded. He could only wish. He looked for the reporter plant from the *Asahi-Shimbun*. This guy was supposed to lob him a softball, and a follow-up softball, but he couldn't see him. The reporters' questions assaulted his ears like nearby gunfire.

"If you ask me questions one at a time, I'll try to answer them one at a time," he said. He held his right hand rigidly above his brow to shield his eyes from the bright lights.

"General Kindwall, will you turn over to Japanese authorities the driver of the vehicle that killed the boy?"

"Once my investigation is complete, if there is reason to believe that criminal negligence was at play in the accident, I will, according to the Status of Forces Agreement, allow the Japanese police to conduct their own investigation and press charges accordingly."

"General, how will this latest accident damage Japanese-American relations?"

"Despite this horrible tragedy, I expect that the Americans and Japanese will continue the rich relationship that has helped, for the last forty years, keep Japan safe and increase her global influence, especially in the area of trade." These were the same questions as ever, but this time there was the sad postscript of a dead boy. Thinking about Yoshida's son darkened Kindwall's mood. He wanted to tell the reporters where to shove their notepads and sharp pencils.

"If you believe that you are here to protect the Japanese from the Communists in North Korea, China, and Russia, how do you explain that the American military is responsible for more Japanese deaths since the end of the occupation than those three Communist regimes combined?"

"If you want to become part of one of those Communist regimes, ask us to leave. It's a very simple issue."

"On the heels of last year's series of rapes by GIs, does this further isolate you and your personnel from the Japanese public?"

"GIs and the Japanese have lived together in harmony since August 1945. Again, I don't expect this to change."

"Are there any clues in the kidnapping cases?"

"The Japanese police have taken the lead in the investigation. The FBI is assisting, and of course, my security personnel will do whatever is asked of them. We are anxious to find the Japanese nationals who may or may not have been kidnapped by North Korean aggressors."

"Sir, is there any truth to the story that your daughter is running with a female criminal group in Shinjuku? That they are responsible for a series of assaults on respected businessmen and that some of the girls in the gang have performed other criminal acts such as prostitution and burglary?"

The room went quiet. Kindwall looked to his left, and then to his right, searching for support, for someone else to answer this intrusive question. The camera flashes picked up again. The reporter who asked the question lurched toward Kindwall and handed him a series of black-and-white photos.

"This is your daughter with Silver Oda, a known Korean gangster and petty thief. Can you explain her association with Mr. Oda?"

Kindwall tore the photos several times and threw the pieces on the floor. He said, "That's her cousin. He's in from Texas. Any other stupid questions?"

Before anyone could ask, he turned his back to the room.

A young man at the back of the press corps yelled, "America still kills innocent Japanese!" He threw a balloon at Kindwall, and it exploded on the back of his blue uniform. The balloon, about the size of a large potato, had been filled with blood, and the reporters at the front of the room were splattered. The cameramen continued to shoot Kindwall's back as he entered his office.

A bloody uniform was nothing new to Kindwall. The shards left from the uniform he'd been wearing the day he got hit in Vietnam were in a box in his closet: the mothers of the dead received flags; the injured kept their blood-tainted uniforms. He removed his jacket and smelled the blood but couldn't tell if it was human or animal. He hated that dress uniform. He threw it in the clothes hamper in his bathroom and put on olive-drab fatigues. He thought of his father, a poor Texas farmer who'd lost it all. The man would marvel at knowing that his son had a private bathroom in his office. His father had grown up shitting in the woods. Kindwall's face burned with shame.

It was only nine A.M. on Monday. He needed a talk with Severin

Boxx, and he might have to get rough, or let someone else do so. This looked like a banner week—his missing daughter and AWOL girlfriend, Yoshida's dead son, and the possible kidnapping of four other Japanese by the North Koreans. Why had he stayed in the military? He could have walked out of Saigon in 1973 and right into a commercial-airline cockpit. Delta had offered him a job in the States; American had offered him even more money and an international route. Stewardess girlfriends in Tokyo, Hong Kong, Sydney. He sat in his chair and thought about the possibilities.

Reality interfered. The press conference. They'd flay and fry him all over the afternoon and evening news and tomorrow's papers. He'd be portrayed as another in a long line of egomaniacal American generals (starting with MacArthur) who considered it their duty to walk roughshod over the Japanese, over any Japanese in their path. The dead high school boy would serve as a metaphor for the entire country. The Japanese are tired of being kicked around by America-*jin,* the butter-headed incompetents who couldn't keep their citizenry safe from the North Koreans. Japanese national morale had soared to new heights in the late seventies and early eighties, and the contrition and apologia that had once defined Japanese attitudes toward America had been altered greatly by the rise of the island nation and the strength of its currency. Kindwall knew that the abuse coming his way had as much to do with his military command as it did with a sea change in Japanese identity. The Japanese were waiting for the American military to falter, and half a dozen times a year, some enlisted knuckleheads provided them with a rich pageant—auto accidents, drug dealers, rapists. They never reported the good deeds: rebuilding a road, stabilizing a dam, supporting local businesses. Good deeds don't make the news. And now Kindwall's personal humiliation over his daughter's disappearance richened the cake for the extreme nationalists, isolationists, and militarists who wanted to do away with Article Nine of the Japanese constitution, the "no war" clause MacArthur had championed that denied the Japanese an offensive military force.

His secretary's voice buzzed over the phone: "Sir, there is a Miss Miyoko here to see you."

Hearing Miyoko's name excited him. One thing would be set right today. "Yes, yes, send her in."

He moved from his desk to the leather couch. She'd never been in his office.

Miyoko walked in. She was wearing her mechanic's coveralls, blue with grease handprints and here and there the outline of a greasy wrench. Her hands were clean because she always wore medical gloves while working. He grabbed her hands and kissed them. He bent down and kissed her cheek, but he felt resistance.

"Oliver, I couldn't sleep. I was so worried about the Yoshida family. I went over early this morning. I tried to offer an apology from you, an unofficial apology. I thought that coming from me, it would help. But it did not. The Yoshidas are enraged. They want to take action."

"What kind of action are they going to take? This morning a kid threw a balloon filled with blood at me. That's as intense as it's going to get."

"I think this is different. Yoshida was a Zengakuren in the seventies. He was the head of the riots in Tokyo, he shut the universities down. He has been neutered by time and people's disinterest. But he is alive again since the death of his son. He wants to crush you and get rid of the American military in Japan."

"Some old tired hippie isn't going to get rid of this base. Anyway, he makes a million bucks a year selling stereos and televisions to GIs. He knows where his honey comes from."

"Japan hippies are not like U.S. hippies. I am telling you, you have problems arising. No matter what"—she paused—"you are my friend, no matter what I think of your military or what happens to us."

Kindwall screwed his face into a question mark. "What happens to us? What does that mean? 'Friend'?"

Miyoko bowed and lowered her voice. "I think it is proper we end the relationship. I am angry you took so long to introduce me to your Virginia, and by the process you did it. I could have been a mother to her seven years ago. But not now. You have wasted time for everyone. You made the clock. But you were wrong, the clock makes you."

A few hours later, Colonel Sussman and Jones entered the general's office without knocking.

"Sussman, why don't you just move in?" Kindwall said.

"My wife thinks I have already," Sussman said. He threw his flight bag on the couch and pointed Jones to the bathroom. "The toilet is in there."

"What is he doing here?" Kindwall said.

"He knows the base perimeter better than anyone except you. I brought him up to date."

"Okay. What's the word?" Kindwall said.

Sussman opened a journal. "This Silver fellow gets more and more interesting. I think we might be obligated to bring in the Japanese police at some point."

"Forget the JPs," Kindwall said. "This is mine."

"Sir, the circle of knowledge is enlarging. Severin Boxx's detention was on the MP blotter last night. The school called about Virginia missing school this morning."

"I'll tell them she's sick. Isn't the flu going around? Just tell me what you know."

"Colonel Boxx will be here in ten minutes with his son. I expect the boy to cry us a river of good intelligence."

"What's happening with these kidnapped nationals?"

Sussman turned to make sure Jones was still in the bathroom. "The embassy dropped a bombshell on me this morning. The kidnapped girl isn't just any twelve-year-old. Her father is the minister of trade."

"Fabulous. We're going to end up dropping a bomb on North Korea. Is that what you're telling me?" Kindwall stood and looked out his window at a line of bombers on the horizon.

"Maybe a small one. Political terrorism. But what do they want with a minister's daughter?"

"They want to send the message that they can reach the highest levels of government, anywhere, at any time. If a minister's daughter isn't safe, no one is safe."

Jones entered the office from the bathroom and stood casually to the side.

"Jones," Kindwall said.

"Yes, sir." Jones approached and saluted the general, way too late.

"I thought you might've forgotten the practice of saluting general officers. I know I'm old guard, but some regulations are still around for a reason."

"Yes, sir."

"Don't think that just because you've taken a seat on my throne, we're old drinking buddies now. I'd hate to hear that you think you're getting intimate with the BG."

"No, General."

"I don't care if your granddaddy assembled the bomb blindfolded and then flew here flapping his arms and dropped the wicked bastard from his teeth. We are not friends."

"Understood, sir."

With a letter opener, Kindwall removed dirt from his fingernails. "If I tell you to, you can push the kid around, but nothing too rough. His father won't object. Boxx wants full colonel like a sixteen-year-old wants a hand job. No marks; I don't need his mother clawing at my face."

"Don't you punish him all the time at practice?" Sussman said. "Some football calisthenics ought to get it out of him."

"Do you see a football field in this office?" Kindwall asked. He looked unhappy with the world.

"His mom slapped him last night," Jones said.

"Good to know."

Kindwall's secretary escorted Colonel Boxx and Severin into the office.

"Sir," Colonel Boxx said to Kindwall, "I'm sorry about all this trouble my boy has caused. But he's ready to set it straight." He pushed Severin toward Kindwall, who was sitting at his desk.

Kindwall kicked his feet atop the desk. "The prodigal son speaks. Have a seat."

Severin sat down gently in the soft leather chair, as though sitting on top of a carton of eggs. He looked around the room at the gathered men. He tried to recall the story of the prodigal son. "Sir, I don't know where Virginia is. If I did, I would tell you."

"Why should I believe you? Numerous of my airmen have come forward to say that they saw you leave a party with Virginia and a Japanese national. Are they lying?"

"No, sir. I left the party, but I didn't go anywhere with them. I met up with some of my friends out in town."

"What friends?"

"Some Japanese." Severin turned and looked at his father, who stood with his arms crossed, frowning.

"You don't have any Japanese friends," his father roared. "What are their names?"

"They're in a band. Sniff and Half Blind Lemon."

"Those are their names or the name of their band? Where did you meet these kids?" his father said.

"Their names. At Yoshida's, checking out stereos. I hung out at Sniff's apartment all weekend."

"Why," Kindwall asked, "would you allow my daughter to leave a party with a stranger?"

"Virginia is a lot stronger than you think, sir. I couldn't tell her what to do. I tried. And the guy was not a stranger to her."

Jones said, "Then I guess that makes you a wimp, if you can't take care of the general's daughter."

Colonel Boxx looked sharply at Jones but said nothing.

"I don't know what else to tell you, sir," Severin said. "I wish I knew more. I can go out in town and ask around. I can go to Shinjuku. I heard Virginia hangs out there sometimes."

Kindwall nodded at Jones.

"We don't need your investigative skills, kid," Jones said. "I'm going to give you a ride to school while the officers have a talk."

"Severin," Kindwall said, standing from his desk and smoothing the crease in his trousers, "you are confined to base. I don't know what kind of punishment your father is going to give you for running away, but whatever it is, however harsh it is, I support it."

Severin stood to follow Jones out of the room. He looked at his father for support, but his father looked away. As Severin exited, his father said, "Have a good week at school. I'm flying back to Taipei at sixteen hundred. I have some pilots to train. Take care of your mother."

The heavy wood door closed with a boom behind Severin and Jones.

Jones said, "You and I are spending a lot of time together in police cruisers. This might look bad on your high school transcript." He slapped Severin on the back, and Severin recognized his menace.

Jones drove the long route to school, around the flight line. Fighter jets and bombers took off and landed. Severin recalled that this flight line had been used by the Japanese as a training ground for pilots during the war. Sacred and profane ground is always changing hands.

Jones pulled off the paved road onto a gravel service road at the end of the runway. "Get out, kid," he said. "We need to chat."

Severin looked at the police radio in the dash. He thought

about calling for help on the system, but instead, he stood from the car. Jones leaned against the trunk, and directly over their heads, planes took off in a deafening fury of screaming metal and fuel.

"I wanted to be a pilot," Jones said. "Like your dad, or a bombardier like my grandfather. That's the coolest job. And those guys get all the hot women. For instance, look at your mother."

Another jet took off, and Severin felt the heat from the exhaust on his face. It might just as well have been his father in that plane, cooking the sky, burning Mach, escaping.

"I need to get to school," Severin said, staring at his dirty running shoes, Pumas, blue with a beige stripe. He needed a new pair: He pushed his socked right big toe through a hole in the sole.

"My vision is bad. And I didn't want to go to college just yet. Ah, dammit." Jones grabbed Severin by the shoulders and spun him around, and pushed him against the car, and cuffed him.

"Does that feel familiar? It should."

Jones sat on the trunk. Severin turned his head away. The cold trunk metal stung his cheek. He had a sideways view of the end of the flight line. Men from the fire crew dismounted their truck and played catch with a football. Lunchtime, he thought. A bird, he didn't know what kind, flew in and out of his field of vision.

"What I'm supposed to be doing is intimidating you into telling us where Little Princess V is. I've been given permission to rough you up a little."

Severin heard him sigh.

"But I'm not going to do that. I think you're an okay kid, and I don't want to make another enemy for myself or my family name. This whole country hates my name. So I'm going to tell Kindwall I rode your ass for an hour and you gave me nothing. Snake Eyes Severin. And that's the end of the game. I'm going on leave tomorrow. Kansas City, brother, a whole month. Best barbecue in the world. Look me up if you ever make it there. Call any Jones in the book. They'll find me. We're all related. Let's get you to school."

He unlocked the cuffs.

The cameraman for NHK held a freeze-frame of the bloodied back of General Kindwall's uniform. Sitting in Silver's apartment, Virginia looked away from the television. Her father had been all over the news. She felt sorry for him. And she had begun to be afraid for herself. It was almost midnight. She'd been gone from home for three days.

Clumps of Silver's silver hair covered the tatami mat. He'd had Virginia shave his head earlier and was now downstairs making a phone call.

Virginia had found a broom in the closet and begun to sweep up the hair when Silver kicked open his door. "We need to go to Adachi-ku. It's the pickup. I can't believe how bad your Mr. America boyfriend screwed me. I had a date with a Swedish backpacker chick."

"Where is Adachi-ku?"

"It's beyond Ueno. We're talking an hour, maybe longer."

She grabbed her purse.

"No," Silver said. "Leave your purse and any identification here. Just take cash. Whatever cash you have."

"I have three hundred American and fifty thousand yen."

"Good girl. Been saving that allowance. Bury your purse under the futons in the closet. And give me your gun."

The stop and go and swerve and swivel of Tokyo traffic made Virginia sick to her stomach. She smoked a cigarette and inspected her nails.

They drove by the Yasukuni shrine, the national war memorial to all of Japan's war dead from 1868 through World War II. A group of South Koreans marched in front of the shrine, declaiming over a loudspeaker in Japanese, Korean, and English that the raping and pillaging that Japan had visited on Korea needed to be paid for with more than a few deep diplomatic bows every year.

Silver yelled out the window, "Go home and get some sleep!" He looked at Virginia. "Japan was over the atom bombs in five years, right? The Koreans are going back to the nineteenth century. I hate the Koreans."

Virginia continued smoking. "You're Korean. Yesterday you hated the Japanese."

"Half Korean." He honked at a bicyclist. "Buy a car," he yelled out the window. "Yesterday I complained about certain Japanese women being lazy in bed. I did not complain about the Japanese people. There's a difference."

Virginia blew smoke in his face, and he coughed violently.

"If crime doesn't kill you, those things will," Silver said, motioning to the cigarette in Virginia's hand. "Public nuisance."

"And being a criminal is a community service?"

Silver leaned in to the steering wheel, his head nearly resting on the horn, and turned toward Virginia. "At least crime gives you something for your trouble. Black lungs are all you'll get from that trash. If America really wanted to protect Japan, they'd stop selling Marlboros here. More people will die of cigarettes in the twentieth century than from ten nuclear wars." Using his forehead, he honked the horn at no one.

"What are we doing?" Virginia asked. "Is there a plan?"

"My plan is to follow the instructions."

"What are the instructions?"

"We go to Adachi-ku. We pick up the cargo. We await further word."

She threw her cigarette out the window. "Adachi-ku is the middle of nowhere."

"Don't litter," he said. "That's a dirty habit. What if a kid picks that up?"

"When did you turn into a model citizen?" Virginia looked at him, truly in wonder.

"I'm proud of my country." He puffed his chest out. "I am a proud *hafu,* no matter how my country treats me. How about you, what is your mother country? You don't even know. Your father hasn't lived in America since you were born. He's never been back. So what are you? American? Japanese?"

"I'm not an American. I'm not Japanese. I have no citizenship and no allegiance to a government or nation."

She didn't think of herself as an American, no matter what her military ID and passport stated. Her father, after leaving Vietnam, had posted to Taiwan for three years and then to Japan; he had Virginia sent to him on a military flight. An air force nurse on orders to Yokota had escorted Virginia from Houston to Tokyo. Virginia was five years old when she finally made it to her mother's country. Naturally, she'd thought the nurse would continue taking care of her, but after the twenty-hour flight, the nurse delivered Virginia Sachiko Kindwall to the MPs at the main gate, a small red suitcase at her feet, a military ID pinned to her coat. Virginia vividly remembered the MPs wrestling a GI to the ground as he tried to regain entry to the base. He'd probably been drunk or committed a crime or both. An MP buried his knee in the man's spine while his partner stepped on the man's head. The subdued man, angry and pleading to Virginia for assistance, stared at her as she sat in the guardhouse with her hands clasped neatly in her lap.

Eventually, her father arrived.

She had no idea who he was. The nurse had wrapped her so tightly in a sweater and coat and scarf that when her father hugged her, she didn't feel it. His whiskers scratched her face, and the tears that ran down his face shamed her. She thought she'd done something wrong. She knew the words "father" and "daddy" and "pop." They were the words that the people who'd sent her here spoke when pointing to pictures of this man now crying and holding her. She cried, too. She rested her head on Fatherdad-

EXIT A

dypop's shoulder and cried, and a man sitting at a desk, one of the
men who'd just stepped on the man on the ground, stared. She
wondered why Fatherdaddypop was crying. In the pictures of him
she'd seen, he'd been stern. Stern with other stern men sitting in a
half circle, the backdrop a thick tapestry of green tents and greener
trees, a landscape she would one day understand to be the jungles
of Vietnam.

Fatherdaddypop took her to a place he called home. The room
he called hers wasn't hers. She'd never seen these things. The
bed had a sheet floating above it, and her bed never had. The bright
yellow walls shocked her. The walls of her real room had been a
faded blue. The toys belonged to some other girl. The man with
the scratchy face continued to hug her and weep and say that he
loved her. And she believed him, but she remained confused. He
put her to bed and she slept.

Now this room was still hers, and the canopy bed remained, as
well as the yellow walls, faded now. But with a shock, Virginia
realized that she no longer owned that room, that she'd given it up,
she'd defied her father and fled his minions, and now she had no
place to call home. Silver's eight-mat room served only as a way
station, a transient flophouse littered with condoms and liquor bottles and cigarette butts and the filth from wasted days. What a
change from the yellow room of her youth.

"Maybe," Silver said, "you can become a Japanese citizen. If you
break enough laws, they'll give you honorary citizenship and a
key to the Imperial Palace!"

"Have you ever 'moved people' before?" Virginia was worried.

"Not to my knowledge. It's just another package. Except these
will be breathing."

"Are you certain they'll be breathing?"

"I'm certain of nothing."

They found the address, a complex with fifteen other buildings
that looked exactly the same, that looked like any of the thousands
upon thousands of nondescript buildings built on the ashes of

the firebombing of Tokyo. They consulted the map at the entrance in order to find the right building.

They rode the elevator to the fifteenth floor. As the doors opened, Silver pulled out the gun. Apartment 1530 was at the opposite end of the hall.

Silver picked the lock and cautiously opened the door. A ceiling fixture lit the bare room. A white business-size envelope was propped up against an empty bottle of sake. Silver looked at Virginia as though she knew what this was all about. She knelt down in front of the bottle and inspected the envelope. Their names were written on it.

Virginia waved the envelope at Silver. "A thank-you note."

Silver put his gun in his jacket pocket and knelt next to her. "Open it."

The note read:

This is a testing of your competence and allegiance. We needed to know that you are willing to do anything we ask from you. Thank you for your cooperation. Proceed to 43–35 Menchenko-tei in Yokohama.

They arrived in the noticeably Western enclave of Yokohama ninety minutes later. The first Westerners to settle in greater Tokyo had been banished to Yokohama. Virginia's ancestor Commander Kindwall was buried at the gaijin cemetery here. Driving through the hills above the city, you might easily think you'd been transported to the Hollywood Hills—many of the houses were International Style, and the slick modern architecture and the cars in the long driveways, multiple Mercedes, Maseratis, and Aston Martins, attested to the kind of wealth that people will do anything to protect.

They found their address with ease. The guard said nothing to them but opened the enormous gate and nodded toward the house. Virginia thought that the guard's body covered enough square meters that they didn't really need the gate: He could just stand in the middle of the driveway and block any car he chose not to admit.

"That guy is a monster," Silver said. "He eats kindergartners for breakfast."

"And grandmothers for dessert," Virginia said. Her palms began to sweat. "I don't think it's a test this time."

As they approached the house, a man who looked like a smaller cousin of the first guard appeared and opened the garage door. He smiled at Virginia as he directed Silver to drive into the garage. His teeth looked like rotten fish in a barrel. Silver stopped the car, and the garage door closed behind them. The garage was dark. Virginia imagined the van windows had been covered with layers of dried seaweed. I'm at the bottom of a black sea, she thought.

"Silver?" Virginia asked.

"I've done some crazy jobs before, but this is tops."

"How long do you think they're going to keep us sitting in this garage?"

"I have no idea."

Virginia's eyes adjusted to the extreme dark. The curtain lifted slowly. She saw the outlines of human forms standing beyond the hood of the van. She heard voices but couldn't tell if they were coming from inside or outside.

What if the goons planned to fill the garage with carbon monoxide? Why would they want to kill her and Silver? Did they know who she was? Maybe she had become the cargo, the package. The general's daughter wrapped tight in a van. Ransom? She'd ask to use the phone and call her father and, in ten minutes, mean American military guys with machine guns would kick down the doors and save her. Yes. But no, she'd forsaken her father.

"Silver, I'm afraid. Everything has been fine until now. Things are no longer fine." She clenched her own throat and breathed heavily. Was it true that breathing into a paper bag would stave off nausea? Someone give me a paper bag, please.

"Virginia, baby. Give it five minutes. You count five minutes to yourself. Let me know when you're done. Then I'll get out of the van and look for a door. Deal?"

"Deal."

Silver patted and squeezed her knee. He'd never touched her before. She found this gesture comforting and then deeply weird.

Harsh fluorescent light burst open the room, and Virginia squinted hard. Men in black suits swarmed around the van. They spoke in quick guttural utterances. Korean. The back of the van opened, and she heard four loud thuds, like heavy sacks of potatoes hitting the rusty bed of a truck. She knew better than to turn around and look. The garage was silent and dark again.

Virginia began to cry.

"Five more minutes, baby. Restart the clock."

The garage door opened slowly, and the garage filled with an inky, reflective light. In the side mirror, Virginia saw the bigger of the two guards waving his hands, directing Silver to back up.

In English, he yelled, "Hurry up," then "Stop!"

The smaller guy appeared at Virginia's window and shoved an envelope in her face. "Follow the instructions or die," he said, grinning, exposing his rotten teeth.

They parked in an alley in Ikebukuro. The instructions were straightforward. There were two alleys for them to drive to at specified times, this alley in Ikebukuro and one in Ginza, where they would wait, probably under surveillance. And then at noon they were to deliver the cargo to a rogue South Korean shipping company that specialized in out-of-date tofu and Russian handguns.

"Welcome to wherever you are," Silver said.

"Are those people even breathing?" Virginia asked.

"One of them is snoring, which means he's breathing. I don't know about the others."

Virginia used her fingers to comb her hair out of her face. "Don't you think we should feed them, and ourselves?"

"Who are you, the Red Cross? What are we going to feed them?"

"Noodles?"

"Do we take their orders?" He pointed to an *udon* shop at the end of the alley. "Or march them down to the corner one at a time?"

"I'll get six orders of shrimp tempura *udon*. If they don't like shrimp, too bad."

Virginia opened the door to the noodle shop, and steam hit her face as though she'd entered a sauna.

It was late, three in the morning, and drunken salarymen and young punks lined up shoulder to shoulder at the bar, bent over their noodle bowls, slurping like madmen. Noodles were the great equalizer. They'd all missed the last train home and were trying to sober up and decide whether to take a taxi home, six thousand yen, get a capsule hotel room, three thousand yen, or go get drunk again before work, five thousand yen.

Virginia liked to slurp her noodles: It made her feel Japanese, but it drove her father crazy. He'd once asked, "Can't you slurp *half* the bowl of noodles?" She did not appreciate this callous reference to her *hafu*-ness, which she'd told him, and he'd apologized. But meals with her father were some of the most intimate moments they shared, the only time they were in the same room for longer than thirty seconds. She thought of breakfast a few days prior, his omelets and his girlfriend. Was that only Saturday? It seemed so long ago.

This morning she'd eat noodles with a petty-thief drug dealer and four kidnapping victims in the back of a dirty, beat-up three-cylinder van.

Behind the counter, one man took her order while another began to prepare the *udon*. He grabbed premeasured balls of noodles from a tray and dropped them in a large vat of boiling water. In a window to the left of the counter, the tempura were stacked in neat rows. Shrimp, squid, fish, green beans, onion, sweet potato, broccoli, zucchini, green pepper, lightly battered and fried golden. As the noodle man removed the steaming mass of noodles from

ANTHONY SWOFFORD

the vat, his partner held the bowl, poured broth over the noodles, and with a flourish and speed that suggested Old West gunfighting, removed tempura from the counter and placed it atop the noodles. In this fashion, the men prepared Virginia's order in under three minutes. She stood at the door, ready to exit, but waited for a moment, relishing the thick steamy heat and the smell of the broth and the human act of replenishment.

She could run. She knew she could run. But Silver was probably watching the door of the *udon* shop from the van. She could tell one of these men to help her. At the end of the noodle bar, near the bathroom, there was a small plastic pay phone, pink, that looked like a rice cooker. She reached into her purse and removed a ten-yen piece. She approached the phone and removed the receiver and dropped in the yen piece. She dialed her home number and held the receiver to her ear. It rang, a small chirping bird.

Her father answered sleepily. "Hello? Hello? Who the hell is this? Virginia? Severin? Sussman? Who is calling?"

She placed the receiver in its cradle.

She knew why she hadn't spoken into the phone, she knew why she hadn't run, and it sickened her: She wanted to see the faces of their captives and to know the results of her evil. Dialing the phone had been a test. She'd passed.

In the van, Silver faced the captured foursome, his gun pointed in their general direction. The four captives sat shoved together on the bench seat in the back of the van. Silver had removed their gags, but the blindfolds remained, and their hands were tied behind their backs. One man wore a rumpled black kimono, and the face paint and hair of a Kabuki stage actor. The man in the beige suit reminded Virginia of her driving instructor, a dour taskmaster. The woman wore conservative office attire, a black suit with a red blouse and no jewelry. The young girl wore her school outfit, a green skirt and jacket with a white blouse, and she gripped a unicycle as though it were a stuffed animal.

Virginia stood outside the van and stared at the cargo—innocent people in bondage—and heard them questioning Silver:

"Who are you and why have you taken us from our homes?"

"Where are my parents?"

"What ransom do you want?"

"Will you kill us?"

"Can I please ride my unicycle?"

Silver refused to answer their questions.

The reality of her evil sickened and frightened her. These people were her neighbors, the fathers and sisters of her friends.

Silver said, "Okay. *Udon* for everyone. But I'm not untying your hands or your blindfolds. So my friend here is going to hold the bowl in front of your face, and you'll eat like dogs."

"What if we untie them one at a time?" Virginia asked.

"No way. They'll throw the hot broth on us and make a break for it. Little missy here will pedal away on her contraption. Anyway, that one looks like she could lose ten pounds."

Silver pointed at the office worker. Probably a secretary, Virginia thought. Nice boyfriend. Small apartment. Happy life. Not any longer.

"Don't say that," Virginia blurted out. "Don't say that to her."

"Mother Teresa has arrived on scene. Sister, feed your flock."

Virginia fed the youngest girl first. Between huge gulps of hot broth and swallowing as many noodles as possible, the girl thanked Virginia for feeding her. After finishing the bowl, the girl asked again if she could ride her unicycle. Silver reinserted her gag. The woman in her twenties remained calm during her feeding. Virginia tipped the bowl too far toward her mouth, and broth spilled over the edge and into the woman's lap; she flinched but said nothing. Virginia knew that the steaming broth must have burned her and that she was in pain. After finishing her meal, the woman hung her head silently.

"Stop," Silver said. "Let's eat before our noodles get cold and the tempura gets soggy. I hate soggy tempura. Those old guys can wait."

"I'll feed them," Virginia said.

"No. Feed yourself, then feed them."

Virginia didn't understand why Silver was being so obstinate. She didn't know what starving the men for a few more minutes would accomplish, but she had to follow his orders.

She slurped the noodles loudly and with relish. One of the male captives scowled.

Silver threw his bowl and chopsticks into the alley.

"I thought you didn't like litter," Virginia said.

"I don't want to clutter the van. Hurry and eat."

He removed the lid from one of the two remaining noodle bowls and held it underneath the nose of one of the men. The man licked his lips. Saliva gathered at the corners of his mouth. Silver moved the bowl underneath the other man's nose. The man stuck his tongue out and tried to bury his face in the broth. Silver slapped him.

"No noodles for you two idiots," he said, and threw the bowl out the door. He grabbed the other bowl and took a loud drink of the broth, then threw it into the alley, too. The broth and noodles spread across the concrete, and steam rose from the spill in the damp light of the alley, and the noodles looked like dead albino worms.

The two men groaned and cursed at Silver in unison.

"If I were blindfolded with my hands tied behind my back, I'd be more polite to the guy with the gun," Silver said.

"What are you going to do with these people?" Virginia asked.

"*We* are going to follow the orders," Silver said.

Silver told the captives to lie on top of one another, and he covered them with a blanket. He tossed the girl's unicycle in the back. He started the van and slowly made his way out of the alley. The early-morning business of Tokyo had begun, delivery trucks zooming up and down the streets, commuters pedaling their bikes toward the station. Virginia tuned in Radio Free Yokota for the morning's unauthorized editorial.

As the last bars of Neil Young's "Southern Man" ended, the announcer said: "This time I think Old Man Kindwall has made too much trouble for himself and the entire U.S. military mission in Japan. A young boy gets killed on your watch, and you've got to come out with a deep bow. He hasn't done enough. Stand by, GIs. Some craziness is going to go down. Time now for some D.C. punk. This is Minor Threat with 'Screaming at a Wall.'"

The punk guitar riffs and screaming that were first recorded on a soundboard in a dirty D.C. basement bar ripped through the van.

Virginia knew she was being a bad daughter. Otherwise she'd be at home supporting her father during this crisis. But he'd abandoned her when she most needed him, when her mother died at the moment of her birth. He'd encoded this behavior in her.

She nervously tuned radio stations in and out. The sound was dubious: Japanese bubblegum pop mixed with American punk and album rock and the news from the world delivered in Japanese. The search for the kidnapping victims had taken center stage in the country. The populace was being asked to look out for a group of Korean men in a silver Mercedes. There had been some backlash against Korean shops in Tokyo, and nationalist groups called for a boycott of all Korean businesses.

"What if we just take them back to the house in Yokohama?" Virginia asked hopefully.

Silver punched the dash. He'd done so enough times now that his knuckles were bloody. He said, "Have you forgotten who we're working for?"

"Tell me, who are *they*?"

"*They* are operators with a lot of money. And you are not going to screw this up for me. For us."

"You don't know who they are! How can you agree to work for invisible people?"

"A voice on the other end of the phone line. That is the nature of the job," Silver said. "The fewer names and faces I know, the better."

"How much money are you getting? What is my share?"

"You've never asked about shares before. I always treat you well. It's worth our while. You can live on this money for a year. Rent an apartment in Shinjuku. Party, beat up perverts with your friends, snort drugs, whatever kind of girl bullshit you want to do."

He turned up the radio volume and punched the dash again.

As they drove through the busy city, the four captives occasionally moaned and screamed through their gags. The two men were on the floor of the van, and Virginia assumed they were roasting from the heat of the undercarriage. The woman and girl were on top of them. Virginia occasionally glanced back at the stack of bodies. She assumed the woman and girl were in shock, because they weren't making much noise. She worried for the young girl's parents. What could they be thinking? She recognized the irony: She herself, a missing person, driving around with four abducted people. She wanted to know their names.

Silver avoided the busy avenues and zigzagged through the city, taking alleys and side streets that only a native would know. The labyrinth that enclosed them seemed to get more complex with each turn, and deeper. Virginia thought of the labyrinth game she'd played as a child. But in that game, she could always remove the white marble and start over. She wondered whose large hands outside of the box controlled her movements.

The Dead Kennedys played on the radio loudly. The guitar riffs ripped through the van, and Virginia's teeth hurt; she realized she'd been grinding them. She heard moaning and cursing from the back of the van.

The young girl was asking for help, screaming through her gag.

"Stop the van," Virginia yelled at Silver.

"Why?"

"The girl needs help."

Virginia climbed over the center console and ripped the blanket off the pile of bodies. Silver violently applied the brakes, and Virginia slammed against the back of the seat.

Silver had pulled into a side street. He grabbed her chin and placed the tip of his nose on hers and said, "You do not touch those people unless I tell you to. I don't care what they want. Get back up here!" His breath was musty and stale.

Virginia said, "You can't let her—"

"I can do whatever I want."

"She needs something."

Virginia defiantly removed the girl's gag, and she said, *"Mizu. Mizu."*

"She needs water," Virginia said. "Do you want to deliver a dehydrated ten-year-old to your invisible operators? They might not be happy."

The girl said, "My name is Masako, and I am twelve years old and—"

"Shut her up!" Silver said. He scanned the street. "There's a vending machine. Get some water."

Virginia returned with water, and one by one, she offered the bottle to the four people tied up in the back of the van. Silver, agitated, cursed and punched the dash.

"Can the girl sit up front with me?" Virginia said.

"No way. Put her back down and throw the blanket over them!"

Virginia followed his orders and climbed back into her seat, defeated. She said, "I could leave. I could walk to the closest police box and tell them everything I know. And they'd find you. I know your itinerary. I'll save the girl. I'll call my father."

Silver reached across her chest and unlocked her door. He stared at her in silence. She had to look away.

"Feel free to exit at your earliest convenience. The second you leave this van, the girl's future is in my hands. I'll kill her. Slowly. When the JPs or your father find this van and the dead girl, I'll be long gone. I can disappear. You don't have that luxury."

"The Koreans will find you," she said desperately.

"They'll find you first. And they will be unkind. Leave, Virginia, please."

She wanted to scream. She felt dizzy, lost, and alone. What had she been thinking? This thing was real. The girl in the back was not much younger than she was, really, and look what Virginia was taking part in, while all the girl cared about was her parents and riding her unicycle. These were real people with bad intentions. Beating up perverts in Shinjuku: fun. Robbing *konbini* stores: fun. Silver had seduced her into further criminality, and the fun had ceased. She'd had no inclination that he was this bad. A bad man, an evil man, the worst of men. How had she been fooled? She'd thought he was, at heart, a good guy. At worst he seemed like a street punk, a romantic freelancer, living by his own rules, committing victimless crimes. "The *konbini* store owners have insurance," he'd always said. "No one gets hurt."

Virginia asked now, "Did you really send flowers to the shop owners we robbed?"

He laughed. "Of course not. It sounded good, didn't it?"

"Were those robberies just steps leading up to this?"

"You're a good student. I couldn't ask you to do this outright. I needed you invested."

"I've done too much wrong," Virginia screamed. "Things are out of control!"

"You've always been in control, Virginia. You've been a part of this from the start, little sister. You will be here until the end."

Silver pulled the van back into traffic.

She could do nothing but sit in her seat and wait. She couldn't abandon the girl to the fate that Silver had described. A life in North Korea would be better than death, right? Someday the government would negotiate a release. She'd be okay.

Virginia thought of Severin. I considered him so simple, a handsome jock, a kid who didn't have a clue. But the night he walked away from me in front of the *konbini* store, he made one of the smartest decisions of his life. And look at me.

SEVEN

That Tuesday morning, Severin awoke in his parents' house: in his own bed, where he knew the soft contours of cotton and spring, where his feet hung off the edge of the bed, and under his head lay the pillow into which he'd dreamed countless sex fantasies and football victories. The day before, when Jones dropped him off at school in the cruiser, his cool factor suddenly jumped fifteen points. Everyone wanted the story, and he lied. And they knew he lied, so they tried to get closer to him. But he was done with this high school. He knew that much. He'd overheard his parents talking. His father wanted to send him back to the States to finish high school. He'd live with one of his uncles, either in Berkeley or New York, they hadn't decided yet. His mother was in the midst of making the arrangements. The first day of Christmas break, he'd be on a plane. Severin knew his father had made this decision: His presence on base would make things difficult for his father at an important moment in his career, when he would either make full colonel or be told to step aside. Severin would be a public reminder of the difficulties the general had been through. A full-bird colonel can't have a delinquent child running around. A general can, because he's already made rank, but not a colonel. Severin felt like a sacrificial lamb.

He walked into the kitchen. His mother was making coffee and eggs. He wore pajama bottoms and no shirt. His heavily muscled body felt tired, his posture was bad from fatigue, he'd been sleeping fitfully, and his tattoo was in the wide open. His mother wore sweatpants and a tank top, and she was sweaty from a run, the tips of her hair wet like paintbrushes after a cleaning, a splotch of sweat on her back looking like a painter's palette.

"Do you plan to go to school today?" she said.

"I might make it for lunch. I really love the spaghetti mash and mystery meat sauce."

"Okay, comedian. Sit down and eat. I'll even let you drink coffee. You look as though you need it. Did you drink the other night? Or do drugs?"

"No, Mom." He shook his head at the ground. He thought, I wish I had. "Some guy gave me a half bottle of whiskey, but I threw it out. And I didn't see the drugs. I have a reputation, you know."

"You had a reputation as a straight kid. That's not so bad, Severin. Now no one knows what to make of you." She turned toward her son and stared for an uncomfortably long moment.

He could sense that she felt she'd lost something. He wanted to tell her, No, I'm still here, same old me, but he couldn't say that.

"I was informed yesterday that I've been kicked off the football team for insubordination." He laughed, and so did his mother.

"I was proud of you," she said. "Someone finally stood up to Kindwall. You know, the bleachers were buzzing for you. Some people were booing, but they were booing themselves because they've never stood up to him. You're a beautiful young man."

"That's weird, Mom." He looked at her standing at the stove. "To call me beautiful."

"No, it's the most natural thing in the world. You are my beautiful son. Don't you think I'm beautiful? Wouldn't you do anything in the world for me?"

"Of course I would. Mom, can you tell me what is going on with school?" He sipped his coffee. He was waking up.

"I'm talking with both of your uncles. I would prefer that you move to Berkeley, and that's how it's looking. I faxed your transcripts yesterday. Honestly, you would have more fun in New York with

Uncle Oren. But Uncle Douglas is going to crack the academic whip and get you in shape for college. He might keep you out a year to catch up, after you graduate. He can tutor you at home or have one of his teaching assistants tutor you, and then you'll be able to go to school anywhere."

"What does he teach?"

"Physics."

"What does Oren do?"

"He's a movie director. He goes to parties five nights a week trying to hustle producers for money and get actors into his films. You'd love it. And you'd never go to college."

"Maybe I'd marry an actress. Faye Dunaway."

"Too old for you. I wish you knew our family better. You don't even know what my brothers do. That's what happens when you live abroad for ten years."

She delivered eggs to him at the table and started to turn away. But she stopped and let out a little scream. She grabbed his arm, his tattoo, and yelled, "What is this? Jesus Christ, what is this on your arm? A gang tattoo?"

He'd forgotten the tattoo was there. But he recovered. "No." He felt his face flush with shame. "It's Virginia's Japanese name, Sachiko, meaning happy child."

His mother shook her head. "Your father is going to murder you." She sat down across from him.

"I got it Saturday, for Virginia."

"Why don't you really do something for Virginia? Are you going to skip school and sit in pachinko parlors all day or find the girl you love? I know you know where she is. Go tell Kindwall. It will be hard for her, but better than anything else that can happen. You'll both go to college in the U.S. Something will work out. But if she's on the street, and if she's living dangerously, she could get hurt."

Severin jumped up from the table and ran to his room. He dressed in athletic gear, not school clothes, and ran out of the house.

Kindwall's house was a mile away. He could make it there in five minutes and ten seconds. The slopes of the canal that ran through base were littered with beer cans and condoms. Severin crossed the bridge that the popular high school girls hung out on before school, and there they were with their preppie hairdos and saddle shoes and pink sweaters and brown skirts, gossiping and being as bad as they would ever get—smoking cigarettes. He heard his name and he heard Virginia's and he knew that those girls knew nothing, that for the rest of their lives, they would chatter about nothing. He hated them and their perfection of nothingness. At the helicopter pad, a medevac copter touched down. The work of the deployed American military was getting under way, jet turbines spinning, men exercising and yelling. This might be one of his final days on a military base. He wanted New York, not California. Fifty yards from the general's driveway, he slowed down and walked it in. He looked at his watch. Good time: five minutes, twelve seconds. He knocked on the door, still breathing heavily.

Sussman, Kindwall's staff officer, answered. "What do you want?" he said.

"I need to talk to the general."

"To talk to the general, you must first talk to me." He backed into the foyer and motioned for Severin to follow.

Severin stood, sweating, catching his breath. The foyer looked like a jungle, planted with thick green plants that smelled of warm earth and decay. Severin attempted to formulate his thoughts. He could see into the living room, where two briefcases were open and file folders and coffee cups covered every surface.

"What I need to say to the general is personal and confidential. I don't know you, sir, so I need to talk directly with the general."

The colonel was a mousy guy, disheveled but with a superior air. He had a comb-over of dirty-blond hair, plentiful nose hairs he didn't trim, and deep acne craters on his chin.

"Did you know the general gave me permission to slap you

around a bit? No one would ever know. All I need is to spill a little information out of you. Virginia is more important than you are. How do you like that news? You think you're important? You are a quitter. You quit football, and you ran home to your mommy when you should've saved Virginia. You're a predator."

Severin was an inch taller and forty pounds heavier than the colonel. The colonel probably hadn't run a mile in twenty years. He was a chair jockey, as Severin's father called the admin guys.

"Sir, I need to see the general. This doesn't involve you."

With two fingers, the colonel tapped Severin hard on the chest. "You talk to the general after you talk to me. Do you not understand English?"

Severin opened the door behind him, grabbed the colonel by the shoulders, and pushed him outside onto the lawn, where the man rolled in the wet grass before landing face-first in a pile of leaves. Severin closed and locked the door with the dead bolt and chain.

He entered the main house. He called out Kindwall's name, but there was no answer. He heard the colonel beating on the front door. He jogged up the stairs and started opening doors. The first room he opened was Virginia's: yellow walls covered with movie and band posters, a canopy bed, and a messy pile of clothes in the corner. He wanted to lie down in her bed, but it seemed like some kind of violation, and not the proper moment. The next room was Kindwall's, a huge master bedroom, spotless. In another room, framed photos and citations from Kindwall's military career covered the walls. Severin walked around the walls, taking a stroll through the general's career. He'd been everywhere and had his picture taken with everyone. Most of the world leaders Severin couldn't name, but he knew they were world leaders from the way they posed and how they shook hands with determination for the photographer. There were many photos from Vietnam, and they looked just like Severin's father's photos from Vietnam. Young men in green fatigues with jungle background.

Kindwall entered the room. "Look who it is," he yelled. "A true diplomat. To what do I owe the honor, Ambassador Severin?"

Severin spun around. "Sir, I'm sorry to barge in like this. I looked for you in your bedroom."

The general hadn't shaved. He wore civilian clothes. "You should've knocked on the bathroom door. My house is yours. My girl, Miyoko, left me, Severin. Your girl left you. We're birds of a feather. Did you ever get to third base, boy?"

"Sir, sir." Severin couldn't believe the general had just asked him that. "No. Never. I'm not here to talk about that. I want to tell you—" He was sweating.

Kindwall interrupted. "Do you want to instruct me how to remove a bra with one hand?" He laughed. "I already know, Ambassador. But thanks for the lesson."

"Sir, you need to listen to me," Severin said desperately. The general seemed crazed, totally checked out from reality.

"I will listen to you the day you burn in hell, because I will be right there with you. I might beat you by a few years, but we'll be together again at some point."

"Sir, I want to tell you."

"Why did you call me in the middle of the night and hang up?"

"Sir, that wasn't me."

"I don't want to hear anything you have to say. You had your chance yesterday. You slapped my face. In front of your father and my subordinates. I'll find Virginia on my own. Get out of my house."

"Sir, please listen to me. I might know where Virginia is."

He heard the sound of breaking glass, but Kindwall didn't seem to notice it.

"Boy, I might know where she is, too." Kindwall's face was heavy with worry and rage. "And I know that you are in trouble. What do you think you can give me now? You have ruined everything. You might even have ruined your father's career."

Kindwall lunged at Severin. Severin dodged his coach and

sprinted downstairs. In his peripheral vision, he saw the colonel in the living room, on the phone. Severin ran down the street, sunshine, light. He was supposedly confined to base, but with Jones gone, there would be someone else on the gate, some guy who probably wouldn't know who he was or wouldn't care. He'd sprint over the pedestrian crossing. He'd take the train to Shinjuku and rescue Virginia from Silver's apartment. She'd be done with robbery. She'd come home. He would insist this time.

On the other side of the pedestrian walkway, the civilian side, a large group of Japanese gathered. They carried white bedsheets suspended between two poles that read U.S. OUT. Some of the people wore construction hats painted Communist red. Down the street snaked a few hundred people. The man in front held a bullhorn, and the woman next to him carried a sandwich-board portrait of Yoshida's dead son. Other people wore T-shirts with the same image. The man with the bullhorn started the chant, "U.S. out, U.S. out," and the crowd made its way closer to the base. Severin ran in front of the crowd, and the people yelled at him to go home. Severin wondered what would happen to the protestors. Tear gas? Rubber bullets? General Kindwall was certainly in no mood to speak to the people, which was why they were there. Severin entered the train station at Exit A, looking for the train to Shinjuku.

Silver pointed to the warehouse, two blocks away. The dilapidated sign read BULK SOYBEAN AND TOFU. They'd pull in, and in a simple exchange of soiled humans for laundered money, the journey would end. This was Silver's version.

Virginia wanted to watch the young girl ride her unicycle, but she knew that was unlikely.

Silver said, "I'm going to see what things look like."

He jumped out of the van and kept the engine running. He pulled the girl from atop the pile of people. He cut the rope from her wrists and removed her blindfold and gag. She slowly opened her eyes, swollen from crying and fear. With a hand she shielded her eyes from the sun.

"Where are my parents? Are we there?" she asked.

"Very soon," Silver said. He told Virginia, "She's my assurance that you won't do anything stupid. We'll be right back."

Virginia turned on the radio. She wondered what kind of music the people in back might like to listen to. Classical music calmed the nerves, right? But she impulsively turned to the news. More talk about the victims in the back of the van. She turned it down low, but she assumed they could hear. How strange, she thought, to hear your story on the news as you live it, in real time. But of course the news is wrong, the news is always wrong, the news is only ever a guess. The victims are not in a Mercedes with menacing North Koreans. They are in a Suzuki van with a scared young woman.

She heard her father's voice on the radio. "The U.S. Air Force, the FBI, and the Japanese police are working together to solve this crime. The criminals will be apprehended, and the citizens will be returned safely to their families."

The radio announcer described the people: a famous Kabuki actor from the Ichikawa line; a middle manager from Sony, known for his dedication to the job and family; a secretary at a printing firm, looking forward to marriage in the spring; a precocious twelve-year-old who rode a unicycle in her leisure time.

Silver opened the side door and jumped in the back of the van with the girl. "They're coming around. They've got a refrigerated tofu truck to put them in."

"Who are they?" Virginia asked.

"Let's see. They gave me business cards. I don't know who they are. Some mean-looking Korean dudes. Meaner than the guys we saw in Yokohama. No sense of humor."

Silver turned the left side of his face toward Virginia, and she saw the beginnings of a huge bulge where a fist had made serious contact.

"Serves you right." She looked away. "I just heard another news report. They identified them."

"I'll be fine. Thanks."

A cargo truck drove up the alley from behind them. In the rearview mirror, Virginia read from the hood of the van: FRESH-EST TOFU, FIRST CHOICE. A man emerged and opened the back of their van. Silver grabbed the Kabuki actor under the arms and dragged him out the back. The Korean grabbed the salaryman, inspected them both, and nodded toward his tofu truck.

Although she could read the signage and knew how to drive in Japan, behind the wheel, Virginia felt like a foreigner. She slowly moved to the driver's seat. Whatever her role in the lives of the four victims, she might never know the final result. She could guess and make excuses, but unless she took action, she'd never know.

Silver and the Korean returned for the woman and young girl. They pulled the woman out first, and the Korean put his hands on her body. She jerked away, but he pulled her close to him. She started to curse him, and he grabbed the gag hanging from her neck and shoved it in her mouth. He laughed at her. He pushed her toward Silver and told him to take her to his truck. He told the young girl to get out. He removed her gag and asked her name.

"My name is Masako. I am twelve years old. May I please ride my unicycle?"

The Korean laughed deviously. "Of course, little Masako. You can ride your unicycle and do other tricks for me as well. Where is it?"

She motioned toward the front of the van.

"Grab it."

From the side door, Masako stepped all the way inside the van and reached for her unicycle. Virginia reacted instinctively: She put the van in drive and punched the accelerator. The Korean began to yell, and Masako fell hard into the backseat, screaming. The side and back doors were still open. Virginia drove fast and straight down the alley, on her way to nowhere. The Korean shot at the van, and Virginia heard the impact of bullets somewhere, but she continued to drive. She didn't know what was happening behind her, what was happening to Silver, but the tofu truck had not pursued. Maybe Silver was fighting them; maybe Silver had been shot. She didn't know. If she never knew, she didn't care. As she drove, she turned to check on Masako. Virginia grabbed the girl's wrist and pulled her toward the front.

"Masako!" she screamed. "Are you okay?"

"I skinned my knee is all," the girl said. "Where are we going now?"

"That's a good question, Masako-chan," Virginia said, using the diminutive of "-san" in order to cultivate a much needed friendship. She focused on the road and the traffic, a puzzle made of pavement and rolling metal.

On the train, Severin had time to think. Silver would be in the apartment with Virginia, and possibly with his other punk friends, and Severin knew they had guns. He could fight them with fists but not with guns, because he didn't have one. Around the corner from Silver's apartment was a police box, so he'd summon the Japanese police, tell them he knew the location of an American military dependent runaway, and they would apprehend her and take her home. What Kindwall could not accomplish, Severin would.

Virginia wound her way toward Silver's apartment. She'd considered driving up to the main gate at Yokota and claiming she'd found the girl, but that seemed like a huge risk. She needed to put Masako in a safe place and then distance herself. Also, she needed to retrieve her purse and identification. She'd take Masako to Silver's, feed her, and then leave and tell Masako her parents were coming for her soon. Then she'd call a radio station or newspaper and anonymously report the location of one of the captives. She'd return to her father tonight, apologize for all of her crimes and stupidity, and let him send her to the Catholic boarding school in Switzerland. Good-bye, Tokyo.

Driving, she kept her eye on the Tokyo Tower, a great navigation tool. She remembered visiting the tower with her father, viewing the entire city from the observation deck. She longed for a tower she could climb where she'd witness the contours of her future: the slums, the skyscrapers, the temples, the riots, and the calm, if it ever arrived.

Right this second, her future was traffic. Masako, in the seat next to her, kept her calm.

"Masako-chan," Virginia said. "My Japanese name is Sachiko. Happy child."

The little girl laughed and said, "Happy child." She playfully poked Virginia in the side, and Virginia laughed.

"Do you have pets?" Virginia asked.

"My dog is named Chew Chew," Masako said. "He is a Shiba. My orange cat is named Bobby. My goldfish was named Mizu, but Bobby ate it." She pretended to cry, rubbing her eyes with her knuckles. They both laughed.

Virginia kidded her for naming her goldfish Water.

"The world is mostly made of water," Masako said. "You, too."

"Yes, I know. What is your favorite class?"

"I like mathematics and English. I want to move to America and attend the Princeton University in economics, like my father."

Virginia lifted her eyebrows. "What does your father do?"

"He is the minister in trade."

Virginia suddenly felt very ill. She began to sweat. Someone had kidnapped a government minister's daughter, and here she was driving the sweet girl around. Why had they not said this on the news? Maybe they were unsure whether someone had targeted the minister's daughter and they thought it best to keep her identity concealed.

Virginia said, "Did you hear the news earlier, before we escaped from those bad guys?" The phrase "those bad guys" was not an accidental construction. She was hoping to distance herself, in Masako's mind, from the kidnapping. I'm just bringing you home, kid, Virginia thought.

"Yes." Masako nodded emphatically, touching her chin to her chest. "They said my name wrong. They said my first name right, Masako, but my family name is not Sugihara; it is Sugiyama."

"I will get you to your family."

"I want to ride my unicycle for my mother."

Virginia pulled into the back-alley entrance to Silver's building. They climbed out of the van and walked toward the exterior stairs. Virginia carried Masako's unicycle.

Masako said, "Can I show you some tricks?"

"Not now," Virginia said. "Maybe later, when it gets dark. Or we can clear the floor of the apartment and you can ride there."

Masako's face brightened. The thought of riding the unicycle inside clearly excited her.

Silver never locked his apartment. It was a weird habit for a thief, but he insisted, ironically, that you must trust people. The apartment looked as though some of Silver's friends had been partying there; bottles were everywhere. Virginia told Masako to stay in the hallway; she didn't want the minister of trade's daughter seeing such a mess. She found her purse and identification in the closet. Also, Miyoko's red shawl, the one she'd taken out of her father's house the other day. Virginia threw all of the garbage and bottles into the bathroom and folded the futons and put them in the small closet. Then she invited Masako inside and locked the flimsy door.

The girl looked at her strangely, obviously confused by the empty apartment. "Where is the furniture? Where are the bedrooms?"

"This is a minimalist space," Virginia joked. The girl still looked confused. "It's a practice room for dancing and unicycles. You don't have a lot of space, but it's good to practice maneuvers and tricks. I'll sit over here, and you show me your stuff." Virginia clapped her hands three times and sat.

Masako bowed with a flourish and mounted her unicycle. She

steadied herself and then moved slowly around the small room. She executed an airborne 360-degree turn that caused Virginia pain in the neck from just watching. Masako did it again, stopped, and began to rock back and forth on the unicycle, the wheel remaining in one place, her thin arms extended at her sides like wings, her entire body swaying forward so that Virginia thought she was about to fall, and then violently jerking backward at the opposite angle, so Virginia thought she was going to bail backward and crack her head open. Back and forth, back and forth the girl rocked, grinning hugely. Virginia was falling in love with Masako. What if she'd had a little sister? she thought. Would she have looked like Masako-chan? Masako rode toward her, leaned forward, and kissed Virginia on the forehead, and then turned abruptly and began to hop around the room on the unicycle. It was a thoroughly engaging show, a true display of physical talent. The girl's smile alone was talent, a big beautiful open smile of love.

Severin approached the police box around the corner from Silver's apartment. It was made of corrugated steel and looked like a large box office outside a theater. On the walls hung maps of the prefecture. The police spent a lot of their time giving citizens directions because addresses weren't standardized, and many streets didn't have signs; some didn't even have names. The police wore crisp blue uniforms and gleaming white gloves and always looked as though they were ready to march in a parade.

Sitting inside the box were a teenage girl and her mother. The girl looked contrite, the mother and the policemen stern. What had she done? Severin paced outside the box, and one of the policemen opened the door and asked if he needed help.

Severin tried to speak in Japanese, but he was too nervous, and none of the words came out correctly. He felt like his mouth was full of steaming rice and he could neither chew nor talk. He repeatedly asked for the price and location of the toilet.

"No, sorry. *Sumimasen,*" Severin said, shaking his head.

The man could sense Severin's mounting distress and that this was not about the price of a toilet.

"Runaway," Severin said. "America-*jin*. Girl. Runaway." He pointed toward Silver's alley. "I know where she is."

The man entered the box and conferred with his partner. Severin cursed himself for his lazy study of Japanese. And Virginia was not America-*jin*. She was *hafu*. How stupid, he screamed at himself. He burst into the police box. "*Hafu*. Runaway. Gun." He pointed at the alley again. The policemen retrieved their batons from the wall, and one of them picked up the radio handset and made a frantic call.

Virginia heard noise down the hallway, but it was a loud building full of young people, so she thought nothing of it. She continued to watch Masako's unicycle show. She'd forgotten about feeding the girl.

More noise and shuffling feet—and someone kicked the door in, a large policeman, with a big foot. Two more officers followed. The door had been knocked off the hinges, and Masako had fallen. Virginia screamed and reached for Masako. The policemen were yelling at one another, confused. Virginia cradled Masako in her lap. She kissed her forehead and stroked her hair.

A policeman yelled, "Who are you, and do you live here?"

Masako struggled out of Virginia's lap, stood erect, brushed at her skirt, and pointed at Virginia. She said loudly, "My name is Sugiyama Masako. My father is the minister in trade."

With both hands, Virginia reached toward Masako's face as though she might be able to gently tuck the words back into the girl's mouth.

Masako pointed at Virginia. "Her name is Sachiko. She kidnapped me."

Severin stood in the street watching the fourth-floor catwalk of Silver's apartment building. He half expected gunfire. He was worried about the policemen who carried batons, not guns. He hoped Virginia would make it out safely. She might at first begrudge him, he knew, but eventually, she'd realize he'd done the right thing. These were his thoughts. The policemen would not answer his questions, and they forced him across the alley. A limousine pulled up to the building, flanked by four police motorcycles. A distinguished-looking man in a black suit walked up the stairs of the building and descended a few minutes later, carrying an adolescent girl. The driver placed a unicycle in the trunk, and the limousine sped off with the man and girl inside, the motorcycle sirens blaring. Severin approached the police once more, and they again refused to answer any of his questions.

A cadre of reporters and photographers arrived, and they were forced behind a police barricade. The reporters argued with the police, but they had no better luck than Severin. He had decided to find a pay phone and call the base operator and get Kindwall on the phone when there was a commotion from the catwalk.

Two police officers were descending the stairs, dragging someone. Severin couldn't see who it was, so he crossed the street to get a better view. He ignored the police yelling at him to stay back. He looked up the dark stairs and saw, in the middle of the police officers, Virginia. She was struggling with them, shouting.

"I saved her! I brought her here for her safety! I can take you to the Koreans!"

They carried her down the stairs, a man at each elbow, a fire of red fabric wrapped around her chest and neck. She looked small and weak, helpless. Severin lunged up the stairs, but a policeman grabbed and restrained him.

"Virginia! Where is Silver? I led the police here for you." He yelled at the police, "She is not the criminal."

She looked at him, crying eyes, wild eyes, shameful eyes. He stared at her but had no idea what he was seeing. The police brushed by him, and the photographers' shutters clicked, and the police placed her in the back of a car that sped away.

One of the policemen he'd originally approached in the police box saw him standing in the middle of the street. He gave Severin a ride home to Yokota.

An armored personnel carrier guarded the front gate. Severin asked a guard in the shack, "What's going on, a drill?"

"Just get home, kid."

He opened the door to his house and saw his mother, not a TV watcher, glued to the television, switching between the closed-caption base channel and one of the Tokyo stations in subtitle. Severin startled her. She ran to him and hugged him and nearly dragged him to the ground. Her voice was gravelly and dry, and he could barely understand what she was saying.

"You have a flight to San Francisco at midnight," she said.

He'd wake up in America.

PART II

Sagashita Prison, January 1995

EIGHT

Virginia's last full day in prison was much like her first: She awoke at five A.M. and worked in the kitchen until six A.M., preparing breakfast for the warden and guards; she took her breakfast alone in the kitchen; she joined the other inmates for calisthenics; she attended her anti-recidivism classes from nine until noon; she ate a simple lunch of white rice, steamed fish, and seaweed; she worked in the greenhouse in the afternoon; she ate a simple dinner of white rice, pork cutlet, and pickles; after dinner, she showered and was allowed to socialize with other inmates for forty-five minutes. They didn't speak of her scheduled departure the next morning.

The warden allowed her to sleep until six A.M., the first time in five years that she had slept so late. After breakfast, the clerk began her checkout paperwork. It was easier to get into prison than to get out, she thought. In the changing room, a guard gave her the box of property that she'd arrived with: a powder-blue linen suit, a cream-colored blouse, black flats, a red shawl. The clothing smelled like mothballs.

"What should I do with this?" she asked the guard. She held the white prison jumpsuit in her hand.

"You can keep that. It's our present to you," the guard joked.

The guard gave her an envelope with one hundred thousand yen in it, about a thousand dollars. These were her wages for five years of preparing the warden's breakfast. The guard led her to the outer gates of the prison. No one greeted her—no clapping, no celebration, only the quiet of a cold blue morning.

The prison was located in a bleak industrial prefecture in the middle of the country. She walked down an alley littered with bald tires and empty liquor and soda bottles. The blue sky burned bluer than it had ten minutes before on the wrong side of the fence. She stacked four tires on their sides and sat on them.

"I am twenty-two years old," she said aloud. "My name is Virginia Sachiko Kindwall. This is the first day of my life."

The beauty of the alley amazed her, the pure vitality of it. She saw life where others might have noticed only decay. In the cracks of the concrete, weeds grew. Grow, she thought. The rich lush greenhouse of the prison was desolate when compared with this alley. She removed a map and directions from the cash envelope and consulted them. These were the directions to the rest of her life. The X marked the warden's home. She was cold, and it was a long walk, but she didn't care.

The warden's wife, Mrs. Fukushima, had been wet-nursing and caring for Virginia's daughter, the three-month-old Hideko. Virginia hadn't seen Hideko since her birth. The father, a guard from Sagashita, had been transferred to a prison in northern Japan. It had been agreed that he would never try to contact Virginia and that she would tell Hideko, when the girl seemed ready for the news, that her father had died in an auto accident shortly after her birth. The romance had been consensual; Virginia had wanted the man every time he entered her cell, she liked him, and in the outside world, she would have dated him. She wanted the pregnancy—she'd timed it, in fact, had watched her calendar—and a year before her release date, she became pregnant. This infuriated the guard and imperiled his career, but Virginia didn't care. She needed someone on the other side. After five years of incarceration, she needed a life to care for other than her own. Otherwise she might turn to crime again. What else did she know? How to make a Japanese breakfast? So did every other Japanese woman.

She found the warden's home without difficulty. Mrs. Fukushima invited Virginia in for tea.

"Where will you go?" Mrs. Fukushima asked.

"I will try Okinawa. Work in a restaurant. Your husband wrote a letter of introduction for me. Very complimentary. My hope is that in Okinawa, my name will not be so easily linked with my past. But perhaps this is a foolish wish."

"You must be foolish," Mrs. Fukushima said. "You have no choice."

Virginia set down her cup of tea. "I am ready," she said.

Mrs. Fukushima showed her to the back room and her daughter.

Hideko slept, her pink face glowing and beautiful. Virginia bent down and kissed the girl's warm cheek.

"Come with me, my sweet," she said.

Tokyo, January 2000

NINE

The twelve-hour shifts Virginia worked in the kitchen at the Hara Museum of Contemporary Art's café were brutal and demoralizing. She switched from kitchen duty to bus service to waitress at the whim of the restaurant manager, Miss Takamichi. Occasionally, she had to serve as bouncer, ejecting a particularly drunk patron of the arts, as was the case this evening. Her Japanese was flawless. Prior to jail, her Japanese had been good, but after daily anti-recidivism counseling, she sounded like a native.

"Sir, you must leave the café. The management requests that you leave the premises. You cannot continue to enjoy the exhibition. Your family must exit with you."

The drunken man was not interested in listening to a café worker, let alone a *hafu* café worker, tell him to exit. Virginia saw this in his face—the gallon of sake he'd drunk burned red blotches of rage into his puffy features so that his face looked like the road map of a wrecked life. His wife sat silently, staring at her folded hands in her lap, and his children stared at their shoes, dangling just above the ground, shoelaces undone.

Miss Takamichi stood near the galley door, watching Virginia.

"Sir, I ask you with respect for you and your family to exit the café and the exhibition. Please comply with the requests of the management."

"Where are you from?" the man asked Virginia.

"Okinawa," she said, lying. "Not that it matters."

"Pig." The man laughed. Disdain for the pork products of

Okinawa and Okinawans was common in Tokyo. "You are a pig eater. I don't have to listen to you. I run the assembly plant in Yokohama for Mitsubishi Motors. You cannot tell me what to do."

The wife's shame increased. She whispered ferociously, insisting that her husband comply with the lady's request. The man beat the table with his fist. The young son began to cry.

"I will leave today. But I will return tomorrow." The man stood and stumbled from his seat toward the door.

The woman apologized to Virginia and Miss Takamichi as she arranged her children in single file, heading toward the exit. She gathered in a pink athletic bag the various commodities of motherhood—stuffed toys, electronic toys, pacifiers, stuffed books, rice crackers, soy milk—and offered the children kisses on their foreheads and soothing lies about their father.

Miss Takamichi descended on Virginia and shouted at her to clear the table, since a line at the hostess station had gathered and customers looked greedily at the just-emptied table. Virginia did as told, and while gathering the plates and the cakes—formed into replicas from the permanent collection, Dubuffet, Tomatsu, and Nakamura—she thought of her own daughter at home and the certainty that she would never put Hideko through such a family wreck. Also, Hideko would never work in a café.

In the galley, Miss Takamichi ordered Virginia to switch places with the dishwasher, a teenage girl who worked only weekend nights when the museum stayed open late for a film series or a music performance or a benefit. The high school girl shrugged, happy with her stroke of luck, but as always totally confused by her boss's vagaries. Virginia donned green rubber gloves that engulfed her arms beyond the elbows, then she grabbed the hot-water sprayer in one hand and a rancid sponge in the other. Later, when she combed her daughter's thick black hair with her fingers, she would have forgotten this humiliation but for the wrinkled skin of her fingertips. The dishwasher left the building second to last, after all the dishes were clean, just a few steps ahead of the security guard. So Virginia washed the dishes as they arrived, tried to keep up. The temperature in her tight corner of the kitchen climbed to over 120 degrees. Food waste splattered her apron and her face and sometimes her lips, where she tasted disgust. Sweat poured down her brow and stung her eyes, and she knew that her eye makeup ran down her face in a psychedelic waterfall. Sometimes Miss Takamichi would find her way to Virginia's corner and berate her for falling behind, screaming about the shortage of teacups, and she'd remind Virginia that no matter what time she finished—ten P.M., like the rest of the crew, or two A.M., in the shadow of the cigarette-smoking guard—her pay would reflect only ten hours of work. Virginia entertained fantasies of stuffing Miss Takamichi into the industrial-size washer. She liked to think of Miss Takamichi's face becoming as shriveled as her own delicate hands.

In the middle of the night, she'd consider leaving her subsidized boarding room. Then she and Hideko would go, first to a shelter, with a story of being battered—once, in Yokohama, the shelter had refused her because there was no physical evidence of a beating, so she punched herself in the eye and returned the next day—and eventually, a new boarding room, two or three tatami mats, never more, a small stove and a toilet/sink combination crowded into one corner like an Isamu Noguchi sculpture, a communal shower in the hall. Virginia knew that posing as a battered single mother didn't help her karma dividends, but she believed herself already doomed and thus unaffected by any forward figuring of such abstract spiritual sums.

Miss Takamichi and all of her coworkers had left for the evening, and Virginia was now near the end of her task. The security guard sat on a kitchen stool, smoking cheap cigarettes and drinking a draft beer. After locking the galleries, the man always proceeded to drink beer and smoke. Sometimes he attempted to flirt with her, but lately, he'd seemed more concerned with accelerating his buzz. Virginia knew that the man was married, but he never spoke of his wife. Virginia imagined a depressing scene at home, the wife wide awake at eleven-thirty with a plate of hot food, waiting for her husband. The woman would awake at five-thirty to make breakfast and begin the household preparation for the day, two more meals for the family, laundry, paying bills, making social calls, perhaps volunteering at the children's school or the local temple where her husband's ancestors were enshrined. Comparatively, Virginia's eleven-hour day seemed like leisure.

Virginia dropped a service platter that shattered against the mud-colored kitchen tile.

The guard said, "For some action, I will forget I saw it. I'll sweep it up for you and discard it down the road. Otherwise, I will tell Miss Takamichi, and she will remove the cost from your check." The man inhaled deeply on his cigarette and extinguished it against the steel countertop. "And I'll tell her you've been smoking in here." He laughed, impressed with his own devious ingenuity.

Virginia said, "If you touch me, I will tell your wife, and I will press charges." She reached toward the last load of utensils that had just finished the drying cycle. The wooden handle of the butcher knife was hot, and the metal rivets burned into her palm. "Do you still want some action?"

The man stood, confused by and afraid of Virginia's violent gesture. He'd been beaten, and he knew it. "We should go now, if you are finished with the work of the evening," he said.

At home, Virginia paid the babysitter two thousand yen. After paying the sitter she barely made enough money to make the job worth her time, but she needed to be out of the small room for her own sanity, and she needed to stay off the streets. She was in fact a vagabond but needed not to look like one. A woman wandering the neighborhood alone with no clear objective, such as grocery shopping or retrieving her husband's dry cleaning, always drew attention. Virginia wanted to be invisible.

After jail, she'd spent four years outside of Tokyo, working in small country inns all over the country—Okinawa, Saga, Gabo,

Amino, Sampoku, Taneichi—but finally, she returned to the city. In the country the single mother was especially conspicuous. Here in the city, if careful, she blended.

Virginia reclined on her small futon next to Hideko, who slept silently. She kissed her daughter on the lips and tasted the young girl's sleepy breath. Hideko wanted long hair like her mother's, so they were growing it out; it splayed across the white sheets like an ink stain on snow. She was five years old and proud of her pretty hair and the teeth that she occasionally lost. Her smile, Virginia knew, as all mothers do, could light the full moon. Because of their transient lifestyle, Hideko attended *gaikokujin gakko,* schools for foreigners that also allowed some Japanese students, usually the poor. The curriculum was less rigorous than at mainstream schools, but so, too, were the standards for attendance, and this made it easy for Virginia to offer fake names for them both. Whatever Hideko lost by studying at foreigner schools, Virginia made up with tutoring. A good dose of propaganda was also offered at the foreigner schools, populated mostly by South Koreans and Chinese. The Japanese needed this growing foreign population to forget that they had visited atrocities upon them over the last 120 years, during the Far East War, the Russo-Japanese War, the Sino-Japanese War, and other acts of aggression. In the future, Virginia would need to counter this revisionist history with a clear view of the empire's warworks. Of course, to be fair, she'd also need to teach Hideko about the firebombing of Hamburg and Dresden, of Hiroshima and Nagasaki, the full-scale targeting of civilians, Dachau, the extermination of the Jews. Couldn't we just altogether forget the last century? Why had her mind wandered to war? Virginia had named Hideko after a nineteenth-century feminist, Hideko Fukuda, who was a human rights campaigner and a pacifist opposed to the Russo-Japanese War, a woman who'd had a few husbands and many lovers and had spent four years in jail for her work in support of Korean nationals living in Japan. Virginia knew that she herself wasn't a feminist, at least not a public one, and never could be, but she hoped her daughter might follow in Hideko-san's footsteps. Virginia lived her future through Hideko.

While she lay beside Hideko, she had slowly emptied a glass of cold sake, and now she was ready for bed. She pulled her daughter close and closed her eyes, the lights in the room still burning brightly. She needed the light in order to sleep.

Tokyo, October 2001

TEN

Virginia hadn't watched television since being incarcerated. But after the terrorist attacks in America and the start of the subsequent war in Afghanistan, she felt she needed to watch television news in order to stay informed. If Tokyo suffered an attack, she'd require access to information sooner than the next day's newspaper. She hated buying anything that cost more than ten thousand yen, couldn't really afford it. They'd lived in the same apartment for six months. Hideko liked their home and the neighborhood, and Virginia refused to jeopardize this stability with frivolous spending.

Virginia thought of Yoshida's, the electronics store near her father's old base at Yokota. Yokota. She hadn't said that word in years. Home of my youth, she thought, home of my ruin. At an Internet café, she looked Yoshida up online; his shop remained in the same place. He might give her a deal, or let her make payments, sell her a used TV. He would definitely remember her. And maybe it was time for her to do a drive-by on those memories.

Haijima station in Yokota had changed radically. There had once been a mom-and-pop candy store and two restaurants at the station, and now the retail section took up an entire block. She avoided walking by the main gate of the air base and, in doing so, went ten minutes out of her way.

She found Yoshida's. The man looked the same, and he recognized her instantly. He nearly skipped across his showroom.

"Miss Kindwall," he said. "It is a surprise to see you."

"It's good to see you, Yoshida-san," she said in Japanese.

"Please, come to my office and we can talk."

He showed her into a large back storeroom and office space. Hundreds of TVs.

"Can I get to business first?" Virginia asked.

"Please."

"I need a television, but I have very little money to spend. I work in a kitchen for a low wage. I barely make my rent. But I need to get the news. And also I think it would be good for educational programs for my daughter. Do you have any used sets that are affordable?"

Yoshida laughed. He kept laughing. "No one buys used TVs anymore," he said. "It is most important for people's self-image to update every few years. This is good for my business, though I consider it wasteful. I still watch the same television since 1969. I might have a cheap floor sample. Let me check with my inventory clerk."

He dialed the phone and told the person on the other end of the line to come to the store immediately. He didn't say anything about a television. Then he reentered the showroom without saying anything to her.

She'd been sitting in the room for a few minutes and was about to walk out front to ask Yoshida what was going on when he walked in the door. A woman in coveralls followed him. She wore a flower-patterned scarf on her head. And she was still beautiful. It was Miyoko, General Kindwall's ex-girlfriend.

"Hello, Virginia," Miyoko said. She hugged Virginia and spoke in her ear. "Please let Yoshida-san and me help you."

That night, Yoshida and Miyoko took Virginia and Hideko to dinner, and they caught up. In the aftermath of Yoshida's son's death, he and his wife had divorced, and a few years later, Yoshida and Miyoko began dating. They'd been old friends from high school, and now they looked forward to comforting and loving each other for the rest of their lives.

It delighted Hideko to meet these people from her mother's past.

Later, over tea at Yoshida and Miyoko's house, they turned to the topic of General Kindwall. Hideko was asleep in the next room.

"He tried to contact me two years ago," Virginia said. "He sent someone for me. I don't know how he found me. Showed up on my doorstep one night. It was creepy. I told this man to never contact me again and that I had no message for my father. That was the last I heard from him."

"We only know that he moved away while you were in prison," Yoshida said.

Before Virginia left, Yoshida and Miyoko offered her a job doing the books for their businesses. They doubled the salary she made working in the kitchen.

That night in bed, Virginia thought: I left the house today looking for a television set, and I might have found a family.

San Francisco, December 2004

San Francisco, December 1994

ELEVEN

Severin and his wife, Aida, stood over their kitchen table in the Pacific Heights Victorian. The table acted as a horizontal filing system. The thickness of the file varied from month to month, depending on what bills were due, what charities were begging for money, and how many magazines had gone unread. It was near the end of Aida's semester, and she glanced at the table once a week. Severin looked through the mail an average of once every six weeks. At the start of their marriage, Aida insisted on taking care of the bills, and no one Severin knew wrote actual letters.

Severin looked at the postcard, flipping between the front and the back, not really reading and not quite looking at the thing in his hands. He held his past between his thumb and forefinger. Aida took the postcard back and said, "It sounds as though your old coach Kindwall needs some help."

Severin snapped the card out of her hands.

He feared his wife, a furious, beautiful woman—alabaster skin and dark hair to her shoulders and piercing blue eyes, five-two and ninety-nine pounds, never less, never more. Sometimes he suspected that she ate roofing nails for breakfast, but in fact, she preferred hot cereal. She considered dried fruits and nuts and six ounces of water a three-course meal. She'd never owned a pair of athletic shoes. She wore black six days a week. She never wore pants. She never painted her fingernails because her mother had once told her that only whores did so. (Severin had never confirmed this information.) Her bra and underwear always matched.

He feared his wife partly because he thought she was always on the verge of leaving him. He thought this even though no evidence supported the assumption.

The postcard: a famous photo of Ho Chi Minh wearing olive-drab fatigues, deep in the bush, visiting the troops, who sat in a semicircle and ate plain rice that had been baked underground in banana leaves. The return address: Hue City Hotel, Hue City, Vietnam. The ink was smudged and the handwriting looked labored, maybe written while exhaling a lungful of tobacco smoke. It read:

Boxx,

This is your general, your coach. I need your assistance with the matter of my missing daughter. I don't know your financials. I might be able to reimburse partially or in full. Ticket to Saigon, three-day stay, reroute through Tokyo, return to Saigon. Time frame undetermined. Much work to do. Doctors gave me six months. I wait to die. We're down by 14. Your defense has failed.

—General Kindwall

Aida took the postcard back. "What's this?" she asked, her voice raising on the word "this." She waved Ho Chi Minh in the air. "I thought you quit the team in a dramatic showing of individual will. Revolt." She pointed at his arm. "What does he want you for?"

"He seems to think I owe him." Severin tried not to look her in the eyes, but she wouldn't allow him to escape.

"Who is the daughter? First love?" Aida said this so that it would sting, and it did.

"First unconsummated love," he said humbly. He sat down at the table.

"Why did you never mention her? Did you love her?" She sat opposite him and laced her fingers. She looked as though a snake were climbing her spine; her eyes were wide and wild, but so blue they still broke his heart.

"How could I love her?" Severin asked. "I didn't even know her. She was an apparition. We hung out a few times. She got caught up in a crazy situation."

"What exactly is a crazy situation?" Aida's hands opened. She wanted knowledge; she wanted him to fill her hands with the truth. It was all she ever asked of him.

"In Virginia's case, a crazy situation involved beating up perverts, robbing convenience stores, and a kidnapping with possible involvement of the North Korean Communist government. Followed by five years of jail time. Minor stuff."

"This is why you finished high school here?"

"I was a threat to my father's promotion. And my mother thought General Kindwall might actually kill me." At this he laughed.

"How were you involved?" She stood and sorted through mail.

"I accidentally turned her in to the Japanese police."

"Accidentally?" She scowled. "Oh, I don't care. You are telling me this only now, and only because this postcard arrived? Otherwise I would've died not knowing this part of your past?" She threw a handful of junk mail toward the recycle bin, but it missed and spilled all over the kitchen floor, a junk mail bomb.

"The subject never surfaced." He looked at the mess and considered cleaning it up.

"Never surfaced?" She dropped the postcard and picked up a three-inch-thick fashion magazine and slammed it on the table. "You told me about every little waitress and bank teller you slept with, the two girls at a time, the girls who only wanted it in the ass, the cutter, the coke head, the brother fucker. And General Kindwall's daughter never came up?"

Severin felt like a fourteen-year-old who'd been busted with a box of pornography. Those were all good memories his wife had just run through. "Honey, I was a kid. Seventeen. This isn't about the girl."

155

"I could've had your child without knowing this?" She slumped back into the chair. "It never came up? Are you crazy? What now?" She grabbed the postcard. "What am I supposed to do with this?"

"Please understand that I didn't think Virginia Kindwall would enter my life again. If General Kindwall is dying, he must want to make peace with his daughter. I know from my mother that Kindwall never visited her in jail. They junked his career because of this. He took his pension to Vietnam, where he'd served three tours. It's probably the only place in the world that makes sense to him. He's dying. He wants me to find his daughter."

"You think it's that simple?" Her lips, normally fixed in a smile, were turned down in a frown.

"For Kindwall, yes."

"And you? Are you going?"

"Aida, you shoved this postcard in my face five minutes ago. When did it arrive?" He reached for the postcard, but she grabbed it first. "I haven't thought about these people in years," he said. "But generally, when a dying man asks for a favor, one complies."

She inspected the back of the postcard. "It's postmarked the middle of October." She affixed it to the refrigerator, writing side out, using a 2001 calendar magnet from an oil-change place. "Who knows how long it's been sitting here. Time is running out, if you're going."

"I need to think about it." He was truly distressed. He flipped the postcard so that Uncle Ho was looking out on their kitchen.

"Why don't you try fixing things with your own father first, if this is about father figures? Did you skip therapy again this week?" She paced the kitchen.

"Of course I skipped therapy. You make the appointments, and I cancel them. That's a different issue. My father is dead. Dead men don't ask for favors."

"But they talk to you from the grave. You can't solve your issues with your own father by reconciling with other fathers."

"I don't think you understand fathers and sons."

"I don't think you understand wives." She walked out of the kitchen.

"Nice, nice," he yelled. "You win the witty-comeback contest for the day, as usual. You can retrieve your prize at the door on your way out."

"This is my house," she yelled from the living room.

He yelled back, "No, it's your parents' house, and we are leasing to purchase. And soon, in my role as houseboy, I will build a rental apartment in the basement. And then you and I will fight over what colors to paint the walls. I can't wait."

"You are so put upon."

In fact, he was not put upon. Her parents had given them a deal on the sprawling house, fifteen hundred dollars a month toward purchase, with part-time cook and cleaner and gardener, furniture and art and library. And wine cellar. Aida taught psychology at the university and had a budding psychotherapy practice. He worked part-time on the university grounds crew and pretended to look for teaching positions.

But the comment enraged him. So he would get her back. He rolled up his right sleeve and walked into the living room. She sat in a leather chair correcting essays in the same style her father had corrected essays for thirty years prior to retiring.

Severin knelt in front of her and laid his arm across her lap. His forearm still retained some of the muscle of his youth. The tattooed characters on his arm were now a faded green, so many years old, faded like his memories of that time, but still present, still a problem.

"Do you mind? I'm working," she said without looking away from the essay in her hands.

"Since I am confessing my past," Severin said, "I should tell you that this tattoo doesn't mean 'revolt.' It means 'happy child,' Sachiko, which is Virginia's middle name."

●   ●   ●

Later that night, he retrieved an old blanket from the linen closet and prepared a bed on the couch. He tried to sleep but couldn't. He stared at the pile of essays that Aida had corrected, working late, as always. She was a great professor, he'd observed her teaching; and she was an impassioned therapist, he'd watched her tapes. Sometimes late at night, alone in the basement, he'd throw in one of her tapes and watch her heal a damaged mind. He could watch hours of her tapes. It was like watching Pollock paint. You had no idea what on earth he was doing, and then bam—light and heat— and there appeared a painting, your mind thus altered. She didn't like his Pollock analogy, but he stood by it. She offered the analogy of constructing a country garden wall—one heavy stone, one heavy burden, released at a time. New parameters, room inside for growth.

His wife was a star, and all he did with his Ph.D. in French history was mow the university lawn and keep it green with the aid of outlawed pesticides he'd bought cheap at auction in Sonoma. "It's like a ree-verse Agent Orange," the bankrupt farmer had told him.

He'd paid his way through graduate school mowing lawns and painting curbs red or yellow and KEEP OUR CAMPUS CLEAN and RESERVED FOR AREA DEAN, and then he finished his dissertation and kept the job. He told Aida he stayed on in order to remain social with a few of his friends and the other strange misfits that made up the crew. His friend Clark was a trust-fund kid: Grandpa had won the Nobel for economics in the seventies and dropped all the prize dollars in little Clark's savings passbook. Clark worked the crew because he liked the smell of gasoline, and he loved rolling across the grounds on a riding lawn mower, said it gave him a hard-on, and in spring, when the skirts shortened and the skin appeared, he could even orgasm, just riding that John Deere nine to five, and looking dark and steamy at the undergrads. He burned so much gas, the chief of grounds ran an investigation into the mystery of the high fuel bills. Severin liked

Clark: Clark was insane. But Clark's money would never run out, and Severin had none to burn. And right now Clark was sleeping with an undergrad. Severin tried not to think about it. And he tried not to think about Virginia because he didn't want to dream of her.

He went down to the basement and watched one of Aida's tapes. It was his recent favorite, number 12A. The girl was supremely twisted. Four or five new partners a week, a minor coke habit, at ten years old she'd watched her father kill her mother and sister and then himself. Crazy world full of savages, Severin thought as he pushed play.

He awoke early from a fitful sleep. The heat had been turned up high all night, deep into the seventies, to keep Aida warm because his furnace legs weren't in the bed; instead, his furnace legs had covered the brown leather couch with a milky sheen of sweat. He wanted to go vegan and get rid of the leather couch; he felt as though he'd slept on the haunch of a slippery, damp cow, and really, he had.

He'd sweated so much partially because he had always sweated a lot and partially because he was about thirty pounds overweight. When he tied his shoes, there was a small roll at his waist. Humiliation. The climb to the fourth floor of the university library left him panting. Humiliation. He was a lifetime away from his five-minute-mile days. Climbing stairs is good for you, he'd remind himself, out of breath. At the start of graduate studies, he'd stopped working out; the logic had been that with so much time spent working his brain, he had no time to work his body, but this was a lie. He knew he'd be lucky to clock a mile under nine. What would Kindwall say?

But Aida still called him handsome, and his thick hair remained on his head. Sometimes he even awoke to her on top of him in the middle of the night. Simply the best way in the world to awake. But hadn't it been at least six months since he'd woken up with her on top of him? And more often than not, his over-tures were met with silence.

Severin knew how to atone for last night, or at least a good way to start the General and Virginia Kindwall conversation anew: fresh-squeezed orange juice, by hand, not machine; French-press coffee, one cloud of cream; rye toast with huckleberry jam (huckleberry jam, invented at the college where Aida had earned her BA, was a must, how did they *invent* jam?); hot cereal with honey.

He expected her to descend the stairs any second. She had an internal clock tuned to the sound of the water kettle. Roughly six minutes after the kettle moaned—it wasn't a screamer but a French brand that sounded like a tired midnight train making entry into a rural station—the coffee would be brewed, and her clock knew this. He heard the slight creaking of the third-floor stairs. She'd be barefoot and wearing a purple piece of underwear; he wasn't certain what it was called, but it had thin shoulder straps and was tight at her small perfect tits with a bit of lace at the cleavage, and it stopped just below the underfold of her ass. A very short dress. He loved that garment. He frantically forced juice from the flesh of the orange, the thick vertically ribbed phallic thing ripping the insides to shreds. Hadn't the French used something like this for torture during the revolution? Go to the Hôtel de Ville and lose your insides.

Aida looked tired, as if she had not slept, either. She turned on the radio, public radio. Those voices drove him mad. And she knew it; of course she knew it. The first words out of her mouth were "End-of-semester minority-scholarships breakfast at nine thirty."

"You aren't a minority, honey, and you don't have a scholar-ship."

"I'm a woman. I'm a minority. And I have students who are minorities and attend college thanks to scholarships that are intended to help them break the cycle of institutional racism and prejudice."

"Sorry." But he liked it when she got serious and radical. Yes, he thought, let's burn the provost's building down! He let a smile creep to his face.

"The answer is no."

She sat at the kitchenette and scanned the backyard. She liked her backyard, he knew. Sometimes she would sit at the kitchenette for hours and watch the plants and grasses. He wondered if she could see them grow. A gardener was paid well to keep the plants in shape, the same gardener for thirty years.

He placed the toast and coffee and juice in front of her. She pretended not to notice.

"I talked to Daddy yesterday. He wants you to have the framing installed in the basement in three weeks. That means you need to clear it out and get to work." She tapped her fingers on the Formica tabletop. Her eyelids were red and puffy, the result of crying in bed. He knew that when she looked in the mirror and saw this, she'd be angry with him. "Last week he mailed a list of what goes to storage and what gets sent to the alley. I've marked the stuff for the junkmen with an A, in Magic Marker."

"I'll be done in three weeks. Clark might help me. I'll pay him with wine." He took the cloth napkin from her table setting and wiped the sweat from his brow. "Can I turn down the heat now?"

"Don't pay him with wine. Pay cash. That's what it's for. Daddy made a budget." She took the napkin out of his hand.

"Okay, then. I'll pay him with Daddy's cash." It infuriated him when she called her father Daddy. "It just seems kind of trashy to pay your friend with cash."

"Then why doesn't he do it for free?"

"Clark does nothing for free. Five points minimum."

"Points." She shook her head. "This isn't Hollywood. You tell him that lately? How is his university-grounds-crew screenplay coming along?"

She finally reached for her toast. He'd wondered how long it would take. The angrier she was, the longer it would take her to reach for the toast. This was not so bad. Morning sex was out of the question, but maybe she'd be okay by late afternoon. He'd cut out early. They'd meet in the library like the old days, underneath the dark, worn pages of philosophers and statesmen, and their romance would burn again.

"Want to meet me at the library at three?" he asked. "I need some books."

She smiled, but only at the corners of her mouth. "Books? What kind of books? I thought you were done with books."

"I want to research Vietnam." He said this without thinking about it.

"New field of study?"

They'd enter the subject slowly. "Possibly," he said.

"This is good toast, Mr. Husband. You are an expert at toast. Don't they give the grounds crew library cards? You guys don't work, you might as well read."

She brushed the crumbs from her fingers, just the tips. He loved the tips of her fingers. He loved his wife.

"How's the coffee?"

She tried it. "Perfect. I wonder how the coffee tastes in Hue City. French, I imagine. Great croissants, too, one would assume."

"And the juice?"

She tried this, too. "Perfect. I wonder what Hue City orange juice tastes like."

"No one thinks the ground crew works. But we do. Just not when you're looking."

"Sounds familiar. The VC said no one looked when they did their good deeds. I might go to Madrid for the end of my parents' trip. I haven't seen the apartment in a few years." She retrained her gaze on the backyard. "I don't know when they'll make it back. They've been eating every night at Los Asturianos. Remember that place?"

"I do. Alberto. A great host. Good God, his mother can cook. I'll miss it."

Severin tried to locate what she was staring at in the backyard. It occurred to him that possibly she scanned the backyard, and always had, for her childhood self. She was a psychotherapist and a closet diarist; like everyone else, she was self-obsessed. "How many times did we eat there?"

"Six times in nine days," she said.

"When will you go?"

"Friday, after I turn in grades. The five-forty-five Iberia flight. Three weeks. Would you mind?"

"Sort of," he said with a pout. "No Christmas, no Hanukkah. I guess it doesn't matter without God and without kids. Someday."

He knew he shouldn't have mentioned kids. They'd lost a pregnancy a year ago. Just a sad red blot in the toilet, so fast, days after the doctor's positive test, but still, they'd chosen a name, Josephine or Joseph, and imagined the room painted blue or pink, with many furry animals and twirling bits of colored plastic dangling from the ceiling and clothes folded in the dresser, socks adorned with bunnies or baseball bats, the sleepy pajama suits, hats to shield the baby from the sun and harm, and the house filled with music and sweet baby crying and family laughter.

She coughed, a fake cough, he knew, her stalling device. She coughed again, a few moments, to divert the topic. "I'll have my mom overnight you a stack of latkes. Turn the heat down."

"Thanks."

He should have pursued a Ph.D. in thermostat control. After setting the temperature for 30 below and then 110 above zero, he regained control of the electronic brain inside the little plastic box and settled on a reasonable and environmentally sound 68.

The rule was: We do not speak of the sad red blot. We do not use the names Joseph or Josephine. Josephine Baker, no; Joseph from the Bible, no. We no longer smile at each other in the co-op when we see children walking through the bulk-candy aisle with choco-smeared faces and grass-stained knees. No baby showers. No birthday parties. No pink or blue paint. No. No. No.

"I want to go to Madrid with you, but maybe next trip," he said as he reentered the kitchen.

She stood at the open back door. "Severin, how will you ever fit Spain into your busy international travel schedule?"

She was gone now, in the backyard. She walked the backyard in her underwear, her very short dress. He ran up the stairs to the fourth-floor terrace. He loved watching her from this height. He was out of breath. Blue skies and sun, but the outside temperature could not have been over 40, her nipples would be hard and her white body covered with goose pimples. She wore her pink bunny slippers, a new pair at the holidays every year from his mother. She hated the slippers, he hated that his mother gave them to her annually, but he could not stop his mother, and Aida continued to wear them, the slippers they both hated. He spotted two alley kids peering at his genius, beautiful wife through the holes in the wood fence, their bikes piled behind them in a tower of plastic and chrome and rust. An unexpected bonus on the way to school! Let them, he thought. May they be so lucky—may they be so lucky as to not know beauty and genius turning from them.

TWELVE

By this point in the year, the grounds crew mostly wrestled with mud and heavy rain. In December, Clark and Severin spent as much time as possible drinking instant coffee in the warming shed, their wet feet resting atop the pulsing orange wall heater. Clark liked to talk girls. He called himself a girl magnet and the university a girl factory, and as of yet, there were no policies preventing the grounds crew from dating students. Clark wanted to take advantage of this oversight with as much fervor as he could muster for as long as the oversight remained beyond the sight of the officials charged with overseeing such things. Clark was not a conventional girl magnet, and he knew it: He was nearly seven feet tall and totally absent any athletic ability, the kind of guy who spends half his life defending never having played basketball. He had no chin; his teeth were bad because he thought dentists were crooks (not because he couldn't afford the 20 percent copay on the university dental plan); and his hair gathered near the crown of his head in a curly, dull spear. When his girlfriends studied late at night, he played fantasy board games with his ten-year-old nephews. But still the girls came.

Severin didn't mind listening to the stories and giving Clark the same advice over and over: Make certain she's not a sixteen-year-old scholarship whiz kid from Topeka; find out who her father is; use a condom; don't give her a key to your house. But this time Severin wanted to do the talking about girls; no, he wanted to talk wife.

He sipped the cold black silt at the bottom of his paper cup. "She's never done it before, but if she wants to take a trip alone, I guess it's her business. We have no kids to feed. It's not like she needs to teach the winter session for extra money. The flight is cheap. She doesn't need a hotel on the other end. She speaks the language. She's a grown woman. Her parents are there. She likes the food and wine."

"You have a problem," Clark said. "Radical behavioral changes in primates suggest cognitive dissonance of a sort bound to cause trouble for all members of the nuclear family. You are the nuclear family. You are bound for trouble."

"What do you really think?" Severin bent over the hot-water dispenser and filled another paper cup with eight ounces of water, which quickly turned the tiny brown coffee crystals into mud.

"I think she's getting cozy with a colleague or a graduate student. Not from her department. She met him at the coffee joint they all go to, the place that doesn't serve this instant garbage we drink. The place where we would be castrated for drinking instant coffee, even though the Europeans do it. Sanka. We need to switch to Sanka."

"What if she just needs a break?"

"She walks into the other room or up to the third floor. You have a big house. Plenty of room for a break."

"You are undermining my marriage and my sanity."

"No. Your wife is undermining your marriage. Your sanity has always been in question."

"Are you still in on the framing job?" Severin wanted to change the subject. "It's just a one-bedroom with a small living room. The lumber is being delivered tomorrow."

"Yeah, man, I'm in. You'll pay me a hundred and fifty a day?"

"If that's your rate. It's four days of work, if you keep up the pace."

"Is Daddy paying?"

166

"Yes."

"Then that's my rate. How much are you going to rent it out for? Maybe I'll move in and lease my house to a dentist for ten grand a month."

"What's your beef with dentists?"

"Torturers. Cruelty to children."

"I got a postcard from Virginia's father."

Clark jumped out of his seat as though it were on fire. "Jesus Christ."

The name Virginia Kindwall had bounced around the walls of the warming shed for many years, usually as the answer to the question: Who is the one girl you never slept with and will thus haunt you until the day you die?

"I think he wants me to track her down in Japan," Severin said.

"Does Aida know?"

"She read it first."

"Well, no kidding. You can't request my counsel on matters of the heart and not give me the full story. General Kindwall drops you a postcard and asks you to track down his daughter? No wonder your wife is leaving the country." Clark sat back down and crossed his arms. "But this changes nothing. She's still sleeping with someone. So you came clean with the whole Virginia story? The tattoo and all?"

Severin shook his head. "I had to."

Clark looked disapprovingly at Severin. "I gotta go, man. Date at the food mall with a junior physical-sciences major. Free chicken fajitas. Her roommate works the Fiesta counter."

"Physical sciences? Isn't that a course you take in third grade?"

"She's a six-foot-five scholarship kid from Baltimore." Clark held his hand at the tip of his nose, displaying her height. "McDonald's All-American. The athletic director's angel. Three tutors, private penthouse in the new dormitory. Pops got a job sharpening pencils in the registrar's office. She's got full-court stamina. Yeow!"

"For never having played basketball, you know a little about the game," Severin said, turning toward the heater as Clark opened the door and let the cold air in.

"Man, you've got to study your girl's passion. Fifteen minutes of sports radio, that's all it took."

The door slammed shut.

Severin closed his eyes and bit his tongue. His ears began to ring. They always rang, the doctors said, but he heard it only when he focused on a thought. The sound brought no comfort. He made a clicking sound with his tongue and lower lip, trying to cover the ringing in his ears. He'd learned this from a Korean friend; it was the way Koreans called dogs.

He thought of Kindwall. Kindwall had once told the football team that in Saigon you could buy a live dog at market just like you might buy a lobster in Portland, Maine. The dogs knew their fate, Kindwall insisted, he saw it in their eyes. Also, there were streets lined with dog restaurants, *thit cho,* where entire families would dine. When Severin asked, Kindwall neither confirmed nor denied that he'd eaten dog.

THIRTEEN

Severin poured the first two glasses of wine and waited at the table for Aida to come down for dinner. Mary, the housekeeper and cook, had the night off, and Severin had prepared garlic soup and a pork loin. During finals week, he and Aida always spoke less and had less sex, but this year, things seemed extreme. They'd slept together only once in ten days. No matter how bad they might be getting along, they'd always had sex, both of them aware that orgasms healed wounds. But this week she spent most of her time in the office. She'd ask him or Mary to make a plate for her and deliver it to her office. But he'd insisted they eat at the table tonight: They needed to talk about Kindwall, and he intended to ask her what was going on in the sex department. Not that it was likely she'd answer. He at least wanted to share the fact that the lack of sex was bringing him down. He'd chosen a great wine from the cellar.

Aida sat down across from him with a pile of papers clutched to her chest. She said, "Intro is killing me. I should do like everyone else and assign fewer papers. I'm going to have to grade as I eat."

"The key is shorter essays, not fewer. Everything the undergrad has to say about a topic can fit nicely into four hundred words. The best thing Professor Byron ever did for me as a student and teacher was assigning four-hundred-word essays."

"We do this every semester." She drank from her wine without offering a toast. "You tell me to assign shorter essays, and I say no. Byron just wanted to decrease his workload."

"Don't you want to decrease yours?" He picked up his glass. "Here's to smaller workloads and more sex. Cheers."

"It all comes down to that, right?" But she didn't refuse the toast.

I do not want to drink nine glasses of wine and forget about it, Severin thought.

They ate in silence. He could ask: Hey, sweetheart, what's going on? A wildly open-ended question, and he couldn't be open-ended with her or she'd start talking about the war in Iraq or supply-side economics or the old standby, borderline disorders. He needed to go straight to the heart of the matter: Why are we not having sex? She would tell him he was overreacting, being too sensitive, that the world did not revolve around him and his cock. All true things, but still, going sexless for ten days was a killer and possibly a sign that the foundation had cracked. She would also say he was using sex to deflect from the main issue at the moment: Happy Child. But she was not talking about Virginia. She was as silent as her glass of wine. Aida graded her students' longish essays, and Severin stared at the Japanese tapestry on the wall behind her, a country scene, women in long robes with farm animals gathered near. He chewed his food and swallowed and drank his wine. If the sad red blot had not occurred, and they'd had their child, the ten sexless days would be no big deal. He knew some married-with-children guys who had sex fewer than a dozen times a year. (That didn't mean that these same poor guys weren't twice daily power-scrolling through endless screens of fornicating twenty-year-olds on the Internet, actively degrading themselves and the dominant technology.)

Aida coughed and stood from the table. "Back to the office for me," she said.

"Care for a nightcap at midnight?" he asked.

"Not tonight."

"When can we talk about Spain and Vietnam?"

"I'm working. I'm working on everything."

She nodded at him and walked upstairs.

Severin sat in his father-in-law's leather chair and worked on the bottle of wine he'd opened for dinner. A 1993 burgundy. In Japan, at the age of seventeen, he hadn't even known what a burgundy wine was. He might have guessed its color as reddish. What had he learned since then? After the collapse of his life in Japan, he'd vowed to live simply. But what teenager's life didn't collapse? he asked himself. Once in California, he had concentrated on studying, and after a year of reading everything his uncle put in front of him, he walked into U.C. Berkeley's open arms. He lived in Oakland, in the bad part, West (Worst) Oakland. He built a community garden next to a liquor store. With neighborhood moms, he sold cakes in the Safeway parking lot to raise the cash to rebuild a basketball court. He talked them into giving the extra money to the library. He lobbied Safeway to deliver the same high-quality produce to its Worst Oakland store as it did to the Piedmont glamour supermarket where they valet-parked your Benz for free and your kids could play unattended in a fifty-thousand-dollar playground while you shopped. He wrote a grant and got forty new computers for the nearby elementary school. He coached Pee-Wee football. He drank and smoked pot and slept with a respectable number of girls. He studied European history and graduated fifth in his class. He started graduate school in French history. One night during his third year, he smoked hash and listened to Charlie Parker's "A Night in Tunisia" one hundred times, volume at thirty out of thirty, 305 straight minutes of Bird. The next day he met Aida. A week later, a military transport plane with his father aboard crashed in Egypt, all forty servicemen dead. A sparsely attended funeral in Spokane, Washington. His father had no friends, and this haunted Severin. His mother bought a bed-and-breakfast on Gabriola Island, British Columbia. She started to write a memoir of a military wife.

Over the years, Virginia's name occasionally surfaced in conversations with his mother. They had silently agreed never to mention

Virginia around Aida. When his parents still lived in Japan, Mrs. Boxx had narrated the Kindwall story. Virginia got five years of prison, a light sentence owing largely to Sugiyama Masako's warmth for her kidnapper. Within six months, the Pentagon decommissioned Kindwall. They took two years and one general rank off of his pension. He bought a bar just outside the base and named it Kindwall's Corner. He changed the name after six weeks of slow business. He vowed never to visit his daughter in prison, and he didn't. His bar failed. He moved to Vietnam.

Aida descended the stairs and entered the kitchen. He heard her preparing a coffee press for the morning, a quiet blow, but one with teeth. In the natural balance Severin prepared the coffee every morning. He woke up earlier than her to do this. She walked upstairs without saying a word. He at least expected the courtesy of a nasty comment from under her breath.

He thought about the task before him: building a basement apartment. He'd become a laborer in his own home. Turning the basement into a rentable apartment had been Aida's father's idea. It was intended to provide investment income for his daughter. Severin knew that this not so subtle dig at his current earning and social status was intended to motivate him in his job search and other professional endeavors. Most likely, it would have the opposite effect.

The items marked with a black A, for "alley," he should stack in the alley behind the house and the freelance junkmen or the garbagemen would get rid of the stuff, whoever found it first.

Severin started his work clearing the basement—dish crates, boxes of clothes, broken or severely out-of-fashion furniture, framed poster art, bed frames, metal bookshelves, and other detritus from Aida's parents' thirty years of making and breaking house. Every night, junkmen went through the alley behind the house looking for good junk to sell the next weekend at a flea market. This style of distribution of wealth and goods seemed peculiarly American to Severin, and he liked the system: a poster of

Georgia O'Keeffe lilies is removed from his wife's wall when she outgrows O'Keeffe at age fourteen, the poster collects dust in the basement, one afternoon it is carried to the alley by her husband; that evening a junkman stuffs it into the back of his 1987 Chevrolet Celebrity station wagon, and a few days later, a recent immigrant working at a meatpacking plant in Fairfield buys the poster from the junkman's wife for $1.25; that night the meatpacker's wife uses a page of the Spanish-language newspaper and window cleaner to wash the black A off of the glass frame, drives a nail into the wall of their apartment, and hangs the print of the Georgia O'Keeffe lilies. Later that night, during intercourse, or the next afternoon, while making chicken mole, the meatpacker's wife will wonder what the black A meant. She will never know.

The basement included what once would have been called servants' quarters. But presently, it was called Mary's room. Mary had been in the employ of Aida's parents for thirty years. She was the woman who'd cleaned the house for Aida's parents, taken care of Aida when she returned home from school, and cooked dinner three to four nights a week, depending on the workload his wife's parents were dealing with at the university. And now Mary worked for Aida and Severin. Mary didn't live in the house, but she kept her work uniforms in this room and took her afternoon nap on the single bed in the corner. She also hung photos on the walls, of her family and a few jazz greats, Thelonious Monk, Charles Mingus, and Clark Terry, and figures from the culture, General MacArthur and Martin Luther King, Jr., and Elvis Presley. Severin would have to move Mary's room to the third floor, to the room he'd always wanted for an office, but so be it. His office would remain in the first-floor stairwell: dark, cramped, crowded. But hadn't Ben Johnson written while on the toilet? And who was he kidding? He was not "revising the dissertation for a try at the university presses." Each day the dissertation rotted further.

In Mary's pictures, she looked like a happy woman with a loving family. One picture on the wall was from Aida's fifth birthday.

Mary sits next to Aida, who is, with beautiful five-year-old cheeks full of oxygen, attempting to blow out the five red candles on the chocolate cake that Mary baked that morning. Severin removed the photo from the wall and placed it in his breast pocket.

He set to the work of dragging junk through the backyard and into the alley.

Later, he assumed Aida wanted him to sleep on the couch again. He heard her above him on the phone but resisted the impulse to pick up the line. He wondered if this was the guy—if the Kindwall issue had emboldened her so that she'd talk to her lover on the home line while her husband prepared a bed on the couch.

In the kitchen, pouring a glass of water, he realized that she'd flipped the postcard so that the writing side was exposed. They'd been engaged in this silent nuclear holocaust all day: him exposing Ho Chi Minh, her exposing Kindwall's faulty, incriminating script. He read the postcard again. *This is your general, your coach.* My coach, he thought. The word had power for anyone who, as a kid, swung a bat or threw a ball or ran around a track with any facility.

Would he go to Hue City and Tokyo? He'd have to wait for Aida to return from Spain. He assumed Kindwall had that much time. He and Aida needed to straighten things out at home.

But he finally admitted to himself that the possibility of finding Virginia thrilled him.

FOURTEEN

The next afternoon Aida packed for her flight to Madrid. Downstairs, reading the paper, Severin could hear hangers sliding across closet bars, dresser drawers opening and closing, shoes slipped on, checked out at the mirror, kicked off in favor of another pair. Different but not necessarily better, the new pair. He tried to ignore the noise and concentrate on the newsprint.

The newspaper was the only way he tracked the news. The continuing battles in Iraq gorged typeface, though the editors increasingly buried this news at page A16 or deeper up the ass of the paper. His boyhood friend Connor was in Iraq. And a distant cousin he'd once lit illegal firecrackers with had lost a leg at a bridge over the Tigris. They'd renamed the newborn daughter Tigris. Jesus. Naming your kid after the godforsaken river where you lost your leg. I need to send a card and some money. Yes, Mom said something about them being foreclosed on. Maybe I can start a college fund for Tigris. Aida will laugh, tell me I am all plan and no action, no money. Where is your leg, my cousin?

How many pairs of shoes is she packing?

He knew Aida was tired, having finally posted her grades to the Internet at three A.M. after numerous technical difficulties, a few Scotches, and much cursing. He'd noticed she was packing a large suitcase, a very large suitcase that could qualify as a shipping crate and would take two men to lift and cost a hefty surcharge to check through at the airline counter. He thought she was supposed to be gone for only three weeks, back in time to hit a few faculty meetings and get the next semester under way. That was not a three-week suitcase. Maybe she intended to keep some clothes at her parents' Madrid apartment and finally follow through on her promise of spending more time outside of the U.S.

He read a new batch of Iraq war names of the dead. They were names like any others, American names, Anderson and Cruz and Washington and Nguyen. In America retailers worried about the pace of holiday gift buying.

The size of the suitcase angered him. Why was she packing enough clothes to move to Spain, not just visit? He'd give it five minutes.

He counted the minutes in his head.

He ascended the stairs.

She was naked when he walked in the room. She grabbed a blouse from the bed and haphazardly donned it. "Give a girl some privacy," she said.

"I've seen it all before, sweetheart. Remember how you say it's mine and no one else's?" He tried to grab her ass, but she escaped his reach.

"That's what I say." She walked into the large closet.

"What else do you say? That's a big suitcase for a three-week trip."

"What has gotten into you?" she yelled from the closet.

He wasn't going to allow the closet to regulate the conversation. He entered the closet, too, and sat on the floor. She looked in the mirror and held various blouses against her body. He'd never noticed how many items of clothing his wife owned. This was her closet, hers alone, and it was nearly as big as a studio apartment, and full. He wondered how she kept track of it all. A numbering system? He thought of the dry-cleaning bills.

"How much do we spend a year on dry cleaning?"

"A few thousand dollars. You want to take it out of my allowance?"

"I asked because I am curious about the domestic workings of this house. Yesterday I asked Mary how much we spend on dish-washer detergent and aluminum foil."

"Are you serious? I can afford my dry-cleaning bills." She smiled smugly. "And all the dishwashing liquid and aluminum foil Mary needs." She rolled her eyes and threw a blouse on the floor. "Have you gone mad? Aluminum foil and dishwashing liquid? What's next, are you going to count toilet-paper squares? If I pee a lot, can I use three?"

"Sorry. I was just curious. I never really knew you had so much clothing. Most of it's black, I guess that's why." He shrugged and attempted a smile.

"Are you saying I always look the same?" She frowned.

"No, I'm saying you wear a lot of black." He knew he'd entered a minefield. There was no safe way out. He spoke slowly. "I believe you wear black nearly every day. And so it would be easy for me to not notice the large number of black blouses, skirts, and sweaters that you own."

"Do you want me to wear more colors? What's going on?" Her voice rose to the fighting pitch.

"Aida, you tell me what's going on. You don't even see me."

"Is this about the sex again? I am sorry we didn't have as much sex as you require during finals week. It's one of the greater tragedies of the year, I know. Tell it to your buddy in Iraq. Tell him you didn't have sex with your wife for a week. See if he has any sympathy. How long has he been there, nine months?"

"This discussion isn't about Connor. Don't deflect," he yelled. He liked using her own terms on her, a freestyle-jazz manner of verbal warfare, sampling, repeating.

"You need to find some way to entertain yourself. Grounds crew not as exciting as it used to be?" Her face was red, and splotches began to appear on her chest. "Maybe you could search for a teaching job and stop playing with garden tools. It's embarrassing. You should hear what people say."

"What do they say?"

177

"That you had so much promise." She lowered her head and sighed.

"Then it was mine to waste. Who else makes jokes about your grounds-crew husband?" Severin closed his eyes. "We only *touched* once during finals week." He didn't want to ask the question but knew he must. "Are you planning on leaving me? Is that what this trip is about?"

She walked to the bed and sat down. He stood from the closet floor and followed her. Her clothes covered the bed, so he chose the floor again.

"I am not leaving you. I requested an emergency sabbatical for next semester, and they granted it."

She took off her blouse, chose another one from the bed, and put it on. To Severin, it looked the same as the previous one.

She said, "You need to figure out this Virginia Kindwall Happy Child thing. It really messed me up. I can barely talk to you without breaking down. What else about your life have you not told me? She was the love of your youth. Her name is tattooed on your arm, and you lied about that. For years! Revolt? You wouldn't know revolt if it slapped you in the face. You know only passivity and quiet defiance. Do you understand what you've done? I am not a stupid woman, and you have made me feel stupid."

"I'm sorry for this. I never thought it would matter. I don't see how it does. I never slept with her. It was high school, Aida, for God's sake." He sat down next to her on the bed.

"People hide things for a reason." She grabbed his arm and slapped at the tattoo. He didn't move his arm, and she slapped him again and again. Her eyes were raw and sad. "You hid this hideous thing in open view."

"We'll figure this out," he said. "You go to Madrid for three weeks. Come back home and we'll discuss Vietnam. I don't even know yet if I want to go." He reached for her chin gently, the way he once would have in order to kiss her, and she would have given.

She slapped his hand. "No, you don't set my schedule. Not

now. You figure out Vietnam and Kindwall on your own. I'm tired of saying those words. I'm staying in Madrid until I decide what to do next. I might apply for a job there. And maybe I'll ask you to join me." She shook her head.

"Who are you seeing that you need to stay in Madrid?" He spun from the bed and looked at her directly.

The look on her face was of horror. "I am not seeing anyone."

"Who you have been screwing matters a lot to me. Tell me who it is, and then we can straighten this out. We can talk it through. I don't care who it is. I just need to know. When it started. Frequency. Intensity. And then we can talk. You can tell me what's really bothering you. I know you weren't sleeping with someone else for better sex, so I need to know why."

"You don't change," she screamed, and clawed at her own chest, and drew blood. She'd done this once before, after the miscarriage.

He reached for her hands and grabbed them. "Aida, please stop."

She pulled away, but he wouldn't let her hands go. "You have falsely accused me of sleeping with someone else, and your main concern is making certain that the sex wasn't better than ours?"

"Then you're not really leaving me." He paced the room and nodded. "You're going to Madrid to figure some things out." It was as though he were speaking to himself. "That's fine. That's okay! We've been married a while. Sometimes people need to figure things out. How long do you need? I can visit you for a few days every month. Long weekends. This will work out. I love Madrid. We've got it."

"Got what? I have my bags packed for an extended stay. I didn't cheat on you. I plan to remain faithful. I need some time."

"Do your parents know?" He scratched his unshaved face.

"They know I'm staying longer than two weeks. That's why I didn't put you on the phone with them the other night. They would've betrayed me with the tremble in their voices. They are afraid of what might happen with us."

This was not the answer he'd been looking for. He wanted to know if her parents knew she was cheating on him. "I need to know frequency, intensity, and duration. If you don't give me those numbers, I will find out who it is, and I will kill him." His face was beet-red now.

"Jesus Christ, Severin! There's no one to kill. Not you, not me, and not the fantasy screw. We're not dying in a trashy love triangle. Sorry to spoil your macho fantasy. There's no triangle for you to break."

"I thought things were going well. I thought we were sailing. I thought we were over the miscarriage and on our way out of the darkness. I should think harder and longer. I should look around."

She kicked a shoe, and it slammed against the wall. "The miscarriage has nothing to do with this. I won't allow you to talk to me that way. Think about the postcard!" She reached for her chest again but stopped herself.

Severin stared at the bloody scratches on her chest. His wife had done that to herself, and he had caused her to do it.

"I've been watching your tapes. That patient Dora, she's leaving her husband for another man, right? Have you become your own patient?"

Her eyes were open wide, with tears streaming from them, and there was snot forming at her nostrils. "Those tapes are my tools for training students and for my own practical education. They have nothing to do with us. I don't mind you watching them, but don't bring my patients into our life."

"Your patients are in our life whether you like it or not."

"Just give me this. Let me take this break." She buried her face in her hands. "I'm sorry I wasn't communicating with you earlier. I should've told you my thoughts on this whole Kindwall thing. I need a break. I'm your wife."

"I'm happy you've remembered you're my wife just as you've finished packing to leave. Did you screw this guy last week?"

180

He began to cry, like a child slapped repeatedly by an elder.

Aida said, "I haven't slept with anyone. I'm sorry to disappoint you. I know it would be easier to understand if I had."

A few hours later, Severin tracked down a neighborhood kid who, for twenty bucks, helped him load Aida's shipping crate into the back of his rusty Wagoneer. The container burdened the rear suspension so much that it looked as though the front of the vehicle were taking off, heading for orbit. Her parents had used the same crate when they moved to Europe for a year after graduate school.

They didn't speak during the haul to the airport, other than her occasional correction of his driving. These editorials gave him comfort because this was how they always drove, him in the driver's seat, her next to him, offering unsolicited advice on lane changes and speed and braking and overall road conditions.

A Skycap helped him hump the crate onto a cart, and Severin burned another twenty in the guy's palm. A cop yelled at him to get his heap of garbage out of the flow of traffic or he'd have it towed in thirty seconds. Rain had begun to fall. He kissed his wife, he kissed her deeply and she kissed him back, and then she pushed him away and ran into the terminal, her heels striking the concrete like a carpenter's hammer against the head of a nail, the sound echoing through the dilapidated frame of a house.

The drive home was rainy and dark, the road a tunnel of gushing water and doubt.

He was certain that inside the truth about her lies, further lies existed. He sat at the kitchen table with a pen and a legal pad and went to work on her story.

Clark was right: It had to be someone associated with the university. Maybe some hotshot in genetics who had given a lecture in the spring and returned to teach a seminar for the fall semester. Or an adjunct bastard, living in a four-hundred-dollar-a-month fifth-floor walk-up, eating dirt and beef bouillon, screwing someone's, anyone's, wife because his contract didn't give him benefits and he needed some kind of bonus. Severin had to figure out who this was.

ANTHONY SWOFFORD

She was right, they weren't going to die in a trashy love triangle, he didn't even own a gun, but he needed to know. He had to know. His head would explode if he didn't discover the interloper's identity.

The best way to find out what's happening at a university is to ask the waitstaff at the Faculty Club. They know it all. They know who eats together when, who shares a burger and fries, who pays for whom, who gets drunk on Riesling at lunch. If a junior professor wants to know whether he's going to make tenure, he asks the headwaiter.

FIFTEEN

Severin entered the Faculty Club. He always used Aida's badge to enter the building, and everyone knew him, so it was no trouble to grab a meal. He had brought the newspaper, so it looked like he was out for a casual dinner alone, when in all actuality he'd commenced a fact-finding mission, a mission for truth. In two days, the campus would be empty except for the high achievers in winter session, so he had to make his move, and fast.

"Good afternoon," the waitress said. "I'm Lisa, and I'm taking your table from Jennifer. Usually, I just work in the lounge, but she needed some help. May I take your order?"

She was probably a junior. Eco-culture major. Christmas yoga camp from the age of eight. Summers spent working on a Tahoe tan. Daddy a lawyer? Her hair was dark black, and her face shone like a halo. She had smoky gray eyes, and she wore mascara thick on her eyelashes; her eyelids were forest green, and her lips were painted deep red with shiny gloss.

"I'll have the Cobb salad," Severin said. "No egg. Extra avocado. A mint julep, too."

"I'll have to charge you for the extra avocado. People think if they cancel the egg or something they can get extra 'cado for free, but it doesn't work that way. Avocado is very expensive, like a dollar per or more, even in bulk." Her hand was on her hip. She looked lovely, as though doing an imitation of a waitress rather than actually practicing the trade.

"I don't mind paying," Severin said. "Whatever the rules are, I'd like to follow them."

"Today's other rule you should know is no alcohol before seven. So you'll have to wait about fifteen minutes for your julep."

"Is this a dry county?" he joked.

"The bartender is finishing an already late final essay. He said he'd be in by seven."

Severin ate half of his salad and paid his bill, and on the back of the receipt, he wrote a note inviting her over to the house for a drink. He felt like a fool, but why not? He had questions for her, and she looked so plugged in.

Later that night, he heard the knock and knew Lisa's knuckles waited on the other side of the door—it was a soft knock, casual, assuming familiarity. He checked himself in the hall mirror: He was barefoot and wearing jeans and a black T-shirt; he hadn't showered in a day. He opened the door.

She said, "Isn't your wife like that professor in the psych department everyone fears?" She smiled. Perfect teeth. Freshly applied makeup. Her windblown hair hung over her shoulders.

"That's her. You should take a class from her. She's a great professor," he said proudly. "But she's gone on a sabbatical."

"That's lame. I signed up for her class. Where did she go? Why would she want a sabbatical from you?" She stared at Severin so intently he blushed.

"I want to know the answer to that same question. That's why I've asked you here. Madrid." He motioned for her to enter. She'd traded her waitress outfit for a short skirt, much too short for the weather, and a T-shirt printed with the word "Pussycat." She walked as though she knew she was being watched.

"I can probably tell you some things you might want to know about your wife. How old are you?"

"I'm thirty-two."

"You look younger, like twenty-seven or -eight. I'm twenty-two. Today is my birthday." She bounced on the balls of her feet while she said this. "I like a good birthday."

"So do I," he said.

She walked farther into the house and sat down on the couch. She picked up the blanket and said, "Who's sleeping down here?"

"We had a house guest last night. Old friend from college."

He asked to see her driver's license. It was, in fact, her birthday, and she was from the exclusive Piedmont, right across the bay. He'd once hated people from Piedmont; now he probably resembled them—a wife's wealth will do that to you. You could live two blocks away from Piedmont and save five hundred thousand dollars on your house, but your kids would go to school in the ghetto and your neighbors would party all night, every night, grilling in the driveway, fistfights on the sidewalk, liquor bottles rolling down the hill.

Poppy was probably a Silicon Valley guy who harvested fields of tech money.

Severin said, "Happy birthday, Lisa. What do you want to drink?"

"I just want some seltzer water. I'm going to smoke some pot, if you don't mind. I'd rather smoke pot. Alcohol is so destructive. It's been killing indigenous societies forever."

"I don't mind you smoking. Let's go upstairs."

She followed him to the fourth floor.

"This is a crazy house," she said. "All the books and art. My parents have this designer buy all their art. They don't even know what it is. And the only books in their house are from the supermarket racks. Might as well pay someone to read the book for you. I show them my books for international postmodern, and they don't even know how to pronounce the authors' names. My parents might as well be dead."

"That's the history of parents. Out-of-touch simpletons. You might be one yourself someday. I hope to be."

"Yeah, I guess so. Who wants hip parents? I know kids whose parents smoked pot with them, and they are the craziest kids on campus." She sighed. "My parents just seem so *dead* in that big house."

They sat on the terrace. They could see to the bay.

"This is a badass view," Lisa said. "If I lived here, I'd smoke on this terrace every morning."

Severin had the distinct feeling he had bitten off more than he could chew. He'd last smoked pot five or so years earlier. Aida was not into it, and he never really had been, going in on an eighth a few times a year with a buddy, taking a few inhalations with a girl, and forgetting the rest of it in the freezer until he moved again. Once a landlord had sent the remaining pot in an envelope along with his deposit refund.

He watched her load the pipe like a pro. Oh well. It might be fun. She inhaled deeply—how could she fit it all in her lungs?— and held it in while she spoke.

"Yeah, I could smoke a lot of pot on this terrace." She handed Severin the pipe.

He felt stoned instantly. His feet went numb. A few minutes passed, or hours. Lisa mumbled on about Nietzsche and Riefenstahl, and he fell asleep in his chair.

He woke up—an hour later? His eyes felt heavy in his skull. He was cold in his T-shirt and jeans, though Lisa had thrown Aida's robe over his legs. Behind him in the bedroom, he heard the television. Lisa was sleeping on top of the comforter, the remote control in her hand. On the screen, men played high-stakes poker. He sat on the bed, and she awoke.

"Hey, dude," she said, her eyes tiny gray slivers. "You passed out. I smoked a lot more to get as high as you. Then I came in here and watched the Gambling Channel."

"I haven't smoked pot in a while. Want to order in some food?"

She brightened. "Yeah. Burritos. There's a place in the Mission that delivers. San Francisco is the best city in the world."

"That's debatable. But not now. What's the number?"

She dialed the phone and ordered. They went downstairs to wait for the delivery.

Lisa knew her burritos, no doubt. He wished he'd ordered another one to eat cold in the morning for breakfast. He still felt somewhat stoned, and his stomach expanded like an overinflated tire. What, was he twenty again—pot and burritos? He could almost hear Aida.

He and Lisa moved from the kitchen table to the living room. She sat down at the baby grand and slaughtered some Mozart. He missed his wife. She could play Mozart perfectly. But she'd left. Or had he pushed her away?

He sat down next to Lisa on the piano bench. He put his arm around her waist. He kissed her neck. The Mozart slaughter continued. He wasn't sure if he was kissing her out of desire or the urge to remove her fingers from the piano keys; probably a bit of both. She was a beautiful young woman. She turned her face toward his, and they kissed deeply and long. Her lips were thick and warm and her tongue was soft. He kissed her lips and bit them and kissed her neck and she kissed his and they followed each other to the floor, laughing. He did not need to help her out of her clothes; she got rid of them herself. He carried her to the couch and undressed on the way. He sat down and pulled her atop him. He knew he'd never forgive himself but didn't care. At first he heard Aida's voice calling his name. But he stared at Lisa and could see nothing but her body and feel nothing but his movement inside of her, and he smelled only her, of all the smells on earth, and all of the noise was theirs.

Two days later, Lisa changed her winter vacation plans. Her family was going to Aspen, but she wanted to stay in San Francisco. This angered her father across the bay, she told Severin, but he'd get over it. All he ever did during the holidays was get drunk and verbally attack any person who wasn't a Republican, including his daughter.

"He was a hippie, you know, during the sixties," Lisa said. "The whole deal, free love, lots of drugs, Haight-Ashbury, demonstrating in the park, any park. And then he got his law degree from Boalt Hall and an MBA from Harvard and he buzz-cut his hair and found a nice virgin to marry, ten years younger than him, a pretty freshman from Smith. I like pulling out the hippie pictures when his business friends are over. 'Here's Dad at Woodstock. Here's Dad wandering the Haight after four hits of acid. Look at the pretty beads in his hair. Did you know he made hemp soap and sold it on the street?' They always get a good laugh, and it pisses him off."

"Do you like to piss off your father?"

"Sort of. It's payback for all the trouble he gave me. He was a tyrant. He made me shine my shoes every morning! I always say he should've been a general. He could've won a few wars. Sometimes I think I hate men, but really I hate my father. That's why I had a girlfriend my freshman year. He said it wouldn't last, and he was right."

Severin and Lisa were naked on the living room floor, on top of a blanket. In the fireplace, a fire burned orange and pulsed and cracked. Their bodies entwined at the hips. The trophies from a few days of leisure and sex collected at the edges of the comforter: DVD cases, three empty bottles of wine, glasses stained red at the bottom, after-sex towels.

Severin refused to sleep with her in the marital bed. Also, he thought he might not be able to get hard with a woman other than Aida in that bed. He really liked the bed, they'd spent about five thousand dollars on it, at Aida's urging, for her bad back, the Swedish or the Swiss, one of the pasty S countries where they were genius about design and sleeping and never went to war. But really, a blanket, the floor, a few pillows, a fire, and Lisa's body could put the bed manufacturers out of business for good.

SIXTEEN

Nine in the morning in San Francisco, six at night in Spain: In one corner of his brain, he waited for the phone to ring. He'd left three messages at Aida's parents' house. Maybe they were on a car tour. Made sense. He wanted to tell Aida that he now knew the truth. He wouldn't tell her that it took two straight days of championship sex for him to coax it out of a star student named Lisa Rich. He wouldn't tell her that Lisa had allowed and even urged him to do things to her body that Aida had always refused. It would be unfair. That would be cruel, and he had no desire to be unfair or cruel. But he needed to tell Aida that somehow, he could not say how, he'd discovered that she'd been sleeping with the student bartender at the Faculty Club and that the kid was spending his spring semester in Madrid.

Lisa Rich had once taken the bartender home, and she swore to Severin that the guy did not get her off and that mixing the best *mojito* in town had nothing to do with laying pipe. It had happened after work, late at night the prior spring, only once.

She said, "He simply could not screw," truly bewildered by this, Severin knew. "I really wondered if it was his first time. I asked him, and he told me off and ran out of my room. I found him downstairs the next morning, passed out in the mudroom. He'd drunk all our rum. Sad case. Work has been tense ever since. And I've had a few classes with him."

Well, aren't we all sad cases, Severin thought. I can't even keep a wife. I wonder what kind of jokes Aida told this bastard about me. Maybe she didn't. I haven't spoken poorly of her to Lisa. I have repeatedly urged Lisa: Study with my wife, change majors, ask Aida to be your adviser. I'll put in a good word. Hard worker, extra mile. Yes, a function of guilt.

He no longer wanted to beat the guy who had been screwing his wife. Anyway, the kid was on vacation, and violence of any sort involving the campus community—as they now called it; even Severin, prince of the shovel-and-rake cadre, was part of the campus community—was investigated and reinvestigated and punished. And Aida's tenure review board, if she returned, convened in the fall. A brawling husband seemed likely to count against her, despite the eminence of her parents and her expert scholarship and teaching.

He felt sorry for his wife. Why had she done it? What had made her turn? The kid was twenty-two. His age surprised Severin. He never would have guessed Aida would go after a tadpole: daddy issues, maybe, an old erudite prof with a beard, but not little-brother-incest issues. It made so little sense. But so did Lisa rubbing her breasts against his chest. This is the way we live, he thought: Lisa rubbing her breasts against his chest, him smiling inside and saying yes, and the distinct and unsettling feeling that he knew her from somewhere. But that was impossible. And had he told her first that Aida was going to Madrid, or had she told him first that Boner Boy was going? No, it didn't matter. He owned the truth.

Clark had, as Severin suspected he might, flaked out on the offer to assist with the framing job in the basement. It was not hard for him to convince Lisa to join his crew. Framing was a relatively simple task, he'd done it one summer during college: lumber and nails and straight lines. Severin bought a red hard hat for Lisa, and she wore an old pair of jeans and one of his white T-shirts. She was a good helper, though she didn't do much but sit and talk and occasionally kiss him. The work progressed.

"Maybe I can rent this place from you guys," she said during the second day of work. "What are you going to ask?"

Her boldness shocked Severin. It took him a few moments to think of a response. "I don't think that would be a good idea. It would be uncomfortable for me."

"Come on." She laughed. "Men would kill for this. Your wife upstairs, your mistress downstairs, *paying you rent.*"

The word "mistress" didn't sound right. Was that what she considered herself? Did this make him an adulterer? He didn't think of it as adultery. It was something else, he insisted to himself, though he couldn't name it.

"I'm sure your dad can afford it," Severin said. He used an air gun to blow nails into studs. "But I think it's a bad idea." She sat on his toolbox and watched him work. After a few minutes of shooting steel into wood, Severin looked up to see Mary standing on the basement stairs. He took off his goggles and tried to act normal.

"Mary," he said. "Oh, hey, I forgot Monday was one of your days."

Mary looked at him with wise tired eyes and said, "Mr. Severin, what kind of work you up to?"

"This is the framing for the apartment. And I'm going to move your dressing room up to the third floor, didn't Aida tell you?" He smiled.

"Oh, yes, sir, I know all about this construction business." She was talking to Severin but looking at Lisa. "I just seen that mess upstairs in the living room, and here's this young lady you hadn't introduced me to yet."

Mary never called him "sir." "This is—" Severin froze. "This is a student helper I got off the campus work board, one of Aida's students. She had to get out of her dorm for the winter break, so she's staying here. She's going to help with some other chores around the house." He set down the nail gun. "I think she had some friends over last night, isn't that right?" He looked pleadingly at Lisa. "Mary, please meet Lisa."

Both women smiled, but neither moved to shake hands or offer a greeting. After a moment, Mary grunted and walked upstairs.

"You are a horrible liar," Lisa said, laughing. "I should teach you."

Severin ignored her and returned to work. Why shouldn't Mary believe him?

Severin worked for an hour and then needed a break. He didn't want to face Mary again, so he took Lisa out the back way, and they jumped in his truck and drove south to Daly City for Filipino food.

Of the many family happenings he'd miss during Aida's absence, the one that most tore at his heart was the first night of Hanukkah. Aida's mother was expert at brisket and potato pancakes, and he enjoyed potato-pancake-eating contests with her father, a large and competitive man. Aida's family followed the Jewish holiday meal traditions laid down by her maternal grandfather. His wife's mother had left the religion after college (her father had been raised atheist), and other than the high holidays, Aida's familiarity with her native religion and ethnic history was scant. In the course of one afternoon's reading of *Basic Judaism* by Milton Steinberg, Severin had her beat on Jewish history.

The first night of Hanukkah, he ordered in from a barbecue joint, brisket and potatoes Lyonnaise, but it wasn't the same. On Christmas night, he and Lisa ate a canned ham, smoked a harrowing amount of pot, and laughed a lot.

Aida finally returned his call.

"What do you need?" she shouted across the Atlantic.

"I'd like to ask you some questions," Severin said. "And I want you to give honest answers. That's all I ask."

"Let's hear it."

"I was told, by a credible source, that you are sleeping with the bartender from the Faculty Club. A student. Is this correct?"

Silence on the line.

Severin said, "Just say yes or no. I don't need a reason, not now. We can talk about reasons later."

"No, goddammit," she said.

"Please, just be honest. I already know the story. He's studying in Madrid for the spring semester. Let's be done with this."

"Okay." She sighed. "Yes, I'm sleeping with the bartender. It wasn't you. It really wasn't. I'd turned thirty. My career was so-so. My tits were starting to sag."

"Honey," Severin said, "your tits are not—"

She cut him off. "Listen to my story. I went for something new and exciting when I felt I was no longer exciting. He chatted me up. Poured me doubles. Asked about my book. Said he'd read it; lying, of course. But I didn't care. At least he'd heard of it. He had a trashy little apartment, dirty laundry and empty beer bottles, and it reminded me of college, and youth, and I loved it. I don't know why I kept it going. The sex was great, though. That must have been it. And I let him do things to me I'd never let you do, things that I thought a husband and wife shouldn't do. Nasty things. I feared that if I ended it, he'd tell you. The department would find out. They'd crush me in the tenure review. And then he told me about his little princess, the one he was going to marry. Pretty simple stuff. Not even worthy of a case study. A boy eight years younger than me broke my heart, and I've left my husband. But the boy and I are going to have one more long fuck session here in Madrid. There it is. Do you like it? What now?"

"Now I hang up the phone."

SEVENTEEN

A week passed. Mary hadn't come back to work after meeting Lisa. Severin had put a call in to Mary's house, telling her he expected her to show up for work as per her regular schedule. Though he didn't have the authority to fire her, he wanted to. She might have called with an explanation, but he refused to answer the phone or check messages. The mail piled at the door, and he never looked at it. With his silence, he wanted to force Aida to return so they could deal with this in person. If he answered the phone or checked his e-mail or the postal mail, and found correspondence from her or heard her voice on the other end of the line, he would feel compelled to deal with the issue of her infidelity right there and then. He wanted her to face the reality of her crimes against him, and in person. He would admit his infidelity, and face-to-face, they would deal with each other and their awful treatment of each other, and somehow they would make their way out of this pathetic cycle. At times he wanted her to walk into the house while Lisa was there, to really shock her.

He and Lisa spent the evening in the library. With a fire roaring, they read, taking breaks for sex. Some of the authors of the books were professors at the university. Lisa read aloud the personal inscriptions to Aida's parents and offered commentary.

"This guy gave me a B-minus. Who gives a B-minus? Just flunk me."

While she held aloft a tome by a well-known literary critic, she said, "I have a friend who slept with him." She spent a lot of time looking at the author photos and fanning through the books.

"I already checked for money," Severin said. "Looking for something?"

"Smelling the old paper," she said. "It reminds me of rooms I've never entered."

"What rooms would those be?"

"The rooms people like your wife enter." She spoke as if to a wall. "That's why I got my job at the Faculty Club. My dad doesn't even know I work. He'd be embarrassed if he knew I served my professors. He says they're a lower class, like actors."

"It's not so fascinating a world," Severin said. He took off his socks and rubbed his toes. "It's rather boring, a lot of regurgitation. What else is there to write about the French revolution? That's why I left. Very little in the academy is original, outside of the cutting-edge sciences."

"Maybe you left because you weren't good enough. That's what I heard."

"Where did you hear this?" He glared at her.

"It's just what people say. 'He couldn't handle the pressure. Now he mows the lawn.'"

"They say a lot about me. And it might be true, some of it. I still don't get your fascination with the university."

"Come here."

And he did.

She brought his hands to her face and kissed them. She was like an animal in the hunt for warmth or safety or an ever vanishing meal. He thought of his hands as a cave. He knew that whatever nourishment he might offer her would not be enough. She was young and beautiful; he did not offer enough warmth, or enough danger, or enough friction. The remaining days she'd give him would be thick with sympathy. Together in this house, they'd breathe sympathy, not oxygen. He knew she'd been writing about their relationship in her journal, and as soon as classes resumed, she'd tell her friends and her therapist about him. She might even tell her mother. The problem—or one of the problems—with sleeping around was the inability to control the flow of information on the other end: Discretion practiced by one party is a waste when the other party talks; in fact, discretion looks suspicious when the former lover talks. It might take years, but at some point a friend of Aida's or Aida herself would be sitting at dinner in a restaurant, among mostly strangers, a meal honoring a visiting scholar, and the story would surface, the story of the professor's husband who'd slept with a student one winter break, and, oh yes, it was a woman in psychology, right, and the student was a bright and crazy academic star, and the wife had gone to Europe for the break, and the husband mowed the university's lawns, a job the wife had found for him, isn't that funny, he'd earned his Ph.D. but he was not suited for . . . And then someone's quick recognition that the wife was sitting at the table, and now everyone at the table knew and remembered. There was no such thing as a private life, all lives were public. And then the dessert menus would arrive, and Aida would excuse herself and take her purse and coat with her and never return to the table. Severin felt awful knowing that the bleak scenario that had just played out in his mind would indeed occur.

Lisa kissed the inside of his wrist. He took off her shirt; she always gave in with the least bit of coaxing. It was a white T-shirt that proclaimed in green lettering, FOXY BLONDE AT YOUR SERV-ICE. But the hair on her head was dark black. She shaved her pubes. What color were they? he wondered. Did it matter? He didn't care. They could be purple, and he'd still bury his face there with love. Her nipples were pink and singing. She turned to him and smiled, removing her pants. Perhaps this was a game for her, a diversion, but whatever she considered it, he would miss it when she took it with her.

She traced his tattoo and kissed it. "Does this really mean 'revolt'? I know some guy who has a tattoo typo in Japanese. He thought it meant 'falling cherry blossoms' but it means 'falling cereal boxes.'"

"The importance of dictionaries can never be exaggerated. Mine means happy child."

"What is that?"

"Who. Who is the question."

"What? Who?" She wanted the story. She pulled herself up on her elbows and looked him in the eyes.

"A girl I loved in high school."

"You still do?"

"A long time ago. But you might say that. I'm trying to decide."

"Where is she?" Her eyes were opened wide, *tell me.*

"Japan."

"Then why are you here?"

Later, she snored lightly and awoke him. The house was cold and smelled like deep winter, like a snowfall, a whiteout, a deadly blizzard. They were on the floor, their bodies mashed together in the fetal position. He could not go back to sleep and went downstairs to watch Aida's tapes. He tried someone new, a random selection, tape 17.

The patient was in her mid-thirties. Her mouth was thin, like the blade of a knife. She wore large round glasses, a disguise. Aware that the session was being taped, the woman proclaimed that she would under no circumstances discuss her sex life. Aida approved. The woman laughed and sighed while speaking. She cracked her knuckles and bit her fingernails. She twirled her hair. She worried that her husband no longer loved her, or was no longer capable of showing whatever love he did have for her. They had two children. The woman feared raising her children alone. She wanted to save her family. Aida urged the patient to think about her role in the recent emotional gulf between her and her husband. The woman admitted to increased frigidity in the last few years. Her husband's sex drive was greater than hers. Okay, she would talk about sex. She had the feeling that sleeping with any woman would satisfy him. He might even pay for it, she feared. What about AIDS, syphilis, what else? She knew that friends of his had paid for sex and that one had been arrested recently in an industrial area. The man had been ordered to advertise his crime and punishment on a freeway billboard. Then the family moved out of state. The patient did not want to move. What mattered most to her was the life of her family. She wanted her children to live in a safe environment, the kind of environment she had not lived in. The woman admitted that sometimes she held back sex in order to feel wanted. Also, she needed proof that her husband loved her for more than just the sex; she needed confirmation that without the sex, they could still get along, still love each other. The woman took the tissues that Aida offered. She asked permission to move to the couch. For the last fifteen minutes of the session, the woman wept and did not speak.

The excruciating sounds of the woman weeping caused Severin distress, but he didn't fast-forward. He stared at the woman, sad that he was unable to help—as if passing carnage from an accident late at night after the paramedics had done all they could, saving no one. Aida informed the patient that the time was up and that they would have to pick up again the next week. He thought that time spent only weeping should be reimbursed. Severin knew that for the analyst, the last few seconds must be the most awkward moment of a session, telling the patient that she must get up and leave and reenter the world. Now that poor woman had to return to a home where her husband chased her around the house, an undersexed teenager ready to screw a knot in a picnic table. For the first time since watching the tapes, Severin felt as though he had broken someone's trust, Aida's and the patient's. He wondered whether he would recognize the woman if he saw her in the co-op with her children.

He put in another tape.

He didn't return to the library until three in the morning. He found Lisa in roughly the same position, still snoring lightly. He joined her there.

EIGHTEEN

Severin woke up late and spent the afternoon in the basement, running some wire for overhead lighting and studying the plans for the bathroom and kitchenette.

Lisa's semester started the next day, so they had a little party that night, inviting Clark and his girlfriend, the basketball star. The women didn't know each other and didn't talk much. Severin and Clark shared various mishaps from the grounds crew over the years: the runaway riding mower, the sprinklers that wouldn't turn off, the time the drinking fountain and nonpotable water lines got crossed. The women laughed politely. They were all very stoned.

At noon Severin and Lisa awoke on the couch, naked. She'd missed her first class, and he was two hours late for work. Today, for reasons he could not isolate, the ten years between them seemed like a lifetime.

Severin came home after work. He went straight to the basement and turned on the nail gun, and he threw steel into wood at an alarming pace. He had to finish this job. The Sheetrock guys were showing up in two days, and he wanted the apartment complete, with a rent-paying boarder sleeping within the walls, by the time Aida returned. This would make him look good, proving his industry and his importance to the family. The apartment would be finished, and Lisa gone. He and Aida would talk about their affairs, it would be very civilized and modern, and they'd reunite, and he'd go to Vietnam.

He emerged from the basement to find Mary in the kitchen, cooking dinner, and Lisa sitting at the kitchen table, pouting.

"Mr. Severin," Mary said, looking up from a stew, "this girl need not be telling me how to do my job. I ain't washing her clothes, and whatever room you have her laid up in, I ain't cleaning that, either."

"Mary, where have you been for ten days?"

"It's very simple. I took my Christmas break." She turned away and concentrated on the maze of pots and pans she had going on the six-burner stove.

Severin knew that was the end of the discussion as far as her absence was concerned. She had trouble with her family, a son in prison and a ne'er-do-well husband who appeared when he needed money, and generally, these two men sucked from her all of her salary and all of her time. Mary gave short answers that rarely touched the surface of the truth of her life. Aida considered her "avoidant." It was a trait that Severin admired.

"Please remind me of what your normal holiday bonus is, and the vacation pay, so I can write you the check," Severin said, aware that attempts to purchase silence rarely worked.

"I'd prefer that I wait for Miss Aida to come home and pay me."

"It might be a while."

"I don't know nothing about that," she said, looking in the oven. "The best bonus you could give everyone is to get that girl out of this house," she turned and hissed at Lisa.

"You old bitch," Lisa yelled. She jumped from her chair. "Girl? You're the girl. You're the one working over the stove. Get on your knees and clean the floor, housegirl."

Before Severin was able to say or do anything, Mary was going after Lisa with a wooden spoon. Lisa ran. Mary was a large woman, but she was fast, too, and halfway through the dining room, she clipped Lisa's ankle. Lisa fell to the floor. Mary stood above her, whipping her hips and ass with the wooden spoon.

"You little white two-by-four, quit disrespecting me. You ain't a woman. You don't even got no breasts."

Severin grabbed Mary from behind and coaxed the spoon out of her hand. "Okay. It's okay, Mary." He turned her and pointed her toward the kitchen. "You can't go beating on people. She's going to apologize for the way she spoke to you."

Lisa had curled into a ball. Severin nudged her with his toe and said again, "She's going to apologize for the way she spoke to you."

Lisa said, "I'm sorry I talked that way to you. I just want to be respected in this house."

"Mary, please finish up with dinner. I'll come down for two plates when you ring the bell."

He peeled Lisa off the floor and carried her upstairs. He took her into the master bedroom because he thought it might make her feel better. Anyway, he'd grown tired of sleeping with her on the couch or on the floor in the library.

Later, Lisa wore one of Aida's negligees to bed.

He woke in the early light of morning. A pine branch brushed against the window, dusting the eaves. That must have been what awakened him. He sat in bed thinking. He looked at the nearly naked girl next to him. The bottom seam of the negligee rested on the small of her back. Her beauty was incalculable. He felt suddenly ashamed. Had he made a wreck of his life? Would his mother tell him to act his age? Probably. Yes. But it felt good. He rested his hand on Lisa's ass. He could feel the muscle. She was wound tight. Ready to take off.

He kissed her neck, and she half awoke. He offered to make her pancakes. Yes, but first she wanted him inside of her. "Give me some sleepy sex," she whined. They made love in a slow and satisfying wave. How could he ever live without her? But he didn't love Lisa. He still loved his wife. It was possible. Yes, it really was.

Naked, he walked the two flights down toward the kitchen. The pocket doors were closed. He heard the sounds of a working kitchen: exhaust fan, blender, and microwave. But Mary never prepared breakfast.

On the other side of the doors, Aida greeted him. She smiled, but it was fake. She looked exhausted; dime-sized dark circles hung beneath her eyes, and her clothes were wrinkled. Her blouse looked like a topographic map.

"Good morning. Pancakes and eggs for you and your friend?" In her hand, she held the same spoon Mary had used to whip Lisa.

He suddenly felt cold. His knees were weak. Had he drunk too much the night before? No, nothing at all: It was the fact that his wife was staring at him, she of another continent, of the twelve-hour flight. Yes, his wife.

"Honey," he managed to say. "Honey."

She threw a red apron at him. "Please cover yourself."

He wrapped the apron around his waist and sat at the breakfast table. He was going to vomit, or weep, like the woman in the patient video. He felt like a patient himself, half naked, weak. In his peripheral vision, he noticed a television and VCR sitting atop the dining room table. He heard a voice emanating from the television. The voice belonged to someone he knew. His confusion mounted.

"There's something playing on the TV for you," Aida said. "I want you to watch it very carefully. I know how you like my tapes. I want you to watch it and think. I'm going to rewind it to the beginning."

He sat in front of the screen. In the upper right-hand corner, in vivid neon green, PLAY appeared.

The female patient stared at his wife.

She said, "First, I think I should make it clear that I'm aware I have some hostility issues. In the past, I have not gotten along with my therapists or authority-type figures, people who tell me what to do."

Severin closed his eyes. He opened them, but nothing had changed, same patient, same therapist. He began to sweat, and his legs shook uncontrollably.

The patient continued: "My father paid for the best people in

Northern California, and they never did a thing for me. I think it's good that you are getting me on video. I think people can learn some things from me. I'm a good patient, really. I'm a model patient. I do what I'm told. I take advice. I learned this from my father. Your students will learn from watching me. I should tell you that I don't like you already. I almost took one of your classes once. I'm happy I didn't, because if I had, I couldn't be your patient now, right? I think it's better that I'm your patient rather than your student. I make a better patient than a student. But I'm getting a weird vibe off of you. I generally do from other women; older women, especially, are intimidated by me. They don't like my body, and they don't like my brain. And the fact that my father has money. A lot of people don't like that. Men, too. They are afraid that I won't need them because I have my father's money. But they don't understand that I don't really need his money. Well, I think you should ask me some questions. I want you to ask me questions and try to figure me out. I want you to get to know me, and I want to get to know you. That's why I signed up for this. I want to know everything about you. I know the house you live in. I know your address. And I know who your husband is."

Her eyes told her story, dark gray, hunting. Why hadn't he noticed this before?

"I see him on the riding lawn mower and painting curbs. Sorry, I don't mean to laugh. It's just kind of funny. I think it's funny. Even the junkmen, you know the junkmen, the guys picking up trash in the alleys? Even those guys make jokes about your husband. It's sad, it's really sad, Doctor. Sorry, I'll stop calling you Doctor. I don't usually do this. I think it's a reaction to you and the video camera. It's really close. I need space. My father was poor when he was a kid, but he moved up. He warned me never to marry down. Didn't your father tell you that? He was a famous sociologist, right? Shouldn't your father have warned you about mating outside of your group? It's one of the major factors in failed marriages, especially when the woman marries down. Men comfortably marry down because they are really, in the end, only interested in their cocks. It's common sense, Doctor. Do you not like it when I call you Doctor? I like it. It sounds official. What we're doing here is going to help someone. Don't you think so, Doctor? Don't you? Doctor?"

Aida stopped the tape. "You never saw this one. You saw another of hers. She didn't mention you in that session. Usually, she mentioned you. I kept the others hidden because of the things she said about you. I didn't want you to hear that garbage. You know who she is, right?"

Severin knew. He knew instantly. Of course he knew. Her blond hair. Her voice. Her attitude. It was Lisa—Lisa of the dyed black hair; of Piedmont, California; of the trust fund and the FOXY BLONDE T-shirt. Lisa in bed now, wearing his come on her stomach and his wife's negligee.

He felt his wife behind him, her heat and fury. She paced the length of the dining room.

"Mary called me in Spain. It took her about two weeks to get up the courage, but she called. It didn't take much for me to figure it out. Yesterday I sat across the street at the Andersons'. I watched this pathetic show you were putting on for the whole world. You thought no one knew what was going on?"

"Who is she?"

"She's a very ill young girl." Aida sat down across from him.

She looked defeated. Was it jet lag or this sordid story he'd dragged her into? He'd never intended to defeat her. He wanted to ask her about her trip to Madrid, the restaurants where she'd eaten, the art she'd seen. They both loved the Prado, but their favorite paintings were quite different. Hers was Velázquez's *Las Meninas,* and his was Goya's *Saturn Devouring His Son.*

Aida said, "She's from Nevada. Her mother worked in casinos. Her father was a drunk and a losing gambler until he killed her mother and her sister and himself in front of her. He told her he wanted her to pass the story on. Severin, what have you done?"

"But no. She's from Piedmont. Her father's a Silicon Valley guy. Wait. I mean—what?"

"You're wrong, Severin. You are so wrong. She's patient 12A."

"What about the story she told me, about the bartender and you? What about Madrid?" He tried to push *play* again. He needed more information from the source, but Aida stopped him. She pushed eject and took the tape.

"What do you think? You're a smart man. You are a smart man! And now look. The bartender is her boyfriend. *He* is from a prominent family. His father doesn't want him to marry her. The father considers her trash."

"When did Mary call you? Why didn't you call me?"

"I called you every day. You never answered. I guess you were too busy upstairs in our bed."

However he'd imagined her reacting to his foolishness, it was not like this. He had crossed the threshold of foolishness into total delinquency and outright criminality. Her warmth and understanding that had colored every fight they'd ever had before Kindwall's postcard arrived was gone. She was a psychotherapist; she was *trained* to understand deviant behavior. But a curtain of ice covered her face. He had lost his wife, and he knew it.

"No. I didn't bring her into our bed until—"

"Please shut up."

Lisa walked through the dining room. She looked at Severin and said, "Nice apron, dude."

"Lisa," Aida said. "We must talk. We'll work together. I'll find you a new analyst. We've made progress. You'll continue to."

"I'm your analyst. You people are my patients. On strings. Thanks, Severin. It really was my pleasure. My girlfriends were right when they said older guys know their way around a woman's body. Have fun in Japan. I hope you find her."

NINETEEN

Severin got a hotel room in the Tenderloin. He heard cars accelerating and drugs-for-sex deals going down all night. Down with drugs and sex, he thought. He didn't sleep. He suffered competing impulses: visit his wife in their home or visit Lisa in her dorm. He didn't even know her name. Patient 12A? Could she be considered his girlfriend? No. He was an object inside of her fantasy, and he'd fulfilled his role, sucker, expertly.

He loved his wife, and he knew she would never take him back. He had risked everything and lost. He got angry with Aida. If she hadn't left for Spain. If she hadn't told him that crazy story about needing time. Time? What is time? We were married. Time was the rest of our lives. And there was the issue of Kindwall's postcard, the dying general. And the foolish tattoo on his arm. Aida was right again: He knew nothing about revolt. He wondered how much it would cost to get the tattoo removed. Maybe he could just burn it off with a propane torch. More pain, less money. Now he could afford pain. He had no money.

He asked Clark to meet him for lunch.

Clark said, "I heard, man. I heard the whole story."

"Where did you hear it?"

"An Internet college gossip site that my girlfriend showed me. Her real name is Amanda Hasher. Super-disturbed. Über-

disturbed. Stalked a chemist last year. I thought she seemed a little off that night at your house. Man, you fell for it."

"Why didn't you say something?"

"Right." He laughed. "'Hey, buddy, the hot twenty-year-old in
your bed is crazy. Pull yourself out of her.' That would've worked."

"I need to get out of the country. I don't feel right taking
money from my accounts with Aida. It's her money. She might
have taken my name off already. I've got a grand in my account.
Can I borrow three thousand dollars? I'll give you my truck."

"That rusty junker is worth about five hundred lousy dollars.
But I'll take it as collateral. Where are you going?"

"Vietnam."

"Kindwall?"

"Yes."

Aida had left a large envelope at the front desk of the hotel. It was
full of bills that were his, junk mail addressed to him, and another
postcard from Kindwall, attached to the first one with a paper
clip. The new postcard read, simply:

I wait to die.

PART III

**Ho Chi Minh City, Hue City,
Tokyo, February 2005**

TWENTY

Severin had taken three sleeping pills during the flight and missed dinner, breakfast, lunch, and the intermittent snacks, as well as all of the beverage service. The flight attendant shook him, attempting to coax him from slumber. His lips were glued shut with dried mucus, and his mouth tasted like a dog's tongue boiling in a pot.

"Sir, we are arrived the Ho Chi Minh City, final destination of this aircraft. You must remove yourself further from the plane."

Severin didn't respond. The woman's face came slowly into focus.

"Sir, the plane is cleaning now. You must admit to immigration."

Admit what? he thought. Admit that I have no idea what I'm doing here, that I banged up my marriage over sex with a college girl, that I have four thousand dollars to my name, and I'm in search of a woman I haven't seen in fifteen years who might be totally uninterested in seeing my face? Okay, I'll admit this to immigration, and then what, get deported? Just throw me in the cargo hold and add the miles to my account. He couldn't even remember changing planes, which he must have done in order to be here in Vietnam.

"You must fill out the immigration forms." She shoved them in his face along with a pen.

Severin blurrily filled out the form.

The flight attendant stood, holding his bag. "Sir, we must now entertain the cleaning. It is certain you exit."

"Yes, yes," he said, smiling, slobbering. He stood on weak legs, took his bag from her, and headed toward the exit, where an impatient pilot was standing, tapping one foot against the other. There must be a company regulation about saying good-bye to every passenger, he thought.

"Sir, your checked luggage will be at Vietnam Airlines carousel number three."

He turned to the pilot, said, "Thank you," and raised his duffel. "This is all I've got."

In the immigration line, he thumbed his passport, looking at the entry stamps for the various countries. In the first years of their marriage, he and Aida had traveled often, and then they'd stopped. Maybe that was their problem: They'd needed to travel more, imprint more foreign images on their brains and in their hearts. Ahead of him, an infrared sensor took a body image and projected it against a large screen. Each traveler looked like an engorged, pixilated sketch of a human. A woman was removed from the line, presumably too warm for the authorities.

Dozens of Vietnamese military men milled about, mumbling at one another. "Fools," were they saying? While the gaggle of soldiers laughed, the men inspecting passports remained stone-faced. Severin felt guilty as charged; for what, he wasn't certain. Imperialist crimes. Sure, why not. He thought of his father landing in 1968. And Kindwall. They'd traveled here for war; what was his purpose? And why had Kindwall returned? Had his memories of war been so intense, so constant, that he had no choice but to return to their source? Inspect for authenticity? Had he been called back by the jungle canopy, or was it his own voice he heard echoing through the jungle and the delta?

The immigration line barely moved.

"Mr. Severin?" a man asked. He was thicker than the soldiers, and older. His girth meant he possessed wealth and that he made his money as a crook or a businessman or in the Party, or all three, and his age meant he'd fought in the war. "I am Banh. James Banh." He laughed, with a delightful twinkle in his eyes, thick creases in his forehead. He rubbed his belly. "I arrive from Hue with responsibility to General Kindwall for your travel. You have not arranged a visa. Please follow."

Banh led Severin to a small office where a man who must have been in his nineties sat in the dark. Banh said, "Give him eighty dollars."

Moments later, Severin's passport was returned with a thirty-day visa sticker for the Socialist Republic of Vietnam.

Banh said, "Here, like in America, money is the grease of everyday life."

The two men made their way out of the airport. A pair of soldiers stared at Severin. Tour guides mustered their groups of affluent middle-age travelers from Britain, the U.S., Australia, Japan, and South Korea. Severin and Banh passed merchant's tables stacked with souvenirs and books. Severin slowed down and glanced at a title: *Memoirs of War,* by General Vo Nguyen Giap. Had Kindwall written a book?

Severin stepped outside, and a thick and gripping humidity clutched his body.

Banh had left his car running in the fire lane—a large blue S-series Mercedes with curtains in the windows, governmental, sinister. He handed a cop a wad of bills.

Severin settled into the backseat. He loved a Benz. A college friend had inherited his father's Mercedes, and they'd driven it everywhere, two times cross-country. The Germans knew how to build a car. The backseat was as large as a Jacuzzi.

Banh said, "We are all sorry you missed the general at his monthly meeting in Saigon. He left two days ago to return to Hue City."

"Why do some say Ho Chi Minh City and others Saigon?"

"Some of us cannot forget the past. Plus, it's shorter."

"Are we flying to Hue tomorrow?" Severin asked hopefully. It was more than four hundred miles to Hue City from Saigon.

"I will gladly drive you this evening," Banh said. "The next

217

ANTHONY SWOFFORD

Hue flight is not until five P.M. tomorrow. The general would like
to see you prior to that."

"How sick is he?" Severin asked.

"He remains sick with the prostate. The doctor's machines do
not offer a positive picture."

Banh merged onto the main airport road. Once they were a
mile down the road, there were no lights.

"Electricity?" Severin asked.

"Only occasionally. The rich people. Some have gas genera-
tors."

"Do you have any water? I'm dehydrated."

"I'll stop shortly."

They drove in the quiet. Severin tried to imagine the country-
side lit with bombs. He was unable to do so. His father had once
told him, "If you haven't been, you don't know, and count yourself lucky."

Severin had last seen his father three years before he died. He'd
missed Severin's college graduation by a week. Made an excuse
about getting the dates wrong, but Severin knew the truth of the
matter was that his father couldn't sit in an auditorium for the
length of a commencement ceremony. Too many people, too much
time, closed doors. He had given Severin a blank card with a
check for five hundred dollars and told him to go to Mexico for a
week and get drunk and sleep with a whore. "It's what I did when
I graduated college," he'd said. Severin had wanted to punch him
when he'd said this. But he didn't. His father had crashed on the
couch in Severin's apartment for a few nights, and then he'd slept
with the manager of the apartment complex, a woman in her
early thirties who'd often threatened to evict Severin and his roommate but, after his father's visit, never did so again. Thanks, Dad.
Severin had never cashed the graduation check. It was in his wallet now. He wondered if he'd ever really had a father. He'd been
nice enough, he provided, he was handsome and strong, and people liked his company. But Severin realized that he'd never *known*

218

the man. They'd inhabited the same space, but he'd never known him: What was his favorite book, movie, car, movie star, song, meal, city? His father had traveled the world, was always on orders somewhere, teaching the military pilots of another up-and-coming democracy or a U.S.-friendly petrocracy how to fly. But he'd never been at home to teach his son how to walk or ride a bicycle. He'd seen the world, but he'd never put a Band-Aid on his son's knee. Still, the son thought of him, the dead father, every day. We die, too, Severin knew, when those we love die.

The darkness of the jungle was unchanging.

Banh said, "Near here, many Americans and Vietnamese dead. Pitiful. Some see ghosts. I choose not to."

"How do you know the general?" Severin asked.

"We fought one another in the war. Now we are friends. Nations cannot break the bond of men. Nations are false, made from banks and borders. Men are blood, bone, and soul."

Severin said nothing. The night rushed by. He lowered his window a quarter of an inch. The wind screamed through the crack. Severin understood why some saw ghosts and why Banh refused to do so. The speedometer read 150 kilometers an hour, way too much speed for the road. If you drive fast enough, perhaps the ghosts don't appear.

Banh turned in to a dirt lot in front of a low, dimly lit building. "Generator," he said, referring to the lights.

Inside the building, no larger than 150 square feet, people gathered around tables, playing some kind of card game, gambling, it seemed. The building was constructed of cinder blocks reinforced with mud.

Someone knocked on the passenger-side front window, and Banh opened the door. The man set a bag in the seat and spoke to Banh in Vietnamese and then disappeared.

Banh said, "Here is some water; it should keep you hydrated for the trip. And here is a plate of rice. The tank is full, and I don't plan to stop. Enjoy the ride."

• • •

When Severin awoke in the morning, Banh was driving a switch-back road. Pine trees jutted toward the sky, rich and vivid greenery.

"Good morning, Mr. Sunshine," Banh said. "We have made the good headway. We are only half an hour away from Hue. Enjoy the view."

The landscape looked like the foothills of the Rockies. Severin hadn't expected this. He wondered if Kindwall and Banh had fought here. He thought of the fighting going on in Iraq. He wondered if, in thirty years, young men and women would visit Anbar Province to tour battle sites where their parents had fought and died. Maybe they'd go to Basra, too, and of course spend a week in the modernized Baghdad, Silicon Sunnis writing code, families on their way to Baghdad Disney. But Saigon had fallen to the enemy, and it was just now slowly coming out of its diplomatic and commercial thaw. Iraq would have to turn out like Japan, with an accommodating populace, if anything modern—government, technology, or travel—were to take hold.

Banh said, "The general has told me a lot about you. He says you were a star of his football team and then you turned against him. You helped his daughter to leave him and then you turned her in to the police."

"I followed her. I tried to help."

"Then you must tell the general so. He's impressed that you have traveled this far to speak with him. Once you see him, I am certain you will be convinced of the proper course."

Severin was hungry. "Any food around here?"

"I would prefer not to stop until we get to Hue. You can have *pho* at the hotel. It is very good. Made by my sister."

"Will the general be awake?"

"If not, I am under the order to disturb him for your arrival."

"What does the general call you?"

"He calls me Colonel, which was the highest rank I attained."

"Is your first name really James?"

"No, that is only the joke. I am called simply Banh by everyone but the general."

"Do you consider yourself at his service?"

"I might call myself his chief of staff. It is the . . . You call it a mutually benefiting situation. We scratch the backs. We nearly killed each other, and now we scratch the backs."

"What does the Communist leadership think of your friendship?"

"I am the Communist leadership for Hue City. There are Party elements who find it distasteful that I commune with a former enemy, but most people don't care. It fails to register. There are American men like the general all over the country. Some of them are on your MIA lists. Sometimes a man would walk away from his unit and never return. He might fall in love with a village girl and make her his wife. He'd offer his protection services to the village, and the village would hide him from VC and the Americans. When you return to Saigon tomorrow, I will give you a tour of what the tourist brochures are now calling the Cathedral District. It has a ring. You will see that there gather some of the children of these strange unions. In the cities, they are outcasts and criminals, drug addicts. No one wants them."

As they made the descent toward Hue, small villages began to appear on the sides of the road. They passed platoons of scooters loaded down with various goods and merchandise and sometimes a cargo of people: five live hogs tied in a long wicker basket; a six-foot-high stack of eggs, two dozen to a flat; a wire basket full of stove coal; and one scooter carrying no fewer than six children.

At the sight of the scooter piled high with people, Banh spoke. "Once we called them buffalo children, those who rode a buffalo to school. Now they are scooter children. Life has softened."

It hasn't softened that much, Severin thought. The villages slowly became rows of buildings; he assumed they were entering the out-skirts of Hue City. As the population increased, so did the poverty. Every home on the street doubled as a shop of some sort: shoe repair, kitchen sinks, televisions, motor scooters, *pho, pho, pho.* And here and there—his father and Kindwall had been right—dog. *Thit cho,* hanging like Peking duck in Chinatown. And why not, it looked good. Farther into town, things cleaned up somewhat, as well as a town with dirt and cobblestone roads can. Some French Colonial homes retained a bit of their former glamour, the Party banner hanging out front as a reminder of who owned the power and the glory. They crossed a river and drove alongside a series of hotels. They pulled in to the Hue City Hotel through the back entrance.

Three of Bahn's associates accompanied them, and one insisted on carrying Severin's bag. The three men showed Severin to his room. They were happy to display the river view. He thought he heard one of the men say that it was the Bo River. Whatever, it was slow-moving and brown. Boats heavily burdened with commerce floated down the brown river. Severin was certain that some of them were on the verge of sinking, because they floated so low in the water. Most of the boats had television antennas. From many of them, the wash hung to dry. A waterborne village.

He took a shower, and when he got out of the bathroom, Banh was sitting on his bed. "Sorry to startle you. I have seen the general. He is anxious to greet you but is suffering low energy. He's ordered that we eat lunch first. Please dress and follow me."

One room had been converted into a dining hall, and the room next to it had been turned into a kitchen. At the table, ten or twelve men sat eating. Some of the men were Banh's age, and others were younger: their sons, Severin thought.

"Please welcome," Banh said to the assembled, "the Mr. Severin Boxx. A great friend to the general and to us."

The men clapped. The table was crowded with plates of food—fried glass noodles and spring rolls, fried carp suspended upright between thin sticks of bamboo, and bottles of a Vietnamese beer, Saigon.

Banh sat next to Severin. "Have you eaten the Vietnamese food other than *pho*?"

"Yes, I have. There is a great Vietnamese place in my neighborhood in San Francisco."

The men nodded.

"Some people say the best Vietnamese food in the world is in California. All the best cooks left and went there. But my sister is a great cook, you will see," Banh said.

Severin rolled a spring roll in a lettuce leaf and basil. It tasted light and meaty, and right.

"These are great," he said.

Banh nodded and smiled. "Save room."

A woman delivered a plate of sausages. Some of the men snickered.

Banh said, "It is near the end of the month, and this traditional flavor is for you to eat for success. We do not eat this at the beginning of the month. Try it."

"What is it?" Severin asked.

"The dog," Banh said. "In the sausage, it is most palatable. You will dip it in the shrimp paste. It is a favorite."

Severin said, "I can't eat dog."

"But you must." Banh picked up a piece and dipped it in the sauce and ate it. He then poured himself a glass of rice wine and washed it down. "It is the light fantastic. The general insists you participate."

"Where do the dogs come from? A dog farm?"

"People in rural areas raise them at home, the good life, and then sell them at the market. They live a nice life until death. In Vietnam, the dog's life is good. It is an honor to be eaten by the humans. They are serving a purpose. In the U.S., you raise the dog to protect your home, to stupidly fetch the tennis ball. What else the purpose? Nothing. Here the dog holds a higher purpose."

This sounded like a relatively solid argument. Severin looked at the men enjoying their delicacy, washing the flavor down with the rice wine. Why not?

He reached across the table and took a slice of sausage with his chopsticks. He felt sick, holding the meat between his chopsticks, but he knew he would not be allowed to leave the room without tasting the dog.

"What is it called?" he asked.

"This we call *doi cho*. The general requested this preparation for you."

The men around the table were staring at him. Severin raised his piece of *doi cho* to the men, as in toast, and ate it. They erupted in a cheer, some of them rising from their seats. Banh poured rice wine all around. Severin finished his glass in one swallow and asked for another. He had not really tasted the dog. He had tasted his revulsion at eating the dog. The sausage was soft; creamy, even. He ate another piece, again to cheers. He felt like one of the crowd. And then his stomach turned. He got up from his seat and ran toward his room, where he managed to make it to the bathroom prior to vomiting. He sat down in the bathroom, leaned against the cold tile wall. He felt dizzy.

Banh appeared at the door. "Sorry, Mr. Severin. I thought you might stomach it. You have the fever?" He touched Severin's red and hot forehead. "This is good," he said. "The dog warms you. It is the intent. Let's go." Banh motioned for him to stand.

Back at the table, a jokester had piled Severin's plate with half a dozen pieces of sausage. He decided to eat them. If he could eat more dog sausage, he could find Virginia. It seemed like a stupid test, but what about his life right now wasn't? When the men realized that Severin intended to eat the dog on his plate, they became excited. More wine was poured. Banh placed six glasses of rice wine in front of him. Methodically, he ate the dog. With his chopsticks, he carried each piece from his plate to the shrimp sauce and then to his mouth. He chewed slowly and intently. The men clapped and pounded their fists on the table and drank with him after he swallowed each piece. Yes, now he tasted the dog. It did not taste like chicken. It had a dark, musty taste, the taste of deep earth, of old civilization. He wondered if, for the Vietnamese, eating dog wasn't one more prideful boast, a message for the "civilized" world: *You say we are inhumane by doing this, but we are just like you, you eat dogs every day, they are different dogs but dogs all the same, in your jails, in your ghettos, in your factories, and on the streets of all of your cities, you slay the dogs and eat them.* He felt that his stomach might explode, and his head. He felt an intense fire taking over his body, from his feet to his forehead. Was this what Kindwall had wanted by insisting that he eat the dog?

Severin stood and offered a final toast to his new friends. He ate one more piece of sausage and finished a shot of rice wine. "You're a local now," Banh told him. The group dispersed, and Severin returned to his room. He was drunk and uncertain what effect the sausage would have on his body. He fell into bed and passed out.

An hour after he'd fallen asleep he awoke to acute pains in his stomach. He rushed to the bathroom and vomited. His body was weak and covered with sweat and he shook all over. He looked at his watch. It was five-thirty in the evening. Exactly nine minutes later, he vomited again. This continued for five episodes. When he was in the throes of a sickness, Banh appeared in the bathroom doorway.

"Mr. Severin," he said. "I heard you being ill. What is wrong?"

"I don't know. Dog poisoning?" Severin regretted eating the dog, not only for the abstract moral principles but also for the very real sickness racking his body. It felt as though someone had tied his stomach into ten square knots. His legs were weak, and sweat poured from his burning body.

"I will make you the cold bath."

That was the last thing he heard prior to fainting.

He awoke in his bed late in the evening. At least it seemed late in the evening, but he couldn't be sure. He looked out his window at the river. There seemed to be some festival going on; lanterns lit by candles floated downriver in a chain of light. He wanted to call his wife. Yes, he really did. He'd apologize. He at least needed to apologize again and tell her he was in Vietnam. No matter what, he was still her husband and she needed to know his location. He walked the halls looking for Banh or one of his assistants. He found Banh in a large suite at the end of the hall, sitting at a table with another old man.

"Mr. Doi Cho," Banh said, motioning toward Severin. The two men laughed. Only when the other man turned to face him did Severin realize that it was Kindwall. The general looked as though his shoulders were folding in, the body enclosing itself in its own envelope. But it was the same man from his past, the large face, hardened, unsmiling, damaged by war. He had no hair. His jaw still looked like an ax.

"Sir," Severin said. He felt seventeen again, in the worst way.

"Please join me for a drink," Kindwall said. With great effort, he rose from his seat and steadied himself with a cane. He reached out and shook Severin's hand. The general's big hand was still a vise. *Doi cho,* Kindwall said. "The monkeyjumpers of Vietnam."

"I need water. No alcohol. I'd rather have done a thousand monkeyjumpers." Severin walked toward the wet bar. He wanted to escape somehow. Why had he come here?

"No." Kindwall pointed to the couch. "Have a drink with me."

"Yes, sir," Severin said.

Banh steadied Kindwall and guided him to the couch, and Severin followed.

"Call me General. Or call me Coach. Call me whatever you please. Call me dead. The cancer is in my bones. Banh is pouring Scotch. Do you have a problem with Scotch?"

"No, sir."

Banh delivered a tumbler for each of them and left the room.

Kindwall said, "I never thought you'd become a weekend warrior. You're out of shape. Please don't tell me you play racquetball. You gave up the weights?"

"I make it to the gym a few times a month. I was a student for a long time. Too many hours at the library."

"Books don't build muscle." The general's eyes moved constantly, checking a room, inspecting the doorways and corners. It was an alarming facet of his face that Severin had forgotten: a constant assessment of the threat situation. But now it took energy to move those eyes, Severin knew. They moved slower, and their vibrant blue had turned cloudy.

"What have you done with yourself?" the general asked, sizing Severin up as though inspecting cattle. Severin hadn't touched his drink. "What are you going to do with that Scotch, drink it or dance with it?"

Severin toasted the general and took a drink. He hated Scotch. "College. Graduate school."

"You work on the grounds crew at a university? This is true?"

"How do you know that? How did you find me?"

"You were sitting wide open for the world to find you. Colonel Banh's son did a search for you on the Internet. The kid found you in about five minutes."

"I'm not hiding from anyone. What do you want, sir?" Severin lowered his head. Looking at the general was beginning to depress him.

"Everyone is hiding from someone," Kindwall said. "What would your father say if he knew you ran a riding mower? I expected more out of you. I'm sure he did, too. God bless him."

"I never knew what my father expected from me. I never knew him, sir." Severin stared hard at Kindwall.

"Nor did I. I respected him and his career. But I never knew him. He was a good man. I sent your mother a note when I heard about the crash. A lot of great military leaders died that day, your father at the top of the list. How is your mother?"

"She's well. She runs a little inn near Victoria. She gardens. Sails. I see her once a year."

"You should see her more often. I was always fond of your

mother. And she saved your ass, boy. She got you out of Yokota quicker than I could find you. I might have killed you. With my bare hands." Kindwall stared at his hands.

"So what now?" Severin asked.

"I want you to find my girl. I want you to bring my girl home so I can tell her that I love her."

"Why did you insist that I come to Hue City first?"

"Because in order to properly motivate you, I needed you to see me. I needed you to look into the face of a dying man and promise him that you would return his daughter to him before he dies. I needed you to be motivated by the face of death. Look at me, Severin. Look at me and tell me that in the next two weeks, you will return my daughter to me. That's all the time I have. They tell me I have two months, but in two weeks, I'll be sucking on morphine, stoned."

Severin stood and looked out at the slow, dirty river. The lanterns continued to flow downriver. "What's the celebration?"

"There's no celebration. It's for the tourists. They do it every night."

"I still need to know why you've chosen me," Severin said. "You know plenty of military people. You know people who do this for a living. Bhan's son could probably find her with three clicks of the mouse, right?"

"I need someone emotionally invested in the mission. Locating is one thing." Kindwall paused and winced in pain. "Persuading is another." He lowered his voice and sounded, for the first time, vulnerable. "You might find her, and she might say no. You must turn that no into a yes."

"What if two weeks isn't long enough?"

"Two weeks is all we have. You failed me once, you must recall." Kindwall rested his elbows on his knees.

It reminded Severin of a sideline huddle, Coach getting dirty, getting down to the business of winning. But what happens if you don't win?

"I was seventeen," Severin said defensively. "I was in love with Virginia, and I wanted to save her. I tried to tell you where she was. I went to your house, and you chased me out!"

"You must find her."

"I'll try, sir."

"Let's make peace, Severin. Let's search for love." Kindwall leaned back and settled into the couch. "I read what happened with your marriage. Is it true?"

Severin looked at Kindwall in disbelief. Halfway around the world, his sins followed him.

"Banh's kid has a file going on you," Kindwall said in explanation. "You're his project. Banh pays him per page. Sounds like you dug your own grave on this one."

"I'd rather not talk about that, sir. Why do you think I'm here? Because I'd rather forget what I just did in San Francisco."

"Pecker trouble, my father called it. You've got pecker trouble, boy. You want a family? You want love? Find the right woman and keep it in your pants. Close the door on the past before you open the door to the future."

Severin couldn't believe he was getting this lecture from Kindwall. Pecker trouble? Is he serious? I traveled halfway around the world to hear about my pecker trouble?

"Sir, can we get back to the matter at hand?"

"I want to die here. I want to die at peace here. And I want to speak to my daughter before I go. I want to kiss her cheek and smell her hair."

"Where should I look first? Tokyo has ten million people."

"Ask around Yokota. The lonely never wander too far from home. Do you remember Yoshida's, the electronics store? Go to his place. He used to know all the local gouge."

"Sir, is there something you haven't told me?"

Kindwall turned toward the window. "I failed, son. I should've given Virginia a mother, but I was too wrapped up in my own grief and in warfare to consider the consequences. I wanted to keep her safe from loss. The thing is, you give your children what you think they need, and it's the wrong thing. And the family explodes like a grenade you're holding to your belly. But it's not a grenade, it's a nuclear bomb, and your family is gone, and your community, and everything you knew."

Severin was agitated with Kindwall; he wasn't answering the questions. "But what about now, sir? What have you not told me?"

"I had a line on her in 'ninety-five, right when she left prison. Because of her involvement with the North Koreans, Virginia was a scourge on postwar decadence and rampant miscegenation, proof for the right-wing radicals that diluting Japanese blood harms the country. They have rallies with posters made up, an X through her face. The Kabuki actor she kidnapped gives anti-mixed-blood speeches in front of the Imperial Palace. It's a regular circus. She smartly moved to Okinawa and dropped out. Kitchen jobs were her way of life." Inside the dying body, the eyes of the old giant lit up. "Then she surfaced again in 'ninety-nine, in Tokyo. She was alone, living in boardinghouses. Then she disappeared again."

"Why didn't you go after her when you knew where she was? Why now and not then?"

"Death's door changes your perspective. Here we are at death's door, Severin. What do you see?"

TWENTY-ONE

The two large steel doors at customs opened, and Severin entered Japan. From the throngs of people greeting arrivals, no one would reach for him or shriek his name. None of the chauffeurs held a placard bearing his name. He had expected this, yet the anonymous reception still depressed him. He wanted recognition, *Welcome back, why have you been gone for so long?*

The sounds of the language attacked his ears—he found and comprehended a word here and there, like a man trying to catch butterflies with a net full of holes. *Love, welcome, hurry, congratulations!* His capacity at the sentence level was zero. The butterflies swarmed and escaped.

Eat, drink, and find a missing woman, that's why he was here. Missing from where and from whom? He exchanged three hundred American dollars for roughly thirty thousand yen. He felt richer than he was: The bills were larger than American currency and colored with vivid ink. Jackpot, casino money, watch it burn.

He bought an international calling card. He'd finally make the call to Aida. *I am sorry still. I am alive and in Japan, I hope you are well and care.*

The earpiece on the pay phone chirped, a ring. He didn't even know what time it was in San Francisco. He looked up at a wall of clocks: Moscow, London, Paris, Istanbul, Bombay, Bangkok, New York, Los Angeles. Seven A.M. on the West Coast. She'd be just awake, making coffee. It went to voice mail, his voice no longer on the outgoing message, her voice now, only her name. He spoke: "I'm in Tokyo. I saw Kindwall in Vietnam. He's dying and has asked me to look for his daughter. And I'm doing this for him. I assume you want a divorce. I'll sign whatever you come up with. I'm staying at the Cerulean Tower Tokyu Hotel in Shibuya. You can find it online. Don't worry, I'm not paying. Kindwall is. I had a room booked at a budget place, but his, well, his assistant booked this room for me. Oh, I don't know what I'm saying. You don't care, you shouldn't care. I'm sorry. I'm really sorry. Good-bye."

Severin looked at the ground-transportation counters and made his way toward the one with the cutest girl behind the desk, Airport Limousine.

Outside, it was night. He found the huge orange bus with AIR-PORT LIMOUSINE painted on the side in eggshell white. A line of Japanese and assorted foreigners waited to embark, their luggage at their sides. Two bellboys loaded the luggage into the belly of the bus. Severin sat just behind the driver's seat. The seats were small, and the windows were partially covered with white lace curtains. Severin remembered this from field trips when he was a kid.

He watched his fellow riders step on: Germans; a few Dutch; two American women trying to figure out exactly where they knew each other from, was it downing tequila shots and Ecstasy at club MX MX in Shibuya, or high school summer stage in Palo Alto, *Twelfth Night, Dr. Faustus, Waiting for Godot;* a smattering of salarymen probably up from Kyoto on business for Kirin or Sapporo, based on their level of yeasty inebriation; three Russian girls who were over six feet tall and destined to work high-fashion slave labor for a Tokyo modeling agency, two months of eighteen-hour photo shoots, half day off on Sunday; two punk Japanese girls with dusty backpacks in tow who had the look of the weary knapsack traveler who has seen far too much of the rudimentary plumbing in too many countries in too little time; and an elderly American couple, the man a veteran of the war—Severin read the stitching on his cap, FIRST MARINE DIVISION, MIDWAY, TARAWA, OKINAWA, the whole bloody machine. Severin overheard the man say to his wife, "They're no taller than they used to be, and the women still have that pretty skin that felt like silk."

The war veteran and his wife chose seats behind Severin. Severin heard him say to his wife, "After the war, the Japs would show respect to GIs, but look at it now, the driver didn't even call me sir, I probably killed his granddad on Okinawa." His wife tried unsuccessfully to quiet him. "I probably killed his great-uncle, too. Why the hell did we come here? I probably paid . . ." He trailed off when she elbowed him in the ribs.

The mortified wife bowed her head. She said, "Because you wanted to."

"Did I ever tell you," he said, "that my best friend lost his cock at Tarawa? Good thing he already had two kids. The Japs took his cock. What a price to pay. I'd rather give an arm, even a leg. You can still hump with a wooden leg. No one wants to talk about those guys. They want to write books about the heroes, not the poor guys who lost their instruments. Tell me, Tom Brokaw, what Viagra is gonna do for Joey Spicone of Far Rockaway, New York, whose penis is forever lost to the beach at Tarawa."

"Please, Henry," the wife said. "What are you trying to do? Isn't Joey dead?"

"I'm making my peace."

The bus entered the expressway. Severin looked out the side window and saw the lights of outer Tokyo. He'd forgotten about the continuous riot of neon, the endless electric rainbow assault. There was nothing in the world that didn't look somewhat enticing when announced in neon. DEATH, flash, flash, flash. WAR, flash, flash, flash. DECAPITATION, flash, flash, flash. No wonder they sold so many electronics here. The church of neon ruled. The god was a tightly compressed gas, colorless and odorless, in the air you breathed, two thousandths of a percent by volume. Other than the screaming neon, this part of Tokyo looked like any midsize American industrial city. Nearby, people constructed products from metal and plastic and nylon, factories burned twenty-four hours as the lives within them expired, burning with the same intensity and doom as the broilers bellowing waste into the sky. Misery and arthritis and an early death were in the contract. The air smelled tired, overdrawn, and underpaid.

Even out here in the suburbs, the love hotels were prominent. Maybe these were constructed solely for the factory crowd: *It's the lunch break. My wife will never know.* King Central Hotel. Lady Queen Plaza. Happy Prince Lodge. The places where people handled each other's bodies on dirty sheets. King, queen, prince, how low can you go? Why not the Lucky Serf or the Prominent Farmer? Because when you pay for a room here, we want you to play like royalty, or royally, this is no tumble in the hay. If the traffic weren't so heavy, Severin thought, I might be able to hear them moan, but from sex or sadness? One could never know.

Now they emerged onto the elevated expressway that surrounds Tokyo. Severin didn't know the neighborhoods, but he knew that he was now in Tokyo proper. Buildings rose five feet from the edge of the road, and everything looked like it had been built yesterday. Tokyo's architectural history was all fake because it had been firebombed and then rebuilt after the war. Art and books and survivors had to tell the prewar story of the country, because the buildings were unable to do so. The neon was even more intense here. Huge two-story LCD screens also lit the night: SONY, TOYOTA, AIWA, KIRIN. The expressway was impacted, with the occasional blue and red necklace of motorcyclists screaming through the lanes of traffic.

The driver announced over the PA system, "Ladies and gentlemen, respected customers of the Airport Limousine, I announce the arrival of our destination, Cerulean Tower Tokyu Hotel, Shibuya. Good evening."

After checking in to the hotel, Severin found the business center and sent a brief e-mail to Aida to follow up on his phone call. Would she respond?

His room looked and felt like a kimono, artful, soft. He wondered how Kindwall could afford six hundred dollars a night. He fell asleep fully dressed, face buried in a pillow, the lights in the room on; beyond, the lights of Tokyo were even brighter.

TWENTY-TWO

In the morning Severin headed to the train station to catch the Chuo line to Yokota. Since he'd last seen it, the city's rush hour had increased in intensity and absurdity. He remembered the first time he'd boarded a rush-hour train. The inaugural Japanese McDonald's had been celebrating its twenty-year anniversary on a Friday morning at eight A.M. in Tokyo station. His father had decided that if they were truly Americans, they needed to take part. That day the Japan Rail train from Yokota to Shinjuku had been no big deal—a crowded train with all of the seats taken and the aisle filled with men clutching the hand straps, either reading the morning newspaper or trying to sleep. Now, at Shibuya, Severin was held back from the boarding area by green ropes of the kind used at dance clubs to keep the line in order. Three officious men in green uniforms made certain that all of the departing riders were off the platform before opening the ropes. The new riders rushed toward the train like a pack of hyenas in search of a felled gazelle. The men in uniform yelled for more passengers to descend to the platform, and they pushed the passengers into the car, increasing the size and the appetite of the pack.

The rush-hour animals in 2005 made his memories of that day in the eighties seem like a quaint Sunday-afternoon hayride. Now they tried to protect the women and girls from perverts: three cars per train had pink stickers affixed that proclaimed LADIES ONLY FROM FIRST TRAIN TO NINE A.M. AND FOUR P.M. TO SEVEN P.M.

Two trains had come and gone while Severin waited for the men

237

in green uniforms to give permission for him and his cohorts to move forward. Most of his fellow travelers were busy typing messages into the cell phone they held in one hand while reading the morning paper they held in the other. This caused an eerie cacophonous music composed of the faint tap of fingers against plastic keys and the flutter of newspaper. Then the command was given, and they forced and fought their way onto the train. Severin was one of the last to board, and as the doors closed, half of his body remained outside until one of the green suits pushed him hard from behind. He made it farther into the train, but two small women next to him popped out, and then they got the treatment, and that worked, and the doors closed, and they were on their way. They were a closed crowd, an insane crowd inside a small box hurtling forward at eighty kilometers an hour. But they knew where they were going. To the next stop and possibly the one beyond that.

The main Yokota American strip across from the air base looked unchanged—signage in English advertised Cheap Cars, American Fried Chicken, Jewelry, Surplus Items, Tattoos, Massage, Massage, Massage, Motorcycles, Top U.S.A. Clothing Brands from Discount, Liquor, Beer, Dance, Dance, Dance. Behind this seedy frontage, a normal working-class neighborhood went about its business in the shadow of the bulky military base. Kids on bicycles rode to school; truants played basketball. Out here, the city was less impacted, and here and there, a building sat empty or in disrepair. The occasional cat walked the street or scaled a fence, looking for food or companionship.

He walked toward the main gate of the base. The pedestrian overpass he had used as a kid was still there, though it wore a new paint job, a vibrant red. He remembered it being a creamy green. At the gate, the MPs saluted and waved cars on. Severin hadn't been this close to a military base since leaving Yokota. All of the buildings were painted the same beige color, numbered with black block numbers, giving the enterprise a vaguely penal-colony feel. Looking at the base, he felt both rage and regret, a sinking sentimentality: The U.S. government owned his childhood home, and he wouldn't even be allowed a look. He knew that because of the war in Iraq, they wouldn't allow nonmilitary personnel on base. He tried to recall whether or not their home had been painted beige. No, it hadn't. His mother had insisted on a coat of blue when they moved in; she'd brought the workers on base herself, bought the paint herself, argued her color case to the general, and won.

The Yokota downtown strip looked like any other in a Japanese midsize town, an equal assortment of textile shops, ramen-*ya*, sushi-*ya*, mom-and-pop shops making their way in the new economy, as families had been doing here for four hundred or so years. Severin saw the sign for Yoshida's, blinking in fierce blue neon. He wondered what Yoshida's great-great-grandfather had sold. He'd loved that shop as a kid. He wondered if Yoshida had recovered, or whether it was even possible to recover from the death of a child. After Yoshida's son was killed, Severin's mother had said, "This is when you are allowed to curse God."

Why, when mentioning Yoshida, had Kindwall not brought up the death of Yoshida's son? Maybe the memory was too dark for Kindwall. Days later, he'd lost his daughter to the Japanese prison system and his own folly. Kindwall must believe in the retribution of the gods, Severin thought.

At Yoshida's, the television screens had grown so large that only a few fit in the window, although the stereos had shrunk, and the cigar-box Walkman had been replaced by the credit-card iPod, so it seemed they might have made up the room. Talk shows with psychedelic stage sets played on the TVs. One TV played news from Baghdad, a bombing at a police recruitment center.

Severin looked into the store and saw Yoshida talking to a GI, selling the kid a TV. Hundreds, thousands, of GIs and dependents had spent millions of dollars in this store over thirty-five years.

Other than his gray hair, which had once been deepest black, Yoshida looked the same: handsome and sturdy in his blue cardigan, khakis, and house slippers.

Severin entered. Yoshida greeted him and returned to the sale at hand. But he glanced at the new customer again. Severin knew that he didn't fit in around Yokota. He didn't look military, either officer or enlisted, and Yokota was not a tourist destination.

Yoshida closed his sale. He clapped the young GI on the shoulder and called his assistant over to complete the paperwork. He approached Severin. "Sir, may I help you?"

"I'm just browsing. Thank you."

"Let me or my assistants know if you need anything."

Severin nodded. He walked into the maze of electronics and felt like a kid again: browsing the store after school, wet dreams about stereos and speakers and TVs, the bigger, the better. A wall of TVs played the same talk shows and news that he'd watched in the front window.

He moved toward the cameras. Banh had given him a credit card and told him to put anything he needed on it. Surveillance. Why not a new digital camera? Aida would get the one her parents had given them.

"Excuse me, Yoshida-san," Severin said. "Could you help me with a camera?"

"How do you know my name?" Yoshida spoke as if he really wanted an answer.

"Isn't that the name of the store?" Severin asked.

"How would you know I am Yoshida? Maybe Yoshida is in the back, counting receipts."

"I used to live here." Severin motioned in the direction of the base.

"I recall," Yoshida said as he pulled a camera out of the display. "This is the best value. And I'll give you twenty percent off for being a native of sorts. Returning son. You look the same. But I can't remember your name. You were a football star."

"Severin Boxx."

"*Hai, hai, hai.* I remember now."

"I never got to say sorry about your son, sir. I got into trouble that weekend. I've felt bad about never saying sorry."

"Your mother was a very soothing presence, a kind woman."

"Thank you."

"What happened to her?"

"She runs an inn near Victoria."

"My girlfriend and I go to Vancouver every few years." He was obviously pleased to know Severin's mother lived there. "Vancouver, Toronto, New York, Chicago, Los Angeles, San Francisco. We should look her up?"

"I'll give you the information. I'm sure she'd like that."

"It's a shame when good people lose touch. One meets few good people in a life."

Severin saw that Yoshida was turning melancholy; Yoshida leaned against a stereo cabinet. He looked Severin in the eyes. "Why are you here?"

"I'm trying to find Virginia Kindwall."

"Why?"

Did he really know Yoshida? No. It was none of Yoshida's business. "I want to apologize for some things I did, for the way things turned out with her and her father."

Yoshida stared at the ground. "I heard Kindwall has been in Vietnam for many years now."

"I don't know Kindwall anymore."

"Only our works live beyond us. Kindwall offered me two hundred and fifty thousand dollars for the death of my son. He thought he could pay me off. I took his checks and burned them at the front gate. But I forgive the man."

Severin thought he'd lie and see what surfaced. "A friend told me Virginia is in Yokota, that she has been seen around. Will you tell me where she stays or where she works?"

"I haven't seen her in years." Yoshida turned away from Severin and then turned back. "I don't know anyone who has. I haven't seen her since as long ago as you. I saw news of her release from prison on television. That's it."

"I thought she'd return to Yokota. She had no family."

"I heard she worked at an inn way up north, in Omu, beyond Sapporo." Yoshida seemed to stumble over this. "The papers followed the story for a few years. That's all I know. Do you need anything else? Video camera? You should travel to Omu, it's beautiful country."

"I don't have that kind of time. Yoshida-san, it was nice to see you. Do you have a scrap of paper I can write the name of my mother's hotel on?"

Yoshida handed him a piece of notepaper.

Severin scribbled. "Please call on her. She'll be thrilled."

Yoshida took the paper and inspected the information. "I will."

Severin said, "If you were looking for a woman you'd once known and you had no clues as to her whereabouts and no one was helping, where would you look?"

"I'm an electronics salesman, not a private investigator," Yoshida said.

Severin handed him a card from the hotel where he was staying. "If you have any ideas, or if you hear anything, will you contact me?"

"Of course," Yoshida said. "My clerk will complete your transaction. Enjoy the camera. Maybe you'll take some photos of Yokota to show your mother how much things have changed?"

Virginia answered the phone on the second ring.

Yoshida said, "There is a young man looking for you."

"That's impossible, Yoshida-san. I haven't had a date in a year." She laughed at her celibacy.

"He's from much further back than a year."

"Korean?"

"No. You don't have those worries any longer. American. I recognized him instantly."

"Who?"

"The boy."

"Severin Boxx?" She stood and absently arranged papers on her desk.

"He somehow has made a connection between you and me."

"Why would he be looking for me? What on earth is he doing in Yokota?"

She threw a short, dull, chewed-on pencil into the metal wastebasket, and the sound was like a cymbal being struck.

"Maybe he's in search of his past. He's the age when men do it, if they are not settled with a family or if they've recently suffered a major disruption in their lives."

"Does the man think of the disruptions he might cause while searching for his past?" She ran her hands through her hair and sat on top of her desk.

"Of course not, dear."

"First my father, now Severin Boxx."

"Your father last tried five years ago. Is it any surprise that Severin would someday appear? I am not surprised."

"Where is Severin?" She fought the excitement that was beginning to build. She fought the excitement with sobering doubt.

"He gave me the card for his hotel. You know it, the new high-rise in Shibuya."

"What did you tell him about me?"

"Nothing. I told you I would never interfere with your life. You found Miyoko and me, and now you have a quiet life. We are happy to provide. You and Hideko are our greatest comforts. It is your choice whether or not to increase the volume. I must get back to the floor."

"*Ja-ne,* bye-bye, Yoshida-san. Talk later?"

"Yes."

In her house, Virginia threw away yesterday's flowers and arranged today's. It was the only luxury she supplied herself and her daughter, fresh flowers delivered every day. Some would call it a waste. So much in this world was wasted—food, drink, bodies; what would a few flower stems and petals at the top of the pile add to the ruin?

Hideko had grown up so fast, the first six years of her life. In many ways, she had taken care of Virginia. Now they were settled. She'd changed Hideko's last name to Yoshida and enrolled her in a normal Japanese school. No one knew her past, Hideko didn't even know her past, only that her father had died on a curvy seaside road in Wakayama. A lie.

Later, Virginia prepared dinner. She sliced a piece of tuna for sashimi and warmed the *gyoza* that the girl from Tamura Butcher had delivered. She'd cook *shabu shabu* in soy milk. Also on the menu, raw sardines, which Hideko loved; though they repulsed Virginia, she fed them to her daughter whenever she wanted them. Virginia placed the thin slick fish on a serving platter, knowing Hideko would eat all dozen, heads, eyes, tails, one bite each. She poured the soy milk into the *shabu shabu* pan and then sat at the table and warmed her feet at the hearth.

She said aloud, "Severin Boxx."

From behind, her daughter said, *"Okâsan."*

Hideko was so light on her feet. It was as though she'd inherited the general's stealth. Virginia had spent her youth constantly terrified that her father was going to jump from behind a door or growl from behind a piece of furniture and scare her to death.

"No, honey, you're not interrupting." She smiled at her daughter.

"Is Miyoko coming to dinner?" The girl excitedly jumped up and down, and her plaid school skirt fluttered at her knees. Hideko wore knee-high white socks and black patent-leather one-buckle shoes. Her hair was ink black and cut in a bowl, catching all of her beauty.

"Not tonight, honey. She and Yoshida-san are having a special dinner alone."

Hideko pretended to pout. She opened the refrigerator and reached for a bottle of iced green tea and a small square of cream cheese the size of a Western chocolate. Her mother told her to save the dessert for later. The girl popped a sardine in her mouth and ran upstairs with the green tea. Virginia remembered that her father had loved chocolate, that his mother would send boxes of it all through the year, some American brand she could not recall, on the top of the box an old woman with glasses, sitting in a rocking chair, the mistress of chocolate. Her father would laugh contemptuously to know that Virginia now considered cream cheese a dessert. She heard his voice: "You're depriving the girl, telling her cream cheese is a dessert!" Where did this memory come from? Severin's appearance, of course. Generally, she tried not to think of her father.

Hideko called down to Virginia, asking if the *shabu shabu* pot was ready. Virginia looked over at the rich simmering soy milk and told Hideko to come down for dinner. As they ate, Virginia tried to ignore the ghosts who'd returned, white and cloudy as the soy milk. How would she explain these figures to her daughter? How do you explain shame? How do you shape your past so that it doesn't offend others?

Severin knew this room. Handcuffed then as well. Fresh paint on the walls, same familiar color; the security apparatus was more advanced now, with color screens, heat imaging, satellite pictures at the click of a button.

An ACE bandage wrapped around his knee held half a pound of ice in position on the throbbing pain.

The MP who'd given him the throbbing pain said cheerfully, "It's high speed, yeah, sir?"

"High speed." Severin nodded, bending forward in his seat to look at the screens.

"Sir, you were here fifteen years ago?"

"Yeah, something like that. You don't need to call me sir, I'm not that much older than you," Severin said.

"Ten years. It's just the rules, sir. This same room, wow." The MP shook his head and whistled in honest wonder. "We found it in the log, just like you said. Lopez had to climb into storage to find the box. Handwritten, can you believe that? Could barely read that guy's handwriting. Severin Boxx, son of Colonel and Mrs. Boxx, runaway, apprehended. Did you get busted?"

"You could say that." Severin shifted in his seat. He was amped up. The pain in his knee was fierce, but he felt alive, electrified. Did it take physical pain to make him feel? He hoped not. He didn't want to spend the rest of his life banging his head against a brick wall. Some men did in order to feel alive.

"Why'd you run away from home?" the MP asked.

"I was in love with a girl."

"Girl trouble."

"Is there bail, or what?" Severin asked.

"Well, you're a new case for me. I've never apprehended an American citizen before—I mean a nonmilitary and nondependent. I regularly arrest dependent husbands and wives. One shoplifting a pint of ice cream. Can you believe that?" The MP shook his head. "Melted in her Fendi knockoff purse. I should've arrested her for that, too. It's against DOD regs to buy black-market goods. My favorite is the woman who stole toothpaste. Said her husband had spent his paycheck gambling online and playing pachinko, and she needed toothpaste for her children. It was probably true, but she still got nailed. 'Lady,' I said, 'you can borrow a tube from your neighbor.' "

"Maybe she was ashamed of borrowing toothpaste."

"You're right. It's sad, isn't it?"

Severin admired the MP's honesty and integrity and wonder at the darkness of the world.

"Do I get a phone call, or can you contact someone for me?"

EXIT A — wait

"Sir, as it stands, I'm doing you a favor. I haven't arrested you. I'm detaining you. So you don't really deserve a phone call. Can you explain again why you were taking digital photos of the flight line and the front gate? It's a serious security violation."

"I don't recall any signs stating that you can't take photos of the base."

"In the current climate, most people understand the facts. You could've just asked. We would've said no, of course. But you could've asked. It's a matter of courtesy, you know?"

"No. I don't know. The courtesy of your baton?"

"Sir, you weren't exactly cooperating. Throwing your camera at my vehicle and yelling a series of profanities does not qualify as cooperation."

"I'm not in the military. I was standing on Japanese national ground. What am I supposed to cooperate with? I'm not part of your system."

"You are. Whether you like it or not."

"I'm an American citizen. You can't just lock me up like this. I was taking photos to show my mother how the area has changed since we lived here."

"I'm flying home on leave next week to see my mother. You know the weather in Omaha?"

"I have no idea, man." Severin laughed. "You're asking me the weather in Omaha? You need some stock tips? Jesus, man."

"Please call me Sergeant Forrester. Just making conversation."

"Sergeant Forrester," Severin said, "any way we can remove these cuffs until your CO gets here and decides what we need to do to get me out of here?"

"Sir, that's a negative. You are a detainee. I mean, this ain't Guantánamo or Abu Ghraib. I ain't suspending your civil rights, I ain't accusing you of terrorism, I ain't shoving a Koran up your butt." He laughed at his jokes, but Severin didn't. "This is a secure area. Once the CO rolls in, we'll straighten this out. You just sit tight. But take a look here. We've got eyeballs everywhere."

Sergeant Jedediah Forrester grabbed the arm of Severin's chair and pulled him in front of the bank of monitors. He crunched some keys on his keyboard, and images from a train station appeared. "This is Haijima station. The Japanese police have given us full access to their local surveillance networks. Man, you should see the beautiful girls walking through that station day in and day out. Exit A is the number one spot. I think they must work in the department store. They look like cosmetics girls. Their makeup and posture are perfect. Their feet must hurt, standing all day. On their way home they buy flowers at this stand." He focused on a flower stand.

"Who are you looking for?"

"We're not spying. We're waiting for incidents. And it will be useful in the case of an emergency, you know, a tragedy, the sarin attack. That's one instance when it was helpful."

"Have you solved a crime this way?"

"Sir, I see the route you're taking. And I tell you we have solved crimes from this chair. We caught a pervert and a purse snatcher this way."

Severin nodded, duly impressed. He thought about Virginia and her friends who had beaten up perverts in Shinjuku. He smirked. "Have you ever gotten laid this way?"

"No, sir, I haven't."

"Why don't you go to the station and talk to a girl rather than watching on the screen?"

"Okay," the sergeant said. "Back to the main gate and pedestrian crossing. That's all I'm authorized to watch. I don't appreciate that comment, sir."

"Sorry. It was an honest question. I have my own girl trouble."

The sergeant ignored him. His fingers danced on the keyboard unsuccessfully. "Shoot," he said, worried. "I need to ask Lopez how to get out of this screen before the CO arrives. I can always get in, and then I forget how to get out."

While the sergeant tracked Lopez down, Severin watched the

Haijima station screen. He looked at the time stamp on the screen, 20:45:37. It took him a moment to translate the military time. He remembered his father giving him lessons in military time, sitting on the porch of their house here at Yokota, his father in his flight suit, Severin wearing his Pop Warner football uniform. Only the stainless-steel band of his father's heavy aeronautical watch had survived the crash. Severin's mother gave it to him at the funeral. It was in his sock drawer. For months after his father died, he'd wake up in the middle of the night, thinking he could hear the watch ticking. He'd open the drawer and pick up the silent, mangled wristband. Nothing. Back in bed, he'd watch Aida sleeping before falling back to sleep himself.

Frustrated, he cussed aloud to no one and everyone.

"Whoa, Daddy, Lopez to the rescue," someone behind him said.

Lopez sat down, and in a few keystrokes, the screen displayed the front gate of Yokota.

"Thanks, bro," Sergeant Forrester said.

"Hey, guys," Severin said. "Can we undo these cuffs?"

"Oh, sure," Lopez said. "Oh, sorry, I forgot, you're a detainee." He danced out of the room.

"Sorry. He doesn't like civilians. The skipper called."

Severin looked at Forrester, confused, defeated. Who on earth is the skipper? What now?

"The CO. As soon as I take the cuffs off and run your paperwork, you're free to go. There's nothing we can hold you for. You're not, like, Muslim or anything. Your passport seems to be in shape. Sorry about the bruise. That's gonna hurt like crazy in the morning. You should try to keep ice on it. It was a clean hit. Thanks for being a good detainee."

"Thank you for your hospitality," Severin said. Forrester filled out the paperwork on-screen, not looking up from his keyboard. Severin would run when the sergeant released him. Everything about the military made him nervous. No, that was a bad idea.

Another blow to the knee. He didn't even know if his knee would work. The duty nurse had checked him out and advised ibuprofen. "Same thing they advise for gunshot wounds and the menses," Forrester had said.

"You ever been to Omaha?" Forrester asked, glancing up from his work.

"No," Severin said.

"I grew up there. It's a cool city. I mean, small. I could never live there again, but I like going back on leave. Mutual of Omaha, you know? Johnny Carson. Made in Omaha. What do you do in Frisco?"

To Severin, it seemed like a trick question. The cuffs were still on. "I'm self-employed."

"You got a wife?"

"I have a long answer to that question," Severin said.

"Many do. I was married at eighteen and divorced at twenty. Short answer." Forrester scratched at a bloody pimple on his pale, muscular neck. He walked behind Severin and unlocked the cuffs.

Severin decided he liked the sergeant, a lonely guy from Omaha, divorced, far from home, talking politely to a civilian he'd never see again.

"Sergeant Forrester, do you think you could drive me by my old house? It's in officers' housing, 154 Cherry Orchard Lane."

Severin could see that Forrester was seriously considering the request. The sergeant walked to a map on the wall. He moved pushpins around and hummed. He flipped through a base directory. He consulted the map again before turning to Severin.

"Well, I'd love to. If you hadn't broken your camera, I might have even let you take a picture." He looked perplexed. "But are you sure about the address?"

"Of course."

"I'll look again." The sergeant scanned the map. "But I know this base like a preacher knows the Bible. And there is no Cherry Orchard Lane."

Severin thought, That's impossible. I can draw you a picture of the house.

"Sir," Forrester said apologetically, running his finger around a section of the map. "I think I know what happened to Cherry Orchard Lane. They bulldozed a section of base housing to build new hangars. All those troop cuts in the nineties emptied the place out. I'm sorry to say so, but that must be it. Dang, what if they bulldozed Omaha?"

"They won't," Severin said. He'd never wanted to return to this base; he'd never wanted to return to that home. "Can we head out, Sergeant?"

"Sure thing, sir. Sorry about that. I guess I could've driven you by another house and lied to you: 'There's 154 Cherry Orchard Lane.' The houses all look the same. I wish I would've thought of that."

On the train back to Shibuya, Severin considered giving up the search. What on earth was in it for him? At this point, nothing. The vague and cloudy concept of redemption was the only value he could attach to the endeavor: redemption for his past at the cost of failure in his present. He'd left his wife for what? A busted knee, the late train home to a hotel, alone? But *had* he left his wife for this? He didn't know anymore. Had he walked into the entire Lisa episode knowing it would explode and propel him here? Kindwall's postcard had unhinged his life. Maybe the general was simply playing out a game of diabolical revenge all these years later: He knew everything about Virginia's life and would tell the truth when Severin returned to Vietnam empty-handed. She lives in the swank hills of Yokohama. Banker husband. Three kids. What have you done with your life, Severin Boxx? Welcome to your ruin.

TWENTY-THREE

The next afternoon Virginia waited in the lobby of the Cerulean Tower Tokyu Hotel. She double-checked the card Yoshida had given her, just to be sure of the name, and she asked the bellboy twice to make certain this was the only lobby. Who knew? Severin might be a VIP entering and exiting the penthouse through a labyrinth of hallways and elevators. Japanese loved their VIPs. Her small house would fit in this lobby ten times. The lobby shops she'd browsed were for people with more money in the bank than she would earn in her lifetime. Did Severin qualify? Why on earth was he here? Wouldn't he have a wife, children, and a job? That made sense: You're here on business, you look up the girl you used to love, check if she's free for a night, shake off the responsibility of home and work. Isn't that what men on business trips do? She had a direct view of the elevators and the front door. She read her newspaper and told the attentive staff, every time they asked, that she was waiting for her father to come downstairs.

First she heard Severin's English, the sound of two boards being beaten together in an empty concert hall. Virginia looked at the concierge desk and Severin, only twenty feet away. This could be a moment from her past, an imagined future, or a long-dead dream. The concierge moved around to the front of the desk and held a map in her hands, directing Severin. He looked the same, yes, but changed. His eyebrows, once dark coal smudges on his forehead, were now a dirty brick-brown, lightened by sun and time. She looked at his large hands, the long fingers he should've used to play piano. Had he ever, just for fun? She'd never told him that she loved his hands. It was so long ago. He hadn't shaved in a week, maybe ten days. She had never seen his face with a beard; that face had always been as smooth as a blank sheet of paper, as young and clean as his youth. Some red blemishes now, from the sun, vacations with a wife? Or from drinking away long nights alone? Would he tell her? He wore black jeans and a black suit jacket. A black T-shirt. He'd never worn black, why now? His right foot beat a rhythm against the floor. His hair was short, but not military short, and kind of scraggly. He fixed his eyes on something behind her. The clock on the lobby wall; he looked right past her. Was she unrecognizable right here in front of him?

The concierge was nodding adamantly, assuring Severin of something. He thanked her and bowed.

Maybe he wasn't in search of her? Stopping by Yoshida's had been a lark, a long shot for a one-night stand, a detour to the out-skirts while on the way to better things. Now he must get to his sightseeing. She thought, I know the list: Tsukiji fish market, Imperial Palace, Yasukuni shrine, Takagi Bonsai Museum. How original! Tourist, she thought sadly. He's a tourist. That itinerary should wear him out for the day. Sore feet, five-star massage later at the hotel. She had her camera in her purse. She'd follow and take pictures of him standing at the shrine or in front of a bonsai and deliver them to his room in the morning. And disappear again. She felt devious, she felt mean, and she felt rejected. She'd planted her-self for discovery, and he'd failed them both again.

At Shibuya *eki,* he fumbled with yen and the buttons on the ticket machine. At the machines on either side of him, three or four people bought their metro tickets in the time it took him to insert his money. She watched. I should help, she thought. Or is he the kind of man who has been handled too often by the women in his life, leaving him helpless? It is such a precarious balancing act, love and nurture, when to give, when to refrain.

He boarded a Ginza-line train. So predictable, she thought.

Ginza line to Ginza *eki,* Hibiya line to Tsukiji and the fish market. But wasn't it too late for the fish market? The fishmonger show had closed hours ago; the catch had been bought and bundled and now was sitting on a plate or a platter. Well, the smell remained. But he got off at Aoyama. Hmm. She followed. This was fun. He was easy to spot in the crowd, not tall, but taller than most Japanese. And he limped. An injury? He got on the Toei Ōedo line, toward Roppongi. More boutiques, high-end shopping: a dress for the wife, jewelry, and specialty rice cakes wrapped in foam. What a fraud.

He exited the train at Roppongi. And he'd figured the fare wrong. Virginia was two commuters behind him in the exit line. He put his ticket in, but the machine spit it back out, and the gates wouldn't open. He looked around for help. The woman behind him annoyingly pointed to the fare adjustment desk. Severin looked disheveled, worn out. The man at the desk simply waved him through, tired of hearing butchered Japanese, tired of speaking butchered English. Virginia fell in fifteen or twenty feet behind Severin. It really was easy to follow a man. Or this man, at least. She wondered what was on his mind.

They ascended the stairs at Roppongi Crossing. Right after the war, this had been the center of the black market, GIs and gangsters making it big with tobacco, booze, rice, and sex. Those same commodities ruled the world today. Severin walked toward Roppongi Hills. The word "hills": a trick. These hills were made of concrete, steel, and glass, two high-rise buildings, a temple of yen.

In the lobby of Roppongi Hills, Severin walked straight to the information desk, the English line. A girl directed him to a bank of elevators. Virginia couldn't enter an elevator with him, could she? No, she'd wait. She watched which one he entered. Then she went to the English information line.

"Excuse me." English sounded stale and heavy on her tongue, as if her mouth were full of year-old white bread. She was spitting crumbs, not speaking.

The girl was Japanese-American.

"My friend just entered this line, American guy," Virginia said. "I missed him, do you know what floor he ascended toward?"

"The thirty-seventh floor. The theater. Elevator three."

"Thank you."

A line had formed in front of the elevator. A number of young Japanese girls were wearing American outfits from the thirties. How strange, Virginia thought. Maybe it's live theater, and these girls are auditioning? She'd never heard of live theater in Roppongi Hills. So this made no sense. New fashion? But hip-hop style still ruled the streets, Japanese boys with Afros, flat-assed teenage girls getting implants to increase the size of their butt. Virginia felt ancient. This was new, the dapper Depression look. She made her way onto the elevator. In the lobby, a gaggle of boys arrived, wearing brown suits, carrying toy machine guns at their sides. The elevator doors closed. Had she entered a fun house, a joke? She stood in the center of the car and took in the girls around her. They weren't all teenagers. Some of the women were her age, a few older. She thought about the men in the lobby; she looked at the women in the car with her. The words came off of her tongue, and she said them aloud before forming the thought: *Bonnie and Clyde*. Clyde Barrow and Bonnie Parker. Outlaws, hero and heroine, dead lovers. The doors opened on the lobby of the theater. She wanted to cry. He'd come here to search for her, he'd remembered her love of this film, in the entire city he had nothing else to go on, and he had come to this theater lobby looking for her. A *Bonnie and Clyde* marathon, twenty showings in five days, live appearances by Faye Dunaway. Virginia remembered now hearing a ticket giveaway on a radio station.

Parked in the middle of the lobby was a replica of one of the getaway cars, a ragtop Ford, a coupe, stolen, as Bonnie would have said. Sitting behind the wheel: Severin Boxx, the car full of women dressed like Bonnie, three or four shoved into the rumble seat, two next to Severin up front, others perched on the fenders and the roof. Severin rested one foot on the running board, his wrist on his knee. Was that a match in his mouth?

Severin bit the wooden match and then flicked it with his tongue. The girl in the passenger seat had given it to him for authenticity, she said. He didn't feel very authentic. He felt like a fool. This was the worst of his bad ideas. A *Bonnie and Clyde* marathon? He'd never find her. He looked around the car. She could be sitting behind him, for all he knew. The girls talked in shattered English, but not in sentences, in phrases from the movie. It was sexy, no doubt about it. He liked best the girls who wore the blond wigs. It looked so wrong, it worked. A man carrying a plastic shotgun approached Severin and motioned with the gun for him to move. He complied. The man handed Severin his camera, bowed, and said, "Picture, please." Severin centered the frame and snapped away. He wanted a copy for himself. He was sorry he'd smashed his camera on the MP's hood. Suddenly, pandemonium broke out, women shrieking and men clapping. From a side elevator, Faye Dunaway entered the lobby, surrounded by three really big black guys. She was mobbed: The muscled bodyguards were stopped in their tracks by a wave of Japanese women thrusting pens and autograph pads at a woman who'd once looked something like them. It must have been supremely weird for the actress, two hundred Japanese women mimicking her in her prime. At the back of the mob, one girl held aloft an old *Life* magazine, Dunaway on the cover in an outfit from her Bonnie wardrobe: gunmetal-gray pencil skirt, cream blouse, blood-red silk scarf tied tight around her thin neck.

The guy with the plastic shotgun offered Severin his seat back, but Severin waved him on and went to the concession stand to buy popcorn now that the line had disappeared.

Virginia fought her way through the autograph seekers toward the car. In the rush, a girl had lost her beige beret, and Virginia picked it up and put it on her head, pulled it down low over her forehead. She sat in the Ford coupe, in the rumble seat, with two other girls. She loved the way Bonnie said coupe: "coo-pay." Every word Faye Dunaway had spoken in the movie fell out of her mouth dripping with sex, even the insults and the craziness.

The girls next to Virginia pulled the triggers on their fake plastic pistols, laughing, striking defiant poses, kissing the pistols, and blowing the nonexistent smoke from the barrels. She wondered what had happened to the real gun she'd once carried. She'd read once that the Japanese police melted down confiscated guns and sank them at the bottom of the sea. Good place for them. People were climbing atop the car, getting their pictures taken. Groups of friends. It made her sad. She'd never really had friends, ever in her life. After prison she was afraid of making friends, afraid of lying, afraid of telling the truth. She had Yoshida and Miyoko and her daughter. Did she need anyone else?

Severin sat down in the front seat.

She wanted this: She wanted to reach out and touch his neck, kiss his neck, and tell him to come home with her. But not yet. She wasn't sure yet. She didn't know what he wanted. She froze.

The actress exited the lobby, and the crowd went wild, furious screams for an icon. The Japanese loved their American icons. Revolt. Revolt, she thought. She'd forgotten about the tattoo that she'd essentially forced onto Severin's skin. She wondered if he'd had it removed. She took a picture of his profile. She laughed to herself nervously. He was so close and had no idea who sat just behind him.

He put his arm around the girl next to him on the front seat, and her friend took photos of them. The girl at his side kissed his cheek and called him Clyde, purring, rubbing his chest. Virginia wanted to slap her: He didn't look like Clyde. Severin jumped out of the coo-pay and headed for the theater. She followed.

She sat directly behind him. She could smell the popcorn in his lap, too much butter. The opening credits, sound of the shutter in the film. She surveyed the truly wild scene: 350 people, almost all Japanese, nearly all of them dressed up like the two main characters. These people were *fans*: It was like being at a rock concert and hearing the entire stadium sing the songs—everyone in the theater knew the lines. On their faces, the images from the screen shone, their lips moved, magic, drugs, cinema. Virginia thought of the man in front of her. She could leave right now, and he'd never know how close he'd been. He'd never find her if she didn't allow it. He could go back to Yoshida's. He could do whatever he wanted. There was no trace of her anywhere. She felt total power, total control. She sat with her power and watched the movie unfold. She felt foolish for having been so influenced by the movie when she was young, making poor Sergeant Focheaux play the film again and again. Now she appreciated it as a piece of art, as cinema. It was beautiful and engaging, a timepiece of both the thirties and the sixties. She'd found the film twenty years too late. Then she'd swallowed it as a manifesto. That, of course, had been her mistake. But nearly forty years after the film's release, what were all of these people doing, rapt? It wasn't simply that it was American. Youth, beauty, violence, vigor. Those were the keys to the film. They would always command a following, in any language and skin color, if done right. Sexy people screwing and crashing cars—certain box-office success and cultural capital. And the triumph of the poor always won the moviegoer's heart. Here was the poor-farmer scene, Midlothian, Texas. Her father's town. Her town, too, the only place in America she'd ever lived, with poor white people who'd loved her and whom she hadn't seen since. Thirty years almost. She started to cry. God, her grandparents must be dead, of course they were dead. She held her head in her hands and wept.

Whether anything came of the *Bonnie and Clyde* festival, Severin felt himself dropping back into Virginia's milieu. He'd looked for her, or a person who looked something like he thought Virginia might look, dressed up as Bonnie Parker. No luck in the lobby. He wished he'd gotten Faye Dunaway's signature. His mother would have liked that. Maybe he'd come back tomorrow for a signature and a second look. He knew that Virginia was taller than most Japanese women; she'd inherited height from her father. Her skin was lighter, her face almond-shaped. Now and again he craned his neck, looking at faces in the theater, looking for Virginia. Could he scream her name? No. It was illegal to scream a name in a public theater. Virginia. For him her name was fire. The injured gang pulled up to C.W.'s father's farm. Louisiana, he recalled. The nail in the coffin. Someone will always turn you in for the right price. He hated knowing the ending. He waited for the rain of bullets. He didn't, he really didn't, want to watch them die. He thought, Give me a new version: the outlaw lovers, old, holding hands on a porch, telling bank-robbing stories to their grandchildren. But that wasn't how the story ended.

Behind him, someone cried.

The credits crawled, and he returned to the lobby.

For a while he sat in the coupe, scanning the crowd. He never would have guessed that *Bonnie and Clyde* was so big in Japan. Someone should remake it in Japanese, he thought, or maybe they had already. He couldn't reach the elevators because of the mob, so he took the stairs. It was a long walk down, but he didn't care about the pain his swollen knee would cause. He needed the time to think about this useless endeavor.

That evening in her living room, Virginia stared at Miyoko and Yoshida.

Miyoko said, "I never had a problem with that boy. I considered him sweet. But why is he here?"

"He is here because he loves Virginia, it seems apparent to me," Yoshida said. "Why do we want to crucify the boy for loving a woman?"

"I don't think we should call him a boy," Virginia said. "He's thirty-two."

"He's still a boy to me," Miyoko said. She kissed Yoshida on the cheek and smoothed the front of his sweater. She was older than Yoshida by a few years but retained the energy of youth. She was still a deeply attractive woman, even in her coveralls. She wore a colorful scarf on her head, printed with spring flowers. The issue of Severin's appearance agitated her slightly, and her face was reddening. What would this man bring?

"Miyoko-san," Virginia sang soothingly. "Calm down. Will you both come for dinner tomorrow?"

"Of course," they said, answering for each other, nodding at each other. Miyoko excused herself to play board games upstairs with Hideko.

Yoshida said, "I think this is all strange for Miyoko. More reminders of your father."

"Aren't I a daily reminder? Is it strange for you, Yoshida-san?"

"No, dear. I respected your father until my son died. And then his actions compounded the tragedy. But see"—he gestured upstairs—"we know that in the strangest way, he gave us all a new family. I feel no anger toward your father. I feel only sadness for him." He bowed his head. "And as for Severin Boxx, I think he has the best intentions. If you invite him to dinner, I approve. He is after love. I understand the impulse."

"When have you chased love, Yoshida-san?"

"I chased a woman when I was Severin's age. All the way to London. I slept in Hyde Park for ten days. In February 1967. I caught pneumonia. She was a photographer. English. She'd come to Tokyo ten years earlier to photograph a friend of mine from high school, a writer who'd just won the Akutagawa Prize and was selling a lot of books and being translated everywhere. I hung about and lusted after her for two days. I was so jealous of my friend, being directed by this woman and her beautiful voice, being allowed to stare at her, at her camera, her hands, her face, all day. Laughing at her jokes. Oh, it drove me mad. I felt like a pervert paying to watch two lovers in a sex club. She left and I forgot about her after a few months. And then, five years later, I ran into my friend at a restaurant in Ginza. For some reason, we'd stopped speaking. He was a writer, and I was an electronics salesman, different lives. We spent a few hours talking, catching up on our families and such, drinking. Good friends from the past, bad company, the saying goes. We'd exhausted our common topics and reached a state of complete drunkenness when he said, 'How was the sex with that English photographer? You owe me, *baka*!' I thought he was mocking me. I got angry, punched his chest with my finger. 'No, really,' he protested. 'She asked me for your phone number. I thought she called you before she left and that you two had a time in her hotel room.' The silent bastard wins again! I thought. 'That's why I stopped talking to you.' I ran out of the restaurant, committed to finding her. The next morning I climbed into the attic at my mother's and found the copy of the magazine with her photo of my friend on the cover. It was a beautiful photo. He was a particularly ugly man, but it didn't matter, she'd erased his ugliness with her lens and talent. She'd composed his ugliness so that it was attractive and compelling. He'd never been so interesting in person. Magic. Her name and my memories of her burned in my mind. I stared at the photo, but I no longer saw my friend, I saw the beautiful and talented photographer on the other side of the image, behind her camera, working. I used my yearly bonus plus my savings to buy a ticket to London. My parents thought I had lost my mind. They tried to arrange a marriage with a girl whose younger sister had recently broken my heart. I landed in London, broke. No money for a hotel, barely money to drink. I slept in the park near the five-star hotels and went through their rubbish for food. Good food. Half-eaten cucumber sandwiches! I stalked the bohemian hotels and pubs and asked around for her. I went to galleries. I crashed parties. I got drunk. I nearly died of pneumonia in a charity hospital. I lost my job. But it was worth the trip. On my last night in London, I found her and spent the night with her. People do foolish things for love. And if they don't, they should regret it."

TWENTY-FOUR

In the morning, when Severin stepped out of the shower, there was an envelope just inside the door: *For the Guest Severin Boxx.* From Kindwall? Had he wanted progress reports? Had Banh checked the Visa and realized how much the room cost? But Banh had booked him here. Severin threw the envelope on the bed and looked out at the Tokyo skyline. It was a gray morning, low clouds. He could see the Tokyo Tower and the Ferris wheel. Did anyone ride that thing? He looked at the envelope. Aida? Divorce papers? That was quick. Impossible. His breakfast arrived. Full Japanese breakfast. Five thousand yen; fifty dollars. He didn't care. He'd decided to call Kindwall and pull himself off the job. He'd tell him to put Banh's kid on the computer for a week. He'd find her. Severin tried the miso soup, and it burned his tongue. Let it sit with the lid off. He'd refund Kindwall for the hotel and the fifty-dollar breakfasts. He'd go back to San Francisco, get an apartment with Clark, date some girls, and look for a job. Be twenty-five again.

He opened the envelope. Five-by-seven photos. Faye Dunaway mobbed by Japanese Bonnie and Clyde look-alikes. What? And then: him, standing a few feet away from a ragtop Ford coupe, taking a picture of a guy pointing a plastic shotgun at him. He threw the photos across the room. He walked to the other side of the bed and picked them up. What on earth? Who? He flipped the photo of himself over and saw, written in pen: *Haijima* eki, *Exit A, 6:00 tonight.*

• • •

Severin stared at the train schedule: numbers, locations, arriving and disappearing in digital green. Now he noticed her. His expression went from frantic to ecstatic. The look was so intense she thought she might collapse. You cannot know me simply by looking at me, she thought. In these ten feet, there are years you might never understand. Why are you here, Severin Boxx, and how did you get here? She could turn around, run. He'd consider this a dream or a nightmare. He might stand there for hours, trying to figure out what kind of drug had entered and altered his mind while watching the train schedule change and, with it, time.

Severin looked behind him, waiting for the door to close, waiting for the bomb to go off, waiting to be ejected from the station. Beautiful still. In her face, though, weariness. She fit into the crowd perfectly, as though she'd become more Japanese, and probably she had. Would they talk about the past or let it melt into the sea of people here at the station?

He must discover the right time to say: Your father is dying, come with me.

She looked professional in a gray skirt and suit jacket, cream silk blouse beneath, and fire-red shawl wrapped around her shoulders. And he? Disheveled, certainly on the inside. Was it that all of the women from his past had grown up and he'd refused? Former girlfriends continually sent memos: married, pregnant, second child, wildly successful career, house in Aspen, house in Maui, condo on the moon.

He stepped toward her, but the flower vendor interfered, grabbing Virginia by the elbow and pointing her toward a dozen roses. Severin stood and watched her purchase flowers. What if Severin and Virginia did this every day, and this just another evening, the loving couple on their way home from work, fresh-cut flowers to liven the home? Dinner, sex, sleep.

Virginia stepped toward him; unmistakably, she skipped. She

264

smiled. She handed the flowers to him. "I bought these for you," she said.

"I come empty-handed," he said, accepting the flowers.

"Didn't you always? Do you need to borrow money?"

"I'd rather not. You tracked me from my hotel?"

She smiled and walked toward her train, and he followed, and then she turned, staring up at his face.

She said, "I don't know where I'm going. Where are you going? Give me my flowers. Why are you here? Jesus Christ, why are you here?" She grabbed his right arm and pushed the suit sleeve above his elbow, exposing the tattoo of her name. "I was certain you'd have had this removed."

"I tell people it means revolt."

She shrieked. "Why are you here, vacation?" Her eyebrows were plucked into perfectly formed soft arches, so thin he thought he might be able to blow the hairs off of her forehead.

"Working vacation." He scratched the back of his head.

"What are you working on?"

"I'm a consultant. Personnel matters, mostly. I folded in a few days off. Can we grab a seat at the coffee shop?" he asked. "Or go somewhere?"

"There's a bar just outside the station. And I need to make a call."

As they walked out of the station, she reached someone on her cell phone, and other than the greetings and pleasantries, he was unable to understand much. He heard eight o'clock. He looked at his watch: It was just after six.

They entered the bar: crude and small, a shot bar, liquor and beer, wooden picnic tables, loud Japanese rock and roll, lovers shoved into every corner, drunk, kissing, shouting for more of everything—volume, booze, and tongue.

They slid into a booth, and she ordered beer and whiskey for them both.

"This consulting job is just a one-off deal," he said. "Opportunity to come back to Tokyo. I thought of becoming an academic, so I earned a Ph.D. in French history, and then I realized that world wasn't for me."

"What now?"

"I'll look for suitable employment." He smiled widely.

She laughed. He was stealing lines from Clyde. "Is that why you went to Yoshida's? But really, why are you here?"

"'Cause you may be the best damn girl in Tokyo."

"Okay, Clyde. It was charming the first time. Give it another hour. Why are you here now?"

"I went to Yokota. Can you believe they bulldozed the street I lived on?"

"They should bulldoze the whole base." She said this with a totally straight face and no humor.

"The radical rises from the ashes."

"I earned a Ph.D.," she said.

"Really?" he asked, totally surprised, and delighted to move the conversation away from his fictional business trip and his real reason for being in Tokyo.

"Are you kidding me?" She smiled in disgust. "I barely finished high school. I went to prison, remember?"

"I thought that afterward, possibly." He leaned back in the booth, as though to avoid the large helping of naïveté he'd delivered to the table.

"Oh, right, the pipeline from Japanese prisons to graduate schools?"

"Hey." He shrugged. "You said it."

"It was a joke. I did, however, receive daily anti-recidivism lessons. I achieved native fluency in Japanese. I could earn a Ph.D. in Japanese if it would make you happy. You're still such a serious guy."

"In my defense, I am sitting across from a woman I loved deeply when I was young. A woman, some would say, whom I helped send to prison. I'm a little nervous." He crossed his arms and looked at a couple across the bar, two people deeply involved in serious tongue acrobatics. He motioned toward the couple. "I thought the Japanese didn't do public affection."

"Did you read that in a guidebook?" Virginia asked. "They're twenty-five. They're drunk in a bar. They're into public affection."

"I'm not opposed, mind you." Severin felt as though he needed to prove some things to Virginia. The last time she'd seen him, he'd been a virgin. He wanted to proclaim, I've had sex tens of thousands of times since then. Of course, so had she. Another reality of your thirties, he thought.

"Severin, you didn't cause me to go to prison. I did. I got caught up in it all, not you. You walked away. And then, apparently, you thought that leading the police to me would somehow help me." She shook her head.

He felt stupid, hearing her say it. "But you must know, I really did think that. I had no idea you were involved in a *kidnapping*. I tried to go to your father. He kicked me out of your house. I thought . . ." He looked at her hands. He wanted to hold them in his. "You followed me? To the theater?"

"It was horribly easy. I hope you're never in serious trouble or need to evade anyone. Or maybe I'm just good. I could've never said a word. You'd still be wandering around the city, lost. But just because we're sitting here doesn't mean anything. We're catching up. And then we'll say good-bye. We have nothing in common."

"Except our past."

"Not enough. Not enough to get my clothes off."

"Is that why you think I'm here?"

"Could be."

"I was walking around, looking for you, totally devastated by my failure, and you were following me, taking photos of my every move."

"Pretty tricky, yeah? I was touched when I realized where you'd taken me."

"The concierge mentioned the *Bonnie and Clyde* marathon. I was planning on taking the day off."

"Why, again, did you show the JPs to Silver's apartment?"

"I thought I was going to be a hero. I thought I was going to save the day. That's what your father expected from me."

"How in the hell could you know what my father wanted from you? He wanted you to win football games. Period. I didn't know what he expected of me other than good grades and upstanding manners. He was a statue." She motioned to the bartender for more drinks.

"Your father meant a lot to me. He taught me discipline. . . ." Severin trailed off. "Not that I've done much with that lesson."

The new drinks arrived, and the bartender turned up the volume on the music. It was a Japanese punk band doing Beatles covers.

"Discipline? You're talking football lingo. I was his daughter." Virginia slapped the table. "Not his star linebacker!"

"But you have to look closely at those guys like your father and mine. They were giants at war. They killed for a living. And then they came home to families. Of course they were screwed up. It doesn't excuse their distance. But it must be recognized. And possibly forgiven. I haven't decided about forgiveness yet."

"I was sorry to hear about your father." She reached for his hands and then didn't touch them.

"And your father?" He wanted to take her temperature on this.

"Entirely past-tense. I haven't seen him since the day of my sentencing."

He took a drink from his whiskey. Stay away from the fathers for now, it's too early, he told himself. "What happened to Silver? I never heard."

"The Japanese police didn't worry with him. I don't know what happened. When they found the people we'd been transporting, Silver wasn't there. They killed the North Koreans in the raid. In prison, I heard Silver had begun working a gang in Okinawa, but prison is so full of lies. I think he's dead."

Severin could tell she felt responsible for Silver, responsible for his disappearance or death, and he knew not to ask any further questions. He wasn't here to relive the past, at least not that past. Prison. The word finally sank in. Virginia had spent five years in a Japanese prison.

Her father had once threatened to send the football team to Sugamo Prison, where the hardest war criminals resided during the American occupation. "Water and rice," Kindwall had yelled. "Three squares a day. Turn you into origami paper. But you won't fold into a crane; you'll be a wet bedsheet, shivering in your own urine and fear."

Neither Severin nor Virginia spoke. He looked around the bar; more lovers kissing. He wanted to stop talking and kiss her for a few years. Then he'd never have to mention her dying father.

She looked at her watch. "I have a train to catch. I'd ask you home"—she looked at him teasingly—"but my living situation is kind of intricate. Delicate." She could tell the brevity of their meeting insulted him.

"When will I see you again? May I see you again? Tomorrow?"

"Let me make a call." She went out to the street.

Was she calling her husband—guess who's coming to dinner? No wedding ring, but many Japanese went without. He wondered what Aida had been doing since he'd left. She'd probably already rented out the basement apartment. That would replace his income exactly. Convenient. Would he ever see her again? He knew how she ended relationships: definitively, no dangling alliances. Why would a marriage be any different? For Aida, the end lasted three letters. For him, the end usually lasted three years. Only when he married Aida had he stopped sleeping with ex-lovers. What comprised Virginia's delicate living situation?

She reentered the bar and sat next to him. "Hey, mister," she said. She put an arm around his shoulder and leaned in to him and kissed his neck. "I know this place for dinner."

"Is it cheap?"

"It depends on what you order." She stood. "You need a one-hundred-and-forty-yen ticket to make it to my station. It's ten thousand yen a head to eat at my house."

"I can afford it," he said.

They walked back toward the station. Virginia picked up Kobe beef at Tamura Butcher. She stopped at the patisserie and bought a proper dessert of truffles. They descended the stairwell at the station, and she wondered what Severin expected from her.

On the walk from the station to her house, she said, "There will be two people at dinner you know, sort of. And one total stranger."

"Let's start with the stranger," he said. Here it is, the unveiling of the husband or boyfriend. I can deal with this. I am not here for her, he thought. I am here to bring her to her father. After dinner, I will give her the news.

"When I was in jail, I had an affair with a guard. I got pregnant, and I have a daughter. She's ten. Her name is Hideko."

"Hideko is the stranger?" Kindwall didn't tell me this, Severin thought. Pregnant by a guard? Jesus.

"What do you think of the fact that I have a daughter?"

"I'm surprised. But I imagine you're a lovely and loving mother. I'm happy for you." And he was. The idea of Virginia being a mother warmed him; it seemed right and good. He wondered why he'd never received the memo. Did Kindwall even know? Kindwall knew everything.

Severin asked, "Is the father—are you with the father? Married?"

"The father is, what do you call it? Absent. It wasn't exactly good for his career when I turned up pregnant. He now works at a prison in Hokkaido. It's like being sent to Siberia. It wasn't love. Do you have children? Or a wife?" Virginia asked. She wanted him to simplify their lives and say yes: Yes, I have a wife I love deeply and two beautiful children who expect me home tomorrow.

He stopped walking. He looked straight into the kitchen of the house they stood in front of. A woman cleaned vegetables at the sink, and two children played a game at the breakfast table, rolling dice, moving playing pieces on a board, laughing.

"I have a wife, but the marriage is ending. We don't have children."

"How long have you been married?"

"Six years and some change. But I recently busted things up rather spectacularly. It's a long story, no time now, but when I tell you, you'll be impressed with my complete disregard for others and my total lack of respect for the institution of marriage and the concept of fidelity."

"I'm sure I'll understand, Severin. In the last fifteen years, I've gained quite a capacity for understanding the folly of others, and my own." She looked at her watch. "We should be on our way. It's a good walk, another ten minutes. Anything closer to the station I couldn't afford."

They passed a temple as a priest closed the gates for the evening.

"How long have you been in Yokota?"

"Over three years."

"And where were you before that?"

"All over the country."

She stepped up to a small, tight porch, lit by a bright yellow light. "This is us. Be prepared for a few surprises. Hideko is extremely shy and afraid of strangers, especially men. She probably won't talk to you all night, though she might address you through me."

"How will she do that?"

"She'll say, 'Mommy, why does that man look so funny?'"

"Good question." He nodded toward the door. "And who are the people I know?"

"Let's find out." Virginia put her key in the lock but didn't turn it. She looked at Severin and laughed, a quiet laugh meant for two, meant for the past, meant for now. "I don't know what you're doing here in Japan, or what it means, or what you want it to mean. I know you're not a business consultant. Wrong clothes, wrong hair. You can tell me later, if you choose. But let's have a nice time tonight. That's what I always wanted with you."

He kissed her forehead. It was all he needed for now.

He heard fast-running feet approach from the other side of the door, and the sound of small hands clapping, and a giggling girl and the word, repeated, "Mommy."

Virginia opened the door to the wide happy grin of her daughter. Hideko said, "Mommy, Miyoko-san and Yoshida-san are here." She started dancing, did a little twirl. She noticed Severin and stopped. She looked at him and frowned, tilting her head sideways and back. She opened her eyes wide, stuck out her tongue, and said in English, "Who is the funny man?" And ran up the stairs two steps at a time.

"Please consider that a warm welcome," Virginia said. "She doesn't practice her English on just anyone. When was the last time you were in a Japanese home? Or were you ever?"

"A friend of my mother's a few times. I don't really recall."

"We only warm the main room downstairs. So the foyer is cold, as you can tell. The rooms are warmed individually with space heaters, only at night, when we sleep. Take your coat off and get in there where it's warm." She pointed toward shoji-screen double doors.

"Wait," he said. He removed his coat and hung it on a peg. "Wait. Did she say Yoshida-san?"

"Yes, and Miyoko-san, my father's ex-girlfriend. They have been dating for years. Yoshida's marriage fell apart after their son was killed in the accident. He and Miyoko get along quite well."

She slid past him and entered the other room.

There was nothing for him to do but follow.

Yoshida-san and Miyoko-san turned away from the low dining table and, remaining on their knees, greeted Severin with a deep bow. His first thought was: I don't deserve that respect. He got down on his knees and returned the gesture. They all stood, an awkward moment. Shake hands now, hug? Smile, smile for now, and nod.

Virginia said, "Severin, you of course remember Yoshida. And this is Miyoko. They are my family. They adopted Hideko and me. And I returned to Yokota. I work for them both, out of my home office, doing their books and paperwork, and they helped me buy this house."

While Virginia spoke, Miyoko and Yoshida nodded.

Yoshida said, "I believe you now have the answers to your questions, Mr. Severin."

Some of the answers, yes. Please don't ask me questions, he thought. This was all a matter of timing. How do you tell a woman who has left her father behind in memory, in her sad past tense, that the man is dying and that his only wish is to see her? And how do you convince her to return with her daughter to the dying man's bedside? Severin felt like the messenger who would shortly lose his head. He did not want to lose his head.

Virginia carried plates to the table. "This isn't a fancy meal, Severo, not like you're used to in San Francisco," she said. "Severo" floated off of her tongue with ease; she didn't even think about it. He liked this. They looked at each other and entered that Saturday-afternoon date many years ago. No one had called him Severo before or since.

But then they were back, here, in her house, with this family she'd made from the fragments of a life. Severin thought of a saying her father had used when a game was tight: *What we break, we will fix.*

Hideko came racing through the room and grabbed a sardine from a platter on the table, threw it in the air, caught it in her mouth, and exited again.

Yoshida yelled, "My little seal! I taught her that!"

"That trick was for you," Virginia said, looking at Severin. "Showing off for a man. I need to put an end to that."

273

The meal began. Yoshida sat at the head of the table with Miyoko and Hideko on either side of him. Severin and Virginia sat next to each other at the opposite end.

Yoshida offered a toast. "Here is to family, and friends who appear like the first blossom, a surprise, after the long winter."

They all toasted, the adults with sake and Hideko with orange juice.

Miyoko said, "Yoshida-san is drunk! Cherry-blossom toast!"

They all laughed, and Yoshida protested, but he was a bit drunk, Severin could tell. Was he celebrating or worried?

They ate the feast: Kobe beef grilled on hot stones, sardines, sautéed lotus root, *goya champuru,* an Okinawan pork and vegetable dish. The adults drank sake and then shochu. When the main meal was done, Miyoko brought out a platter of roasted chestnuts, fresh from the oven. As she set the platter down, one chestnut exploded, blowing debris about the table and making a mess. Hideko jumped up and danced around the table. She said it was good luck. She made up a song about exploding chestnuts and good luck, and she sang it to great applause.

Virginia clapped and leaned in to Severin, and she put her hand on his leg, and he covered her hand with his.

Hideko saw the touching. She screamed, "Mommy wants to kiss the funny man. Mommy wants to kiss the funny man." She grabbed the last sardine and threw it up in the air and caught it in her mouth. Severin saw that her impulse was to run. She stared, wild-eyed, at her mother. Virginia returned the stare, and Hideko, as though overpowered by a supernatural mother force, sat at the table and straightened her skirt. She bit her bottom lip and looked at Yoshida and Miyoko and then her mother. "Mommy, if Yoshida says it is okay, you can kiss the funny man."

"It is okay," Yoshida said. "It is preferred." He offered his glass for anyone to toast.

"Severo," Virginia whispered in Severin's ear, "she has never approved of a funny man before."

Severin said, "I have never been this funny." He toasted Yoshida.

Hideko ran to the refrigerator and returned with a box of cream-cheese squares. Virginia was at first mortified. "Honey, I have real dessert, truffles! Put that back."

"I want creamu-cheesu. Creamu-cheesu," she sang.

She walked around the table to Severin and bashfully handed him a square. He unwrapped it and ate it in one bite. *"Umai,"* he said. "Creamu-cheesu. Excellent." The girl shrieked with excitement and handed everyone else at the table an allotment. In his life, he had never heard a more lovely and pure sound than Hideko shrieking with joy over creamu-cheesu squares.

Together, Virginia and Severin cleaned the dishes. Miyoko and Yoshida watched the news, and Hideko fell asleep, sprawled across their laps.

Virginia said, "They're taking her home with them. They live around the corner. You'll spend the night, won't you?"

TWENTY-FIVE

Virginia slept in an eight-tatami-mat room. She turned on two heaters situated at either side of the head of the futon.

They moved toward each other, fast enough to close the past, erase time lost. They kissed on the lips and then kissed each other's faces, chin, cheeks, eyelids, forehead, nose. They fell onto the comforter, a field of down. It was still cold in the room, but they did not need that heat. They might as well have been in a spring field of wild grasses, a shower of sun. This is every kiss, he thought. This is all of my love. This is the rest of my life. He removed her shirt. No bra underneath.

"Small," she said, referring to her breasts, touching them, making cleavage.

"Perfect," he said. Goose bumps rose to her flesh. He buried his mouth in her body. He clutched her back and pulled her in to him, one body, he thought, one love.

She rolled on top of him. She grabbed his shoulders and arched her back, removed his shirt. She kissed his chest, laid her face against his chest, and felt his warmth, heard his heart, that uncertain organ. She wondered if this was what she'd been waiting for, if he could do what he'd once wanted: save her.

They took off the rest of their clothes in a rush, awkwardly. She was on top of him again, and she felt him deeply and completely, she forced her body against his and he held her at the hips, his hands guided her hips as though they were meant for only this.

And they did not stop. They would sleep, and then one would wake the other with a touch, a kiss, a word.

"Love," she said. It was three or four in the morning. She reached for him. "Oh, God. Come here."

Sunlight entered the room. Her hair was a mess, a beautiful mess, lovely dark knots. He put a knot into his mouth and sucked on it, chewed on it. I could live on this, he thought, dark straw at the bottom of the cage. She still slept, her head buried in his armpit; he felt her breath there. He had been awake for an hour or longer. He knew he shouldn't leave the house in the morning without telling her about her father. But he convinced himself to give it one more day. Yes, they'd spend the day together in Tokyo, free still from the weight of the dying Kindwall, and then another night like this. He couldn't find the right first sentence. He'd been working on the first sentence for days.

She awoke and bit him lightly, lovingly, at the soft flesh of his side.

"Morning," she said. "You're still here?"

"Do you want me to leave?"

"Some do leave."

"I won't."

"I don't know that. I want to eat you," she said, biting him again. "I want to tear you apart and bury your bones and dig them up whenever I want."

"You buried me once already."

"What now?"

"I move in?"

"You have to get a job and learn Japanese. Maybe you can be a salesman for Yoshida?" She was totally serious.

"I know as much about televisions as I do about business consulting."

"Seriously." She kissed his chest and looked him straight in the eyes. "Did you come all this way just to sleep with me and then leave? Couldn't you have just found someone new in San Francisco?"

"I didn't think this would happen. It was not my mission. My intention."

"Mission?" she asked. "What is your mission? Jesus, you sound like my father."

The phone rang, and she sprang from bed. "They probably forgot Hideko's backpack last night. They always do!" She answered the wall phone in the hall.

She hung up the phone and said, "I'm going downstairs to give them the bag. It might be a few minutes before they get here. Take a shower?"

"I will."

He ran the shower hot. The room was full of steam, sweat, heat, his confusion. The first sentence. He stayed under the water for fifteen, twenty minutes. He was awake and refreshed. They'd eat breakfast and make a plan for the day.

When he entered her bedroom, she was underneath the comforter, only strands of hair visible. Her body was moving. Convulsing. She was crying. What had happened?

He knelt on the futon and reached for her shoulder, pulled her near him, but she shrugged him away. In her fist, she clutched his passport, opened to page nineteen, the page affixed with his visa for Vietnam.

"What were you doing in Vietnam?" she screamed. "I was going to have some fun, look through your passport, see all the countries you'd been to, think about the trips we would take someday. The cities we'd show Hideko. I wasn't snooping, I swear."

"I was there." He stopped, sat down, and buried his head in his hands.

"You don't have to answer. You were there to see my father.

You're not the first jerk he's sent after me. Just the first I've had sex with. How much did he pay you?"

"Virginia," he said.

"Don't call me Virginia. My name is Sachiko. Virginia is dead. Say my name. Say it."

"Sachiko." He pulled the towel around his waist. "Your father."

"I know. My father loves me. That's why he never visited me in prison. That's why he didn't pick me up when I left prison. That's why he's never seen his granddaughter, because he loves me."

"You don't understand."

"Since you're so smart with your Ph.D., explain it to me. You know I'm just a girl with a high school diploma from prison. So teach me something, smart man." Her eyes were red and mad, and she pulled at the knots in her hair; she yanked at her hair.

He didn't want to say it. Saying it would make it true, would bring the dying General Kindwall from Hue City, Vietnam, to this little room in Yokota, Japan. And what if Virginia said that she didn't care? What if she told him to go back to the dying man and tell him that his daughter didn't want to see him? That was what he'd been afraid of; now he knew that had been his fear from the beginning, from the moment he'd read the general's first postcard, initiating the demise of his marriage. He'd feared standing in front of this woman, holding a dying man in his hands, and hearing her tell him to take the dying man elsewhere to die alone.

"I have nothing to teach you, Sachiko." He wrapped his arms around her body and pulled her to him, close, and he bent down until his lips were touching her ear, and he said it.

"Your father is dying. Your father is dying."

She jabbed him in the ribs with an elbow. She did it again, but he didn't let go of her, he made no noise because it wasn't painful, and he held her as she continued to jab him in the ribs.

"He is not," she said. She shook uncontrollably. "He can't die. That man will never die."

"He will," Severin said. "He is now, today, right now. You have to come with me." He kissed her temple, he kissed her hair, he held her elbow in the palm of his hand. "You have to come with me to Vietnam. Tonight."

TWENTY-SIX

They took a taxi to the airport. Virginia's face was red and raw from crying, and her eyelids were puffy, like oysters. Hideko was unaware where she was going or why her mother was sad, but she was excited because it would be her first airplane ride. Every few minutes she asked Severin or Virginia what kind of food they ate in Vietnam and proudly displayed her passport.

Banh had arranged for the trio to fly to Hue City rather than put Virginia and Hideko through the exhausting drive from Saigon. He picked them up at the airport.

"Miss Kindwall," Banh said. "It is a great honor to meet you. We will provide you and your daughter with all the comfort. The presidential suite is prepared. Your father will move about in the afternoon. There has been the slight improving in his energy since Mr. Severin left us. Mr. Severin, you have the same room."

"Thanks, Banh. Virginia and Hideko are tired." In fact, Hideko was already asleep in Severin's lap. "So we'll let them sleep, right?"

"That is certain."

Virginia held Severin's hand underneath her daughter's head. She was still unsure about being here, and unsure about having Hideko along, but Yoshida and Miyoko had insisted that she must come, too, and meet her grandfather Kindwall. Virginia's anger with Severin had not subsided. She felt betrayed. She felt as though he'd treated her like a whore, really, sleeping his way into her confidence, promising her diamonds but handing her dirt. And yet she knew he'd had no choice.

The arrival at the hotel was rushed and confusing, too many people wanting to shake her hand, too many people offering praise for her father, but she understood none of it. What on earth did he do for you? she thought. Is this the classic case of the neglected child of the doctor who meets her father's patients, all of them grateful for the cure and telling the sick and neglected child what a fantastic doctor her father is? If I am the sick child, she thought, what kind of doctor is he?

She put Hideko down on the queen-size bed and took the king for herself. She fell asleep instantly.

Banh entered Severin's room without knocking. "It is a soldier's habit, sorry," he said.

"No problem, Banh. I'm used to it. Just don't feed me dog, okay? No dog for the ladies, either, promise?"

"It is already the general's order against dog. That was a test prepared specifically for you and your constitution."

"Did I pass?"

"The general wants your audience before talking to the ladies."

Kindwall did look better than when Severin had seen him last. The cane was not at his side but leaning against the wall, and he sat upright.

"Severin Boxx," Kindwall said. "You did it, boy. Don't tell me how. I don't want to know. Just tell me it's true that my Virginia and her daughter are down the hall."

"It's true, sir."

"Come here and hug me."

Severin bent over the general and embraced him. The general held on tight.

"I'm sorry," he said. "I'm sorry I didn't tell you about her daughter. I thought that, in case part of your motivation was romantic, which I would understand, the matter of the daughter might complicate things. There are some elements of Virginia I thought you should discover on your own. Some men are averse to women who have children from other men."

Severin sat down next to Kindwall. "I think you'll find your granddaughter to be quite an angel. Your daughter as well."

"That is what I expect."

"Sir, I need you to be honest with me." Severin turned and faced Kindwall. "Have you sent people after her in the past?"

The general looked out his picture window at the dirty river. "Yes, boy. I'd sent a few people after her. But they'd all come back empty-handed. I tried about five years ago, when I first had a cancer scare, but she wouldn't even talk to me. I never told her I was sick. You were my last-ditch effort, Severin. Sure, I knew where she was, but I needed you on the trail, don't you see? I needed you to fix things on your own."

"What we break, we will fix?"

"Yes, son." The general clearly liked hearing his own words spoken back to him, so many years later. For a moment Severin saw the entire man appear in the sick body, his posture ramrod, his eyes filled with color, his cheeks flushed rather than ashen. This man is about breaking and fixing, Severin thought, but he never perfected fixing. He'd always had others do that for him.

"I need to rest before the ladies' visit," Kindwall said. "Severin, you have saved my life, for as long as that's possible."

Severin walked toward the door and then stopped and turned back toward the general. "Sir, you might've saved mine, too."

"You see there? We have fixed some things after all." Kindwall looked out at the river.

Severin opened the door from the anteroom to the hall, and Virginia elbowed her way through the security detail and the protestations of Banh, Hideko in tow.

She said to Severin, "I can't sleep. Let me see him. Don't you try to stop me, too. You are totally responsible for everything that happens here. I'm not sitting in my room waiting for the emperor to call for his robes. I have a life."

Hideko looked confusedly at Severin: What have you done to my mother? her face asked. He thought: I am no longer the funny man. He stepped aside and opened the door to the main room.

The general watched the slow dirty river.

Virginia reached for Severin and found his arm. She grabbed tightly, steadied herself. Hideko wrapped her arms around her mother's waist. Virginia hugged Severin. She leaned in to him and rested her head on his chest and watched her father watching the river. She began to cry, and Severin did, too, and she cried into Severin's chest and watched her silent, dying father. For some time she watched him, and everyone was silent, the men who'd tried to keep her out of the room, her daughter, her new lover, they were all silent but in tears, while the old dying man looked for himself on the river.

"Daddy," Virginia said, so quietly that Severin barely heard her. Again, louder, "Daddy."

"Sweetheart." He turned from the river to look at his daughter.

Severin saw the life again, the giant alive inside the unforgiving and unreliable body. Kindwall's teeth were as white as paper, and his dry lips stuck to his teeth as he smiled. He looked at Hideko, and he looked at Virginia, and he opened his arms for his family. Virginia urged Hideko forward, and she complied. The general wrapped his long thin arms around the girl. He looked at Severin and Virginia. He could not stop smiling, would never stop.

"So you are Hideko?" Kindwall said, leaning back and taking her in completely.

"Yes, that is my name," the girl said. "Who are you?"

"I'm your grandfather. Your mother's father. I've been gone."

"We don't live here," Hideko said. "I miss Japan and Yoshida-san and Miyoko-san." She crossed her arms and looked at her mother.

"So do I," Kindwall said. "You are a lucky girl to know them."

Virginia sat down next to her father and pulled Hideko onto her lap.

Hideko rubbed the general's head. "Your head is like a lizard," she said.

Kindwall rubbed his bald head and said, "You're right. I want you on my team."

The girl beamed.

"Daddy," Virginia said. "The past doesn't matter now." She said this, surprised herself it was true. "It's erased. Here we are. We will be here until the end. Whatever you need."

Kindwall bent at the waist, rested his head on his crossed arms, and his daughter rubbed his back and so did his granddaughter and he leaned in to them.

Severin backed away—he backed himself against a wall and watched the mother and daughter soothe the giant. He wanted to answer Virginia: This is why I appeared in Tokyo. This is why I reentered your life. But he knew she knew these answers now. He wanted to find answers to other questions, too, some of his own, some of hers, but they would answer those later. Together.

ACKNOWLEDGMENTS

I wish to thank Colin Harrison; Sloan Harris; Sachiko Tamura; Oren Moverman; Shigeyoshi Hara; the Murai family in Adachi-ku, Tokyo; the librarians at the Tachikawa Public Library; and the Corporation of Yaddo. And Teresa.

ANTHONY SWOFFORD, a graduate of the Iowa Writers' Work-shop, won the PEN/Martha Albrand Award and the Pacific Northwest Booksellers Award for *Jarhead*. He lives in New York City.